Heart of FRANKENSTEIN

LEXI POST

Heart of FRANKENSTEIN

ACKNOWLEDGMENTS

To Bob Fabich, the model for this hero's kind acts and one of my excellent resources on Alaska since he was stationed there. Thank you so much for Timber.

And for my sister Paige Wood, who always finds the time to help make my stories better.

For some very special readers: Veronica Westfall, who is a huge fan and a wonderful lady. Ashley Clark, who has been with me from my first book and has been patiently waiting two years for me to write this story.

I want to thank Lisa Fishback for her help with Angela's profession and for giving me Sturge. I also want to thank Pamela Todd and Kate Schieber for taking the time to go through this story with a fine-toothed comb.

As always, I could not have kept on schedule without the help of Marie Patrick, a great critique partner and a fantastic friend.

HEART OF FRANKENSTEIN

Can a monster find love?

In 1718, he was abandoned then betrayed, spurring his relentless desire for revenge against his creator, Victor Frankenstein. It is now the 21st Century, and despite his fervent wish for death, he still exists, tortured by his crimes, searching only for peace.

Angela Ellis would have frozen to death in the harsh Alaskan wilderness if not for the man who found her on an icy ledge. He calls her Angel, but has no name himself. He is kind, caring, handsome, and scarred both outside and inside. The more she learns about him, the more she wants to know…and the more she falls in love.

He is unworthy of love unless he can confess, but his secrets are buried deep and to reveal them would be to rip out his soul and lose his Angel. Unfortunately, he is given no say in the matter. Nature has a way of revealing all.

For updates, sneak peeks, and special prizes, sign up to receive the latest news from Lexi at
http://bit.ly/LexiUpdate

AUTHOR'S NOTE

Heart of Frankenstein was inspired by Mary Shelley's novel, *Frankenstein; or the Modern Prometheus,* published in 1818. When the story opens, it is the 18th Century and Victor Frankenstein is in the Arctic Ocean on a ship, which has rescued him after finding him on an ice float. He explains to the captain why he is there, chasing after a creature he created.

Victor Frankenstein had a burning need to discover how to reanimate the dead. Upon his success, he built a man that is larger and stronger than any other, and who he describes as "beautiful." Yet, as soon as he is successful and the man opens his yellowed eyes, Victor runs away, now fearful of what he's done.

The creature is left on his own to discover sunlight, fire, clothing, and food. He finds refuge in a shed attached to a poor family's house and by listening and watching through a crack in the wall, learns language and how to read. When he reveals himself, he is chased away, but due to his experiences, he has a resentment toward his creator and kills Victor's brother, framing the family's servant for the murder.

The creature then confronts Victor, tells him his side of the story and asks Victor to build him a mate, promising to leave him and all mankind alone if he does. Victor finally agrees and takes months traveling before settling on a lonely island in the Outer Hebrides of Scotland to build a woman. He creates the woman, but before he animates her, he sees the creature staring in the window with a smile on his face. Victor interprets the smile as evil and fears a species of murderers would be forthcoming, so he tears apart the woman before the creature's eyes.

The creature promises revenge and fulfills that promise by killing Victor's best friend then later Victor's wife on their wedding night. Enraged, Victor makes it his goal in life to kill his creation. The creature leads Victor all over Europe and into the Arctic, but at this point in his story, Victor dies on the ship never fulfilling his goal. The creature comes to the ship and finds Victor dead. He tells the captain of his doomed soul, promising to go to the top of the world, build himself a funeral pyre and set himself on fire.

But what if the creature followed through, only to find he could not die? How would he live his life for the next three hundred years? And what would he do about a mate now that he was the only one of his species?

CHAPTER ONE

He stared at the almost naked woman frozen on the ledge of the mountain. She was breathtaking, especially to him. The women in the far northern regions of Alaska were bundled up so much that he couldn't tell they were women. This woman had shed most of her clothes.

Her face, turned in profile, was white from the cold and her light eyelashes reminded him of dried cotton grass in the late summer. Her long neck revealed no pulse and her golden hair, spread out on one side, appeared as if it had been frozen while blowing in the wind.

He needed to move her, but he couldn't help staring. Her breasts were covered by a thin white top that left her toned arms bare. Her waist was narrow, but her hips flared out in the shape that was the epitome of woman. She had long, tight pink leggings that disappeared beneath her socks, but her boots were thrown amongst her scattered outer clothes.

She looked like a fallen angel. If she was alive, they would make a good match because his past made him closer to Satan than any other angel in man's lexicon of religions.

He looked back along the route he'd come. His tracks were obvious and unless a heavy snowstorm came in, they would remain so. Images of being attacked in Geneva sped across his mind. If anyone found her dead body here, he would be accused of murdering her.

With no choice, he crouched down, his heart heavy that such a beautiful woman in the prime of her life was gone. At least with hypothermia, her mind would have slept before she felt the final breaths of life leave her. Unlike his mate, who was gone before she could take her first breath. The age-old rage that used to fill him barely caused more than a stutter of his heart now.

Unable to resist, he stroked his bare finger over her cheek. At its softness, he drew back as if stung. Her cheek should be hard.

Hesitantly, he set his finger beneath her nose. Was that breath? He couldn't be sure. If it was, it was so shallow that she would die soon. Taking her delicate wrist in his hand, he felt for the pulse he couldn't see in her neck.

Nothing. Disappointment and sorrow rifled through him. Was he so enamored of her looks that he wished her alive? Doubting his own senses, he lay two fingers along the side of her neck. At first, he couldn't concentrate, her skin so soft it distracted him.

Finally, he forced his mind to cooperate. Thump————— thump—————. Elation swept through him almost toppling him over. He had only felt so once before. Now, on the heels of his euphoria came panic.

He *had* to save her. His mind raced as memories sped by of a search party he'd participated in years ago, shortly after he'd settled on his mountain. He had found the young male and thought him dead as well, but a rescue crew had taken over. He'd asked numerous questions, fascinated by the human body and how his own was different.

Taking off his coat of bearskin fur that he donned when traveling anywhere he might be seen, he laid it on the ground next to her. Carefully, he moved her light form onto it and wrapped her tight. It was critical in this late stage that she not wake and try to move on her own or it could kill her.

Lifting her in his arms, he was thankful for the extra strong limbs he'd been given and carefully strode down the mountain to his home. It was a simple one room cabin set against the mountain, hiding the cave he'd originally lived in when first arriving in the region.

Having moved about the arctic for almost three hundred years, he was always careful to keep his presence a secret until he could determine where the closest inhabitant was and who or what they were.

After entering his home, he laid the angel on her back on his handmade bed. Wrapped in his grizzly bear coat, she looked small. He thought back to the young man that he'd found. The rescuers had used warm rubber containers at the man's neck, on his hands, under his arms, and between his legs.

Quickly, he grabbed the smooth rock that he used to hold the door open when carrying supplies inside and set it in the coals of the wood stove. Striding outside, he grabbed up five smaller ones from his porch that he used for chasing away wolves and added them to the fire.

The marten skins he had drying wouldn't be large enough to wrap around the rocks, so he unbuttoned his shirt, pulled it off, and ripped it. The material was flannel and its texture was perfect for her soft skin.

Retrieving the rocks from the fire with his bare hands, he wrapped them in the material and carefully positioned them against her in the important areas. He placed the largest rock between her thighs then wrapped the coat around her again. He took the quilt hanging on his wall and laid that over her as well before standing back.

What if he was too late? What if she'd been there too long? What if she was already dead, slipping away while he prepared the rocks?

Then you'd be no worse off than you were before.

But that wasn't true. Before he didn't know of her. Now, her path had crossed with his. Only twice before had he gazed upon such femininity with awe. The first time was while still in Germany when he'd watched Felix and Agatha, the people he learned to speak from while living in a shed attached to their house. They never knew he was there until the day he tried to befriend their blind father.

He fisted his hands and tore his gaze from the face of his angel. The ensuing attack upon his person when he was found inside with their father was only the second betrayal of his miserable existence. It was less the stick Felix raised than the fact Felix raised anything against him that hurt, though it was less painful than his first betrayal, but a true harbinger of the exile to come.

Turning back to the woman, he focused on the memories of what else the rescuers had done. He glanced at the wood stove. It might be too cool in his cabin. Immediately, he walked to the wood pile set against the wall and added two more split logs. They caught as they landed on the red coals, filling the stove with yellow flames.

He returned to his bed and knelt down. Once again, he positioned his index finger beneath her nose. His stomach loosened as a faint breath stirred the tiny hairs below his knuckle. She lived.

To help the body warm from the inside out, we use warm sugar water until we can get the victim to a hospital. The words of the rescuers ran through his head, his memory sharp, and in *this* case, he was grateful for that.

He rose and moved to his long counter to pour fresh water into a small pot. He didn't have sugar but he had birch syrup he'd boiled down himself. Pouring a liberal amount of his late season harvest into the water, he set it on the wood stove to warm.

If he hadn't seen the sun reflecting off something near her, he would have never spotted her. She must have been lost, which meant someone would be looking for her. He'd had no choice but to leave her clothes where they lay. He would need to go back and retrieve them for her.

Though he understood he couldn't keep her, nor that she would want to stay, he wanted to be sure she lived long enough to make that decision. If she died while under his care, he would be hunted down…again.

Pulling the pot from the stove, he poured a small amount of the sweet water into a tin cup. Dipping his finger in, he guessed at its warmth before picking up his spoon from the counter and moving toward the bed. Kneeling on one knee once more, he dipped the spoon into the sweet water and lifted it to her mouth.

Carefully, he dripped a little on her chapped lips, but it rolled to the side and down her jaw. Emptying the spooned water into the cup again, he used it to part her lips, but they closed again.

He hesitated to touch her face. The action seemed too intimate. Moving her body to warm her was like any other body, but her face, so smooth and unblemished, was what made her different just as her brain and heart made her who she was. Who was she?

Angela Ellis luxuriated in the warmth, a hot tub one of her favorite guilty pleasures. Letting her head fall back, she looked up but there was only fog. Where was she? Moving her gaze toward the ground, she couldn't see it. She closed her eyes again. She must be in heaven.

She chuckled. With a job that took her around the world, it wasn't a surprise she couldn't remember where she was for a moment, and really, how much did it matter? She was warm and happy and alone. Life couldn't get any better than this…except on her next adventure vacation.

She lifted her head as excitement thrummed through her. That was coming up soon. A month-long cruise along what she referred to as the people-less frontier. She loved the idea that there were billions of people on Earth, yet there were still places devoid of human life—except for visitors like herself.

She moved her arms through the bubbling water. Or was she already on her vacation? She tried to think. Images of a dark bar with round outside windows flowed through her mind. More followed, standing in formation in a life jacket for a muster drill, eating fresh caught salmon, staying up to see the lights of the Aurora Borealis. She let her head fall back again. She must be in the hot tub on the outer deck, the ecological ship's only nod toward the cruise industry. They must be traveling through fog.

No wonder she was a little disoriented. She wouldn't even be able to tell which way was up if not for the hot water. The fog didn't seem to move. Why was everything so fuzzy? Did she drink too much last night?

He steeled himself and gently forced his angel's lower jaw down, effectively opening her mouth and dribbling a little of water into it before releasing her. He watched, but she didn't swallow. Not wanting her to choke, he turned her head toward the wall and lowered her chin so the water could leak out.

She was in too deep a sleep. What if she never woke? The thought sent a chill through him far greater than simple cold temperatures. There had to be something else he could do.

A conversation he'd overheard at the outpost came to mind. A woman had been joking with her husband about sharing body heat with his hunting partner. The man had fallen through the ice and needed to get warm.

He could do that for his angel. Standing, he quickly removed all his clothes. Since his sensitivity to temperatures had lessened over the centuries, he had no idea if his body would give off heat, but he had to try.

He folded the quilt down, and careful not to dislodge the heated rocks, moved her toward the middle of the bed. He opened the coat and lay next to her, quickly pulling the quilt over them. Gently, he lifted her head onto his arm and wrapped his other across her stomach.

Her body felt cold even to him. Would she ever warm? Moving his leg against her to make contact all along the side of her body, he carefully covered her legs with his other one, bending it at the knee to avoid putting any weight on her.

She smelled like the Arctic air and a faint hint of mint, her hair beneath his nose already softening. Her curvy body yielded to his hard one. He let his warm breath pass by her nose, hoping she'd bring that heat into her lungs.

As he lay with her, a new sense of how fragile she was

penetrated his brain. She wasn't like most of the women he came into contact with. Though she was a nice size, her face was not weathered by the harsh elements of Alaska and her skin was far too pale to have been hit by the northern sun for years.

She was even more beautiful than he'd originally thought. She was precious, like an angel. Fate had brought her to him. With her, saving her, he might finally find peace. Despite his newfound hope, or maybe because of it, his body came alive with the sensations of touching her.

Though she retained a layer of clothing, he'd shed all of his. His cock, nestled against her hip began to grow firmer. The skin on his arm where it touched hers, prickled with pleasure. And he couldn't resist stroking his nose over her cheek.

His body wanted to mate, but he never could. He wasn't a man. He was something else, something reprehensible, something other than human. The only hope he had for his existence was peace. But it didn't keep him from yearning for what could never be.

Though he was regulated to finding snippets of comfort in the mundane, with her in his arms he found a sense of happiness. Even if just for a fleeting moment in his timeline, he would treasure it.

He held her a little tighter, enjoying the feel of his hard cock pressed against her and the silkiness of her hair upon his arm. As desire built inside him, he embraced it for the oddity it was, reveled in its sensations.

The heat in the room finally began to cool as the wood he'd added burned down. Despite the unmet ache in his loins, he was loathe to move from her side. Not only did he enjoy having her in his arms, but he didn't want to undo what he may have accomplished by sharing his body heat.

He remained where he was, ignoring the movement of the sun that now hid behind an adjacent mountain, covering the cabin in a half-shadow. Instead, he watched his angel breathe, confirming she still lived.

Then her lips parted, and she took a deeper breath.

He froze, afraid she would wake immediately. When her eyelids didn't open, he carefully extracted himself from around her. Wrapping the fur coat about her, his concern increased that she might look upon him and be horrified. With his heart racing in near panic, he quickly replaced the quilt and grabbed up his clothes.

He dressed in his jeans and boots faster than a wolf snatching up its prey. With his flannel shirt now in shreds around the rocks keeping the woman warm, he needed to cover his torso before she woke. He didn't want her to fear him.

Moving to the chest at the end of his bed, he pulled out another shirt. It was wool, which would be far too hot once he added more wood to the stove. Digging beneath it, he grasped a white linen shirt he hadn't worn in decades. Donning it, he buttoned it high enough to hide the horizontal scar across his chest, yet it still remained open at the collar.

Stepping before the triangular piece of mirror he'd found in the Savik dump, he checked to be sure the leather choker with Inuit symbols on it still covered his harshest scar. The one on his forehead was concealed by his hair, but the one under his right eye was visible. He once tried an eye-patch for that, but with his height, it seemed to cause more fear.

Confirming the leather around his neck was still in

place, he strode to the wood stove and added two more logs, watching as they were engulfed in flames. He returned the pot to the stove top and waited for it to steam before pouring it into his tin cup again and walking back to his bed, back to Angel. That's what he would call her. Men and women liked names, and in the Arctic wilderness, they took on names that meant something.

Once again, he sat next to her and carefully opened her lips. Spooning in a small amount of the sweet water, he waited, anxious to see some sign of life in her. Excitement hit him as her throat worked to swallow the warm liquid. Since she didn't wake or choke, he repeated the procedure, this time letting more from the spoon drip onto her tongue.

She groaned, and he pulled his hands away, but she didn't wake.

He quickly gave Angel more sugar water. This time her tongue darted out and licked at her lips. His gut tightened with yearning. The need for companionship spiked hard through his chest. He had little time to recover before her lashes fluttered. He held his breath, anxious to see the color of her eyes.

"Oh." Her lids, which didn't appear to open, squinched together. She tried to lift her hand, but it was caught beneath the blankets and fur coat.

"Don't." He whispered the word because his normal voice was very deep and scratchy. He didn't want to alarm her, but he couldn't allow her to move. "Don't try to move yet. You could stop your heart."

Her sudden intake of breath was the only sign that she'd heard him. That, and she ceased her struggles, much to his relief.

"Am I in a hospital?" Her voice, though soft, flowed over him, loosening his tense muscles.

"No. You're in my cabin. I discovered you on the mountain."

Her eyelashes fluttered again followed by a moan of pain before she closed them tight. "My eyes. Burn."

She must have become blinded by the snow. She'd had no eye protection. He should have realized that. "Don't try to open them. You're snow-blind."

Her head turned toward his voice. "Blind?" The one word was choked out.

The fear in her voice caused sympathy to rise in his chest. "It's not permanent, but it could last a couple of days. If you'll allow it, I can bandage your eyes so they can heal."

Her tongue darted out to lick her chapped lips again. "Please."

At her request, he rose. Striding toward the corner of the room that held the wood stove and cabinets, as well as a sink with cold running water, his mind quickly inventoried what he might use. He didn't wish to use the tape he had as her skin was already sore from the cold. He could wrap her eyes with a scarf, but he needed something hard beneath it to protect her eyes from light.

Jar lids could work if large enough. Quickly, he chose two from the cabinet and went back to his chest for the scarf. As he approached the bed, he purposefully shuffled his feet so she wouldn't be startled by his voice. Laying everything next to her, he pulled his only chair from the table at the center of the cabin and set it next to the bed.

"I'm going to wrap your head and protect your eyes.

Don't lift your head or move. It's very important you remain still. Your muscles don't have the proper blood flow yet, and the strain could cause your heart to fail."

Her brows lowered. "Are you a doctor?"

"No, but I have lived in the coldest regions of the Earth for most of my life. I understand what has happened to you." He sat on the chair and lifted the jar lids.

Her tongue darted out to wet her lips again. "I guess that's the next best thing."

He didn't respond, too focused on soothing her. Her eyes would simply take time to heal. As gently as he could, he laid a lid over each eye socket, resting the edges on her eyebrows and cheek bones. Slowly, he lifted her head with one hand while he maneuvered the scarf beneath it. The silky strands of her golden hair made it hard to concentrate.

Finally, he had the scarf where he wanted it and he tied it around her head to keep the lids in place. "Now if you open your eyes, it shouldn't hurt, but I would suggest keeping them closed for at least a couple of days."

"Thank you." Her soft voice came out in a throaty whisper.

"You're welcome." He stared at her. How long before her body warmed enough to cause her excruciating pain? He had nothing he could give her to take it away, but sleep might help. Rising, he headed back to his counter.

"Where are you going?" Her panic in her voice stopped him cold.

"I'm just across the room. I'll make you warm tea to help your body heal though it may not be the most pleasant."

"Tea? I think a shot of whiskey would be more beneficial."

He quickly pulled out his small herb box. Mixing valerian with hops, he poured it into the pot of birch syrup water still simmering on the wood stove. Then he retrieved the cup and emptied the cooled water into the sink. "Alcohol will hurt you in your condition."

"It sounds like you know a lot—" she coughed.

He was beside her in an instant. "Don't." Laying his finger against her throat, he stroked it, ignoring the pleasant feel of her skin. "Coughing will hurt your heart."

She swallowed against his finger. "Got it." Her tongue came out again to lick her lips.

He tore his gaze away and pushed back the chair, uncomfortable with the desire pushing through him. He stepped to the stove and poured the liquid into his cup, small pieces of crushed herb floated within it.

As he returned to the chair, her lips lifted in a small smile. "I guess I'm lucky you found me. Do you have a name?"

"I have the tea, but don't lift your head. Allow me to do it for you." He tested the liquid with his finger. With his sensitivity to temperatures less than hers, he hoped he had it right.

"Okay, but when will I be able to move again?"

He lifted her head with his hand. "Tomorrow. Until then, you should try to sleep." He pressed the lip of the cup to her lips, and she didn't flinch, which was a good sign. Very slowly he tilted it. He pulled it back to allow her to swallow.

"That tastes weird. Is that herbal tea?"

He nodded before remembering she couldn't see him. "Yes. It will help you sleep so you can heal, but you need to finish it all."

She lifted her lip at that pronouncement, but as he tipped the cup again, she drank. When she'd finished it, he set it aside.

"Okay, I was a good girl and took all my medicine. Now can you tell me your name?"

He walked away and rinsed out the cup. Over his shoulder, he answered. "You need to sleep now.

"I'll sleep if you tell me your name."

He took a deep breath. "I don't have one."

Angela opened her mouth to argue, but she heard a door open and close. "Are you here?" Fear at being left alone and unable to move sliced through her. What if she could move and he had lied to her? What if he made it all up to keep her with him? What if he was a madman?

Then again, what if everything he said was true and she killed herself out of panic? According to him, she only had to wait a day. That wasn't too long. But if he told her she shouldn't move again tomorrow, then she'd ignore him and run like a crazy woman.

She took a deeper breath, but the urge to cough afterwards was strong, so she swallowed hard against the itch before taking rapid shallow breaths. Her body felt like lead and her thoughts grew hazy. What was it she wanted to know from him again?

The warm waters flowed by her. Now THIS was a hot spring. She could just make out the mineral deposits on the rock next to her. Her stay in Tuscany at the Terme Di Saturina spa was turning out to be perfect. All she needed was a dinner companion, preferably a handsome Italian, who wouldn't mind some company on a short-term basis. She definitely had the best job.

She stretched her legs out in front of her as she held on to the rock ledge behind her, the water pulling her forward, relaxing her body. It must be early morning because the fog obscured the multi-level pools. The smell of the hot springs was muted, perhaps due to the fog. It were as if she floated on a cloud.

Michael didn't know what he was missing. She'd invited her brother to come with her on this trip, but once again, he'd refused. If anyone needed a vacation, it was him. He just didn't get that there was more to life than his job. He'd only left Oakland three times since he'd taken the position as comptroller at Manderson Exports Inc. and all three times it was because she'd practically bribed him to come with her. He was far too ambitious, pushing off life until he had time.

She mentally patted herself on the back. She'd managed to land a job that allowed her to work and have amazing experiences at the same time, plus it had great benefits and literally months of vacation time. Her next vacation was all planned. A cruise around Alaska and then a trek across the arctic. Mikey may think she was an adventurer, but she never vacationed without a guide. She couldn't wait to be pulled across the snow by a team of sled dogs or to see her first polar bear from the safety of a snow caterpillar.

Bringing her legs beneath her, she pulled her arms off the ledge and let her hands fall into the water. Ow! Her right one started to burn. How could the water be too hot around her hand but fine around her bo— Ow. She lifted both hands above the water, but they continued to burn. She stood, but too late, her feet felt like they were on fire.

"Wake up. You shouldn't move."

The voice floated to her from somewhere else. It was low and scratchy and recognizable for some reason.

"Wake up, don't move."

She opened her eyes but all was black. "Oh God, I'm

blind." Tears formed, making her eyes sting. She swallowed against them.

"You aren't blind. I covered your eyes so they could heal from their sunburn. In a couple of days, you'll be able to see again." The man held her left wrist as he smoothed something over her hand.

Her memory returned. "That hurts."

His voice lowered. "I know. You have frostbite. Your hands are the worst, but your feet didn't completely escape damage."

She took shallow, rapid breaths against the pain, not wanting to cough again as her memory returned. "How long did I sleep?"

He set her hand down and covered it with a blanket of some sort.

Shoot, she wished she could see. "It must be bad because I feel like my hands and feet are burning."

He laid his large hand on her arm, more to soothe than restrain. "Half a day."

Despite her efforts to be brave, her eyes teared up, causing more pain. "It hurts so much." She could feel wetness against her cheek. If only she was at a hospital, and they could give her morphine or something. "Do you have any pain killers? I'd even take aspirin at this point."

"I don't have anything to take the pain away. Would you like more tea to help you sleep through it?"

She could feel the empathy in his voice. It was as if he hurt for her. Who was this man? And where was she? Maybe when she felt better she could tackle those questions. Right now, she just wanted relief from the pain. "P-please." She couldn't stop the choke in her words.

She heard him move away and tried to concentrate on the sounds he made instead of the pain she was in.

As if he guessed her thoughts, he spoke from across the room. "Think about icebergs and snow and a polar dive into the waters of the Arctic Ocean."

She forced herself to bring to mind her last cold trip. She'd taken a helicopter ride to a two thousand-foot mountain, Revaltoppe, in Greenland National Park. There had been only three of them, a fellow employee, herself, and the guide. She'd thought she'd dressed warm enough, but when they jumped down to the frozen ground and ran away from the beat of the helicopter blades, she'd felt no relief from the wind. Her face was frozen in seconds.

"Here." Her savior lifted her head and brought the cup to her lips.

The liquid wasn't hot, but warm, enabling her to drink it quickly. At his kindness for her, a complete stranger, she began to tear up again.

He let her head rest on the pillow before he laid his hand over her forehead. Did she have a fever? Would she die out here, wherever here was? She tried to remember why she had frostbite, but the burning in her extremities made it hard to concentrate. Or was it the tea?

How could she ever repay him? She had a nice nest egg saved up for when she retired and if it wasn't for him, she would never even make it to fifty-eight. Was Mikey at her apartment in San Francisco? Was he looking for…

CHAPTER TWO

He sensed the minute Angel gave in to sleep. The tension in her body, steeled for pain, eased. The stress of that pain would tax her heart. He was relieved she'd allowed him to make her more tea.

If he could, he'd take her pain on himself, but he couldn't understand what it felt like. He'd been burned the first time he encountered fire, having had no one to teach him that it could hurt, but as the decades had gone by, his sensitivity to temperatures and pain had been dulled.

He no longer feared what man or beast could do to him. The knowledge that his misery would continue into eternity, his just punishment for his early years, kept fear at bay…with one exception. But to feel pain as she did, her tears leaking past the scarf and wetting her cheeks, was beyond him. If only he could spare her that as well.

And her pain had just begun.

Since he'd treated someone for frostbite before, he was confident in his ministrations on that level, and on the progression her hands and feet would take, but the only hypothermia victims he'd come across were either dead, had soon died, or were air-lifted away. He had no idea what the procedures were once they were taken to a hospital.

For the first time since he'd met his closest neighbor, Timber, he wished for his company, if only to plot out Angel's care. Rising, he lifted the tin cup from the bed and walked across the cabin to set it in the sink. He returned to her and gently removed the flannel wrapped rocks from around her body, their temperature no longer warmer than her. Turning next to the wood stove, he added the last of the split logs to it.

He needed to bring more wood inside and he preferred to do so while she slept, so he shucked off his shirt and folded it neatly before returning it to the chest. Grabbing up his axe, he strode outside and around the corner of the cabin to where his wood was stacked. The ledge his cabin was built on was large with a sloping decline on one side, an incline on the opposite northside and even ground directly across from the cabin.

He didn't need as much firewood as men did for staying warm, but with Angel requiring greater heat, he would have to fell a few more trees before winter set in. The logs he had stacked were too large for the wood stove, so he set one on the stump he used and swung the axe.

Lifting one half of the log onto the stump, he swung the axe down again and split it in half. He continued to split logs into quarters, the physical activity easing some of his anxiety over his guest.

While he'd help people in the wild, he'd never taken care of anyone for more than a day before. He'd owned a dog once, but it hurt too much when it died. Everyone and everything died…except him.

Loading the split wood into his wood box, he carried it into the cabin. As he entered, he was careful to be quiet. He'd rather Angel slept. He hated that she was in pain and there was nothing he could do to help.

That she had pain was a good sign. It meant she was healing, but the process would be agonizing.

Her hands were far worse than her feet. He had no doubt that blisters would occur. She must not have had insulated gloves, but her boots had been good until she'd taken them off.

He'd gathered all her belongings while she'd slept earlier and laid them across his table to dry. It was a strange phenomenon of hypothermia that people disrobed. She must not have disrobed much before he found her. For that he was thankful.

Quietly, he stacked the wood and checked the fire before sitting in the chair by his bed. Angel was so fair, her skin, her hair. It made him anxious to see her eyes. He'd never seen the eyes of his mate, but she had been dark, her hair the black of night, her skin in the tallow candles appeared dusky.

His mind drifted back to that night almost three hundred years ago, while his creator yet lived, his memory sharp with every detail. He'd stood at the window watching Dr. Victor Frankenstein work, gazing at the creature that would be his mate. He'd promised to quit the company of man and leave Victor in peace in return for being given a female creature like himself. All he wanted was another like him. Man had woman and every beast had its mate, but he had nothing. He needed a mate.

It was not much to ask. Victor had abandoned him when he'd taken his first breath. The man owed him. Progress had been slow on the cold rock in the Sea of the Hebrides, Victor vacillating between walks along the windy beach and work in his small croft. The doctor seemed to prolong the process.

One night he looked in the window and knew she was almost complete. He'd smiled at her from outside, his joy building. He was anxious to have someone to share his life with, to end his miserable lonely existence. But Victor had seen him, and for no apparent reason destroyed her before his very eyes, ripping her apart like the monster Victor claimed him to be.

He closed his eyes at the remembered pain, the wail of anguish, and the terrible deeds he'd gone on to commit for the sake of revenge. Opening his eyes, he gazed down at Angel. Could she be his salvation?

Angela woke to pain. At first it was so intense, she wasn't even sure where it emanated from. Slowly, she was able to distinguish that it came from her hands and feet. Opening her eyes didn't help. It was pitch black.

She took a deep breath before remembering she shouldn't, just before she coughed.

"You're awake." The deep, scratchy voice was strangely reassuring.

"It hurts." She sounded like a five-year-old who wanted a band aid instead of the thirty-year-old she was. "The pain."

"I know. It's part of the healing process. It means you'll live."

Her breath caught at his statement. She would live? The relief in his voice made it clear he had doubted that she would. She released her breath and determined to find her backbone.

She was in the middle of nowhere with a man who said he'd lived most his life in cold climates. She'd been lucky. What if he hadn't found her. Despite the pain, her head had cleared considerably since she'd last woke up. "How long was I asleep this time?"

"Half a day." From his voice, she could tell he'd moved closer.

"Can I move now?"

She felt him lift the blanket and pull her arm by the wrist before replacing the covers and setting her arm down. "Yes, you may move, but start with small movements and avoid—"

She tried to curl her fingers to ease the pain, but it made it worse. "Ow! Shoot that hurts."

"As I tried to tell you. Don't move your hands. Your frostbite is serious."

She heard his words, but her brain was still dealing with the stinging that seemed to radiate from her fingers to her shoulder. "How long?" She took shallow breaths as the extra spike in pain subsided, and her hands simply throbbed.

"They will hurt for days and then they will blister, which will cause a different kind of discomfort."

"You're just full of good news, aren't you?" Her sarcasm didn't make her feel any better and when he didn't reply, she felt guilty. "I'm sorry. I know you're trying to help and I *am* grateful."

He still didn't say anything, but she heard him walk across the cabin. He had to be a big man. Based on his voice, she would guess he was in his fifties with a big bushy white and black beard. His steps were hard but confident, like a man who'd seen a lot in his years, but they were heavy as if he had a significant paunch. From what she'd read about the northern areas, people were perfectly happy with carrying a bit of weight into the winter.

When he strode back toward her, she gave him a sightless smile, hoping he'd forgive her short temper. She was usually easy-going, but her hands were agony. She hadn't even tried to remove the other from beneath the blanket. She barely felt the sting in her feet compared to her hands.

"Are you hungry?" His voice came with the scent of food.

She took a deeper breath, but not too deep. She wasn't sure what it was, but her stomach immediately told her the answer to his question. "I am. What do you have there. It smells good."

"It's chicken soup." From the sound of his voice, he'd sat down as he said it.

Chicken? She would have expected venison stew or fish soup. Did he have chickens? She listened for a moment but didn't hear anything. "You made me chicken soup?"

From the way his breathing rippled after her question, she guessed that he chuckled silently. "Yes, I opened a can and heated it on the wood stove. I can't take credit or blame for its taste, but it seemed appropriate for the occasion."

She smiled before grimacing as she accidently moved her hand and caused the stinging to spike again. Sucking in air through her teeth, she held herself completely still, waiting for the pain to go back to its normally high level of intensity.

"Would you like me to put your hand beneath the quilt again?" His concerned voice gave her something else to focus on.

"No. Call me a coward, but the idea of having it moved scares the crap out of me right now."

"That's understandable, but I wouldn't call yourself a

coward. The fact that you're still alive is proof that you have an inordinately strong will to live."

"I don't know about that, but I do like to get the most out of life. It's so short, you know? I want to experience so much." Talking to him helped her ignore the worst of the pain. "You still haven't told me your name. I can't believe you don't have one. Everyone has a name. Some of us are happier with what our parents picked out than others." She gave him a smirk. He probably didn't like his name.

"I thought you wanted chicken soup, but if you prefer, we can talk instead."

Her stomach tightened at his words, reminding her she was hungry. "No, no. Please. Food first." She couldn't see him, but she imagined him smiling at her and feeling pretty proud of himself for bringing her back on track. But he didn't know her. If he thought she'd forget what she'd been asking, he was in for a surprise.

"I think it best that you sip at the soup like you sipped the tea, so I will hold your head up."

She smirked. "I hope it's not too heavy for you. I do have a big head." At least her brother was always telling her she thought too much of herself.

"Your head is perfect and very light." He didn't give her time to reply to his compliment before he lifted her head and placed the cup at her lips. As with the tea, he judged how quickly she could sip and swallow and did an excellent job.

When he lowered her head, she'd finished all of it. "I know it was canned, but it tasted wonderful. Was that all of it?"

"No, there is more, but your body is just starting to

function again. I don't think you should eat any more right now." He paused as he wiped her face with a wet cloth. "Do you know how long you were out in the cold?"

Did she? "I'm not sure. What's today's date?"

"Today is September twenty-seventh."

"What? That can't be right? Are you sure?"

He didn't answer her immediately, which convinced her he was right.

"I am correct."

At his words, she groaned. "The ship left Seattle on September twentieth. We were only three days north when I took the helicopter to the glacier. It was not the experience I expected. There were at least a hundred people there with helicopters coming and going. I walked away from it, certain I would hear the helicopters and easily find my way back."

"But the snow carried the sound and it rebounded between the mountains."

At his words, she sighed. "Yes."

"You lasted four days." The surprise in his voice was evident. "Did you have food and water with you?"

She thought back on her trek. When she'd first regained consciousness, she'd avoided doing so, not sure she could face it. Apparently, it was time. "I left on the excursion with my pockets pretty full of snacks because I planned to take another tour when I got back to Wevok. I'm what's called a grazer. I eat a little all day. I was on an ecological adventure tour of the arctic region. The ship was nice and even boasted a hot tub, but the itinerary focused on nature. That's why I didn't expect so many people."

"It was the last week of the season before tourism shuts

down for the winter. If your ship had waited another week to start the trip, you would have been alone."

And then someone would have noticed she was missing, but her tour wasn't like that and with all the people, no one would miss her until the four weeks ended and she didn't return to work…unless— "Do you have a phone or radio or some way to communicate with the nearest town?"

"I don't. I have no need to." He walked away from her.

She could hear him cleaning the cup she used. Did he have running water? Did that mean there was electricity? "What is the name of the closest town to here?"

He finished washing her cup and probably something else by the sound of it. When he was done, his footsteps drew closer. "There is no town. We have Savik, which is an outpost. The closest 'town' is Tavva, but that is on the other side of the Noatak River. I've never been there."

Her heart sank. It sounded like the nearest town was too far. She'd have to figure out something else, but the pain in her hands was taking all her concentration and her patience. "I want to sleep now but my hands are throbbing. Do you have any more of that tea?"

He laid his hand on her forehead again.

"Do I have a fever?"

"Yes, but it's not high. I have the tea heating now. Is there anything I can do for you in the meantime?"

Yes, take away this awful pain. She wanted to scream it at him, but the fact she was even alive to endure it was thanks to him. "Yes, talk to me until the tea is ready. It helps take my focus from how much it hurts. Tell me about you. How long have you lived here?"

"Nine years."

She waited for him to say more, but he remained silent. Maybe living alone, or as alone as he lived, did that to a person. "And where did you live before that?"

"I lived in the Queen Elizabeth Islands of Canada."

"Are you Canadian?"

"No."

Okay, this was just frustrating. She needed to come up with a better question, but half her brain was still on her hands. "Tell me about this cabin. I can't see it. What does it look like?"

"It's one room. The wood stove is in the opposite corner from this bed. Next to it are the cabinets and a cold box for items needing to stay cool, but that I want easy access to." His voice sounded like he was looking in the direction of the area he spoke about.

"My bed, where you are, is in the northeast corner. The wall behind your head backs up to the mountain and my chest of clothes is at the foot. The table I eat at is in the middle of the cabin against a supporting post. Cattycorner to this bed is where I store my tools. Opposite the foot of the bed is a couch along the west wall and between it and the bed are the bookcases I made."

She envisioned each area and filled in her own décor. She pictured the couch with deep red cushions, the chest as an antique, and the bookcases filled with trophies from his hunts. It would be a very manly abode.

His bed was comfortable as far as she could tell, but she hadn't moved beyond lying on her back and she didn't plan to. The pain in her—No, she wouldn't think about that. "If I'm in your bed, where are you sleeping?"

The chair near the bed that he often sat on scraped back. "On the couch." His footsteps moved to the other side of the cabin.

This mountain man, deep in the wilderness of Alaska had saved her life and continued to care for her, but wouldn't tell her his name. Was he a criminal? If he was, she couldn't understand why he would save her. Even after she woke, he'd been nothing but kind.

Maybe he was just odd, like a hermit. Though, he didn't seem strange, except for not having a name. His voice sounded cultured despite his rough surroundings. Maybe a discussion on Shakespeare would be a good test, though she might embarrass him or herself. She wasn't exactly an expert in that area.

Metal scraped against a hard surface. Ah, the stove top… the wood stove top. That probably meant no electricity. She was getting good at this detective work.

He poured the tea into the cup. She could hear the liquid as it hit the tin at the bottom, and the scent that wafted over to her made it clear her tea was ready. The thought of sleep and relief from the constant pain in her hands made her anxious. "I'm beginning to love that smell."

His footsteps travel across the floor, purposeful and long. Either the cabin was small or he was tall. She would guess tall simply based on the deepness of his voice, though one had nothing to do with the other. She couldn't wait to see what he really looked like and how close her guess was to being correct.

He sat down on the chair, its creaking making that clear even before he spoke. "Sleep will help you heal as well as take you away from the pain." He lifted her head and held the cup to her lips.

For the first time since waking, she took control of how much she drank and when, pulling back after a sip at the heat. "It needs to cool a little."

He lowered her head and sat back, the creaking of the chair letting her know.

She was disappointed she couldn't swallow down the whole cup immediately because her mind immediately focused on her burning hands. She forced herself to find a question to ask. "Do you have any children?"

"No."

Shoot, he was back to one-word answers. "I'm not trying to pry. I just need to think about something besides the pain. Can you tell me where you were born, where you lived before here?"

At first, he didn't answer. Was he ashamed of where he came from or was he hiding something?

"My first home was Germany, but I moved to Geneva, Switzerland. I lived in Austria, Holland, England, Scotland, and France before returning to Geneva. I then began my journey north to Greenland and various places across the Arctic Circle. I lived near the north pole before heading south to Ellesmere Island, Inuvik and finally here."

His answer left her speechless. She couldn't reconcile the raspy-voiced Alaskan man with someone who'd traveled and lived so extensively.

He took advantage of her momentary loss for words to lift her head again and entice her to drink.

She was quite happy to. The sweet liquid was cool enough to drink comfortably and it both tasted and smelled good to her. Almost as if conditioned to it, her body started to relax.

She pulled her mouth away, and he lowered her head for her. She wasn't sure she'd be able to lift it on her own. It wasn't as if she'd had much to eat in days. She hadn't even had to use a bathroom since she woke up. Was that yesterday? She paused at that thought. Her caregiver didn't say anything about there being a bathroom.

"You need to finish this if you want to sleep soundly." His voice, so close, redirected her thoughts.

Now she understood why he sounded cultured. If she could get him to talk more, there was a lot he could tell her.

He lifted her head again, and she obediently drank, the pain in her hands already fading as her body relaxed. If she could just get her mind to stop spinning over what he'd just revealed.

She finished the last of the tea, and he lowered her head to the pillow. He was so gentle, yet she was sure he was a big man. Just the size of his hand under her head told her that. She needed to give him a name. She couldn't keep thinking of him as simply a mountain man.

The question was what type of name? Should she pull one from Germany where he was born or should she come up with something more American? Or maybe she could make up a name or...

"It's time to go home, Angie."

"But I don't want to go. Our vacation just started. I haven't seen anything yet."

"I know, but mama is very sick. She needs a doctor."

"A doctor?" Her stomach tightened. "Will he make her better?"

Her father looked away. "I want that with all my heart." He turned back to her. "Don't forget your shovel and pail." His eyes glistened with unshed tears.

That frightened her. She grasped his hand. "It's okay Papa. I'll leave them for Cindy. She doesn't have as many toys as we do."

Her father didn't say anything, but he held her hand tight as they walked off the beach toward the car. When they came to the parking lot, he didn't have her wash her feet by the spigot like he usually did. Instead, he opened the back door for her to climb in without telling her to buckle her seatbelt or to keep her hands inside.

She looked at her younger brother, but he was busy sucking his thumb and clutching his stuffed dog. Her mom didn't say anything either. She always asked about her day.

When her father got in, he didn't say a word. He didn't even look at mama. Were they mad at each other?

When they arrived home, her Aunt Ginny was waiting for them.

Panic set in. "I want to go to the doctors, too. Don't make me stay home, Papa."

"You go inside with your Aunt now, Angie."

"But I want to go to the doctors." She covered the seatbelt buckle with her hand so he couldn't unbuckle her.

Aunt Ginny came to the car and took Mikey out of his car seat.

Her father crouched down. "Angie, I need you to be a big girl now for your brother. You need to help Aunt Ginny, so I can bring Mama to the doctor."

"No, I need to help Mama, too."

Her father's eyes were so sad, she started to cry.

He stood and bent over her, easily unbuckling the belt.

She yelled. "I want to go to the doctors! Take me to the doctors!"

Her father pulled her from the car. "Stop it. Your Mama doesn't need to hear this. Think about someone besides yourself."

His harsh tone stunned her, even as he pulled her toward the house and forced her inside. Then he strode down the walkway to the curb and opened the car door. He didn't look up before getting in. Within seconds the car was driving away.

She ran out the door after them. "I want to go to the doctors! I want to go—"

"Shhhh. You will get well. I promise."

The deep, scratchy voice pulled her away. She blinked her eyelids open but it was still dark. As the dream faded, her memory returned. She had snow blindness and the comforting voice and arms around her were the mountain man.

Somewhere in her foggy brain, she questioned her position, her head on what she believed to be his biceps and his body against her side, but since he was on top of the quilt, she relaxed into the solace he offered instead.

She hadn't dreamed of the day her mother went into hospice since she'd become an adult. It was weird that it would suddenly reoccur. Maybe it was fear over her own condition that had it resurfacing. Being held certainly helped the dream dissipate. It would have been pleasant if her hands hadn't started to throb.

"Do you believe me?" There was a vulnerability in his need to have her trust him that tugged at her heart.

"I do believe I'll heal under your care. It was just a dream from when I was a child. Probably because my hands hurt so much."

Was it her imagination, or did his biceps relax beneath her head?

"I'm relieved to know you were dreaming. Worrying about your condition will slow the healing process."

With statements like that one, he sounded so old, as if he'd had too much experience with people being sick or in pain. It was a sad thought, and she brushed it away.

"I will let you return to your sleep."

"No." She said the word too loud and too quick, betraying her residual fear. "I mean, could you stay a few more minutes. In the middle of this cold wilderness with no sight, it makes me feel better to know there's someone else out here."

"Of course." He seemed pleased by her request. "I have lived alone for so long that I sometimes forget man is by nature a social being."

He spoke of man as if he was something else. How odd. "Why have you lived alone?"

She could picture his shoulders slumping as he sighed, though she didn't actually feel any movement on his part.

"I have found it better that I do so."

"What about brothers and sisters? Do you have any?" Before he even spoke, she sensed sorrow, maybe in the way he shifted. Were her other senses really honing in on such subtleties?

"I have no family." The words were said carefully, as if he wished to hide his own emotional pain.

For the first time since she'd regained consciousness, she was thankful she couldn't see. She was learning so much more about her caretaker than she would have if she was distracted by her sight. She was absolutely sure of that. "Have they all passed?"

"You should rest now." Before she could react, he slipped his large arm out from beneath her head and lowered her back to the pillow.

"Why? Is it night time?" She hoped the answer was no because she wanted to learn more about him. It was better than focusing on her own predicament.

"The more rest you have, the faster you'll heal, and yes, it's night. It will be four more hours before daylight."

Shoot. There was no way she could keep him talking. The poor man had been taking care of her twenty-four seven and he was sleeping on what must be a short, uncomfortable couch instead of in his own bed. Still, she had one more request. "Could I have some water before you go back to sleep?"

"Yes." He moved away from the bed.

She listened to the noise made by the water pouring into the tin cup and then his footsteps returning to her. Within seconds, he had lifted her head and helped her drink. "Thank you."

He moved away again. "Good night."

She listened as he cleaned the cup before he walked to the couch. The frame of the furniture creaked as he settled on it. She readjusted her image of him now that she'd felt his large arm and hard chest against her shoulder. Despite his age, he had to be very strong, probably from cutting down trees and lugging his kill back for food.

That brought to mind a much younger man, but his voice, experience and the many places he'd lived still placed him in her mind at about sixty years of age. The idea of finally seeing him, maybe as early as tomorrow, made it hard to fall back to sleep. But somewhere between imagining what he looked like and wondering about his past, she did.

He waited until Angel's breathing turned regular then he quietly donned his boots and slipped outside. The moon was almost full and the snow on the surrounding mountains glistened in the bright light. How many times had he escaped into the wilderness to bury his pain?

The urge to run through the forests, over the mountains and across vast tundra rose within him, almost choking out all reason.

Not this time. He couldn't leave the woman inside or she'd die. He'd sworn over three hundred years ago that no one else would ever die because of his actions. The lives he saved could never atone for the ones he'd taken, but he was determined never to add to that number, no matter the circumstance.

It was her need to talk. Without awareness, she dug at age old wounds, something the men of the arctic didn't do. Everyone was here for a reason. Here, being alone, was accepted and respected. Angel, though, didn't live here, and as therefore, sought conversation.

He understood her need to escape the pain, but he needed to redirect her and keep her from learning too much. He didn't want to arouse her curiosity because he didn't wish to lie to her. She stirred feelings in him he'd never had.

At first, he thought she cried for a doctor because he'd hurt her when he changed the padding beneath her. That she had urinated in her sleep had pleased him greatly, and the plastic and towels he'd set under her the first time she fell asleep after drinking tea had worked well. He hadn't thought he moved her too much, but when she cried out, he'd grown anxious. It was a relief she'd only been dreaming.

Looking back at the cabin then up at the sky, he calculated the time until dawn. He could take a short run to assuage his restlessness and still have time to work on the chair he planned to make her.

Turning south, he took off at a quick jog, jumping over logs and scaling rocky hills before he came upon Two Beaver stream. Jumping across in three lunges, he continued his run. Night was the only time he dared make a naked run, the bracing cold the only thing that made him feel alive, almost human.

After Victor had died on the ship of the explorer, he thought his life over. He had no purpose and expected to die. The revenge he'd sought had rebounded back upon himself, first when Victor died and left him with no focus and completely alone, then when he'd discovered he could not die himself.

He scaled a black spruce tree, hoisting himself up between the branches until he reached the thinner top. The trunk swayed under his weight, but he ignored his precarious position to enjoy the view. The moon's white light made deep shadows among the under growth, but the snow reflected it, making the entire landscape appear black and white.

Looking back the way he'd come, he found his mountain. A quarter way up was his cabin, which was cast in shadow by the moon's location behind the towering peaks. From here, there was no way for man or beast to know an angel slept there.

He'd learned so much in his extended existence. He'd finally discovered how to hide his scars and yellowed gaze, both having faded with the passing years. After numerous attempts to end his life, to no avail, he'd come to know how to live with minimal discomforts.

Most of all, thanks to an Inuit elder, he'd finally understood right from wrong as it applied to man and beast. Unfortunately, that had shed a clearer light on his own depraved soul…if he had one. Akiakook was convinced he had one because of his feelings of guilt, but sometimes he wasn't so sure.

A wolf crossed a small clearing not far away, its coat appearing black against the moonlit snow. It was joined by two more. He couldn't tell if it was the same pack that occasionally visited him when he had marten skins drying. Night was the wolves' prime hunting time.

He didn't mind sharing his space with the wolves or bears or eagles. He preferred their company to man's. Still, there were a few men he'd met that had shown him not all were as self-involved as Victor.

A dull ache lodged in his gut, so old now it was like an old friend. He'd asked only one thing of his creator. Though he'd wanted a father and all that relationship entailed, he'd only asked for one thing. The denial, though over a century old, still hurt—more penance for his wrongdoings.

The alpha wolf sniffed the air before trotting off to the west. The other two followed. He lifted his own nose to the air and inhaled the crisp spruce scent deep into his lungs and dared to dream. What if Angel was his salvation and reward? Would she be willing to stay or would she want to return to civilization? She was a tourist who'd lost her way, but he believed he was meant to find her.

Despite his habit of suffocating any hope, the tiny flame Angel ignited refused to be extinguished. But a memory of that feeling came sharp and angry to blur his vision. He'd felt the same when Victor promised to create a mate for him only to destroy her.

He was a fool if he thought Angel would do anything but

leave once she'd healed. There could be no salvation for the cursed creature he was.

Angrily, he climbed down the tree, ignoring the scrapes and stabs of the branches and needles. The stings were fleeting since any evidence of damage disappeared almost immediately from his skin. Jumping the last twelve feet to the ground, he headed for home. Despite the hopelessness of his life, Angel had the rest of hers before her, and it was his responsibility to insure she lived to enjoy it.

Once again, he crossed Two Beavers stream and loped across the snow laden boulders and through the not-yet coated forest until he reached his mountain. He paused and looked opposite to the place he'd found Angel. Even in the setting moonlight, he could see his tracks up to the spot. He wouldn't rest easy until the next snowfall.

Winter was fast approaching, so his wait shouldn't be long. He had prepared well for his solitary existence, but if Angel remained throughout the winter, they would need more food.

A strange peace settled in his chest at the thought of caring for her over a long period of time, and his confidence grew. He may not be worthy of her, but he could take care of her until she was able to return to her family. *That* he could do well.

Striding up the slope toward the large shelf where his cabin sat, a new purpose formed. He hadn't had a purpose beyond existing in decades, and it felt good. So good, it brought with it an equal measure of guilt, but for once, he ignored that.

Arriving at the front of the cabin, he unlaced his boots and left them on the steps. He walked barefoot across the snow around to the south side of his home where a set of pipes directed the mountain run-off toward his sink inside, to a barrel high above him, and to a spout that dropped the water down the mountainside to resume its regular course to a small stream that ran along the base. He pulled a rope to open a door in the barrel and freezing water rushed over him.

Letting the door close, he pulled the soap he'd made from the outside shelf and quickly washed. The cold always invigorated him, lightening his mood. After rinsing off in the frigid shower from his barrel, he shook himself of excess water and walked back to the front porch where he grabbed up his boots and quietly entered the cabin.

The warmth hit him and he ignored the towel he kept by the door to stand next to the wood stove to dry, adding more wood to insure Angel didn't grow cold. He stilled. She'd also ask to urinate soon. She'd had enough to drink that she would need to. He usually went outside, but she couldn't. He needed to prepare the chair he had in mind.

Anxious to fulfill her needs, he lit his main lantern, pushed open the door that covered his storage area, and entered the cave.

He stood staring at the piles of supplies and odds and ends he'd accumulated since arriving in northern Alaska. He'd studied much on female anatomy and understood how everything worked, but creating something Angel could use could be a challenge.

His gaze fell on the refrigerator he used to bathe in during the coldest part of the winter. That would work for Angel. He picked it up and set it next to the pantry door, but didn't open it. It would make too much noise, and he wanted Angel to stay asleep until he solved the issue of a toilet.

As quietly as he could, he moved aside extra boards, baskets of potatoes, a crate of onions and a barrel of smoked salmon. Buried behind those items was an old chair with a woven seat. He'd taken it in trade from Timber when the mountain man had run out of fish last winter and had a "powerful craving" as he put it.

Pulling the chair out, he examined it. Three-quarters of the weave had come away from the seat frame, which he'd planned to take off anyway. Gripping the decaying material, he ripped it from the chair. It would need some modification, but he could get it done before sunrise and hopefully before Angel woke.

CHAPTER THREE

The scent of some kind of fish with unusual spices woke her from her dreams. She opened her eyes before remembering that wouldn't help her identify the mouth-watering smell. Was it dinner time? Her stomach certainly thought so.

It was so hard to determine the time of day when she couldn't see. She had a whole new appreciation for those who were blind. At least she would have her sight back soon, or so her caretaker said. Was it today or tomorrow she could find out?

She didn't hear any sounds beyond the occasional pop from the fire in the wood stove. Had he eaten and left? She swallowed the panic that rose at the thought of being helpless and alone. She wasn't helpless exactly. She could probably sit up and find her way across the cabin if she had to.

She should test her theory. She pushed on her hands to leverage herself up, but a burning pain traveled straight up her arms and to her heart, causing her to catch her breath and let out a startled yell. Tears filled her eyes as she took shallow breaths to avoid intensifying the throbbing running through her.

Her helplessness coupled with her total dependence on a stranger threatened to overwhelm her.

The door opened, bringing with it a wave of fresh cold air and the distinctive scent of spruce she associated with her mountain man. It calmed her panic.

"You're awake." His distinctive voice further assured her.

Though she'd like to smile in gratefulness that he had returned, her pain made it impossible. "I am."

He strode directly to her. "You've been crying. Why?" His voice sounded so concerned, she needed to reassure him.

She opened her mouth to answer, but his finger gently wiped the tear track from one cheek. It amazed her how such a big man could be so gentle. He was an odd mix of cultured and roughness. "I tried to use my hands. I know, stupid, but I woke up and forgot about them."

"What did you need to use them for? I can help you."

Again, her heart softened at his kindness. "I was going to try to sit up, just to see if I could." It had been nothing more than panic, but she didn't want him to know that. She prided herself on her adventuresome spirit and she'd completely lost it. It was embarrassing. "What smells so good?"

He was silent for a moment as if he read her mind and knew why she'd changed the subject. "It's yugyak or arctic char, as you may have heard of it. I made it for breakfast. Would you like to try it?"

At his offer, her stomach tightened with hunger. "I've never had it, but I would love some."

Instead of responding, he moved off to the opposite side of the room. As she listened, she could picture everything he did. She'd always heard that when one sense was closed off, the others were heightened. Still, she was anxious to see again. "How many days has it been? I've lost track. I thought it was dinner time since I can't tell if it's light or dark."

"You have been conscious for two days." He came closer and sat on the chair next to her.

The fish smelled even better up close. "Do you think I could sit up to eat?"

He set the plate down somewhere nearby. An end table maybe? He stood and from the sound of his footsteps, he'd walked past the foot of the bed toward where he said the couch was located.

She could picture him picking up extra pillows or folding a blanket so she could sit. Who was this man who cared so much to see her well, yet was so alone in the world? She definitely wanted to know more. "You said you've lived in many countries. What did you do for work? I know in the arctic surviving is your day job, but what about when you were in Geneva?"

If she had had her sight, she was sure she would have missed the hesitation in his step as he approached.

"I think you should focus on sustenance right now and talking later." His voice held a sterner tone than usual. Maybe there was something in his past he wasn't proud of.

Before her vacation began, she'd read that while some people liked the challenge of being self-sufficient and getting down to the basics of life, others came to Alaska to escape their past and still others fled the restrictions of civilization. Was he escaping? And if she pried, would he ever let her leave?

For the second time since she woke, she felt uneasy, but it wasn't something he'd said, just her own thoughts going around in circles. If he wasn't so closed-mouthed, she would have a lot fewer guesses. Then again, how many mountain men were talkative?

He carefully lifted her shoulders before he arranged something soft yet sturdy behind her. When he let her lean back, she was sitting up.

That small change in position had her excited to be alive all over again. "This is perfect. Thank you."

"You're welcome." At his lack of movement, she imagined him blushing beneath a scraggly salt and pepper beard.

She lifted her hand as if she could take the plate of food and immediately moaned as the burning started all over again. "Shoot, that hurts."

He picked up the plate and sat in the chair. "It's best that you don't move your hands and feet. That will only cause you pain."

"You think?" She immediately regretted her sarcasm. "I'm sorry. The pain makes me irritable."

"Then maybe food will make you less so."

She nodded. Anything to take her mind off her hands.

"Open your mouth."

At his command, she did, and he placed a small piece of warm fish on her tongue. She closed her lips around the fork and enjoyed the flavor for a moment. It tasted sweet with a significant rosemary and lemon sauce. As she moved it with her tongue, it flaked apart, its texture pure heaven after only having tea and soup. "Hmmm." She savored every last flake before opening her mouth.

No sooner had she done so then he deposited more fish into her mouth. She'd never had char, but right now it was her new favorite food.

"I'm pleased you like it."

She remained silent, too focused on the fish and her belly to bother talking.

"Last piece."

His pronouncement had her stifling a grown even as she pulled the fish from the fork. It didn't seem like much. Maybe seven bites at most. She lost count, enjoying the flavor too much. "Do you have any more?"

He stroked a wet cloth over her face. "I do, but your body has just started to process food again. You don't want to overwhelm it and become sick."

He was probably right, but she still didn't like it. "Are you sure you were never a doctor?"

"I would never be a doctor." His voice dripped with disgust.

Had he lost someone he loved in surgery? That would definitely account for his barely disguised hatred. "I'm not particularly fond of them either. They make it seem as if they can fix you and then they don't." Like her mother, who was supposed to be "all right," and she wasn't supposed to "worry." She never had time to worry or treasure her moments with her mother because they never told her that her mama was terminally ill.

"I don't know if I can make you well again, but I promise you I will do everything I can to make it so."

His earnestness pulled her thoughts back to the present. "I know I have no choice but to trust you, but I do. I wouldn't even be talking right now if it wasn't for you."

Her caretaker stepped away and moved back to the sink. As the sound of running water broke the silence, her bladder woke up. Oh no! This would be completely embarrassing. She couldn't use her hands at all, so how could she get to the bathroom?

Shoot, he didn't say there was a bathroom in the cabin. He must have one somewhere. Was it an outhouse? She groaned aloud at the thought of walking outside.

He strode across the room so fast his voice surprised her. "What's wrong?"

She turned her head toward his voice. "I need to use a bathroom."

"I don't have one, but I did create something for you."

She was still trying to wrap her mind around the fact he didn't have a bathroom when she heard him set something heavy down next to the bed. "What is it?"

"It's a chair with an opening in the seat and a bucket beneath it, so I don't have to take you outside in the cold." His voice had just a hint of triumph in it.

A chair with a bucket. This is what she'd come to. If she wasn't so embarrassed, she could appreciate his ingenuity and thoughtfulness, but she couldn't imagine how this would work. She was dependent on him for literally everything. "But I can't put weight on my hands." Now she was whining, which was very ungrateful, but the whole situation was upsetting and awkward.

"I will set you on the chair."

There was no way he could pick her up like that. She'd just have to accept that her hands would be in excruciating pain, but what choice did she have?

The weight of the quilt went away as he removed it. Then something else she had on that was very warm. If only she could feel what it was with her hands, but from the way he moved her arms, she'd say it was a coat of some kind. Though he'd been careful not to touch her hands, the burning started simply from the movement.

She could feel she had clothes on, but she wasn't sure what she wore. She couldn't even remember what she wore the day she'd become lost besides the coat and boots.

"Can you bend your knees?"

Good question. She moved her legs slightly, but her feet reminded her they were also frostbitten and she gritted her teeth to keep from crying out.

"I have you." He burrowed his large arm under her knees and placed another one behind her back.

She started to lift her arms to grasp his neck when the burning stopped her. "I can't help." Tears of pain and inadequacy started.

"I don't need you to help. Let me do everything." He was as good as his word, lifting her as if she wasn't five foot-eleven and over a hundred and fifty pounds of dead weight. The man was seriously strong. As he lifted her, she felt cool air on her butt. Had she had an accident?

He set her down on the chair which was surprisingly not as hard as she suspected. It had arms where she could brace herself with her forearms. The burning in her hands was intense and her feet where they rested on the floor vied for her attention, but luckily her bladder was far more persistent.

She could do this. She said she wanted to experience life and this was part of it. Time to stop acting like a baby. "Do you have toilet paper?"

"I do." He brushed it across her forearm. "I'm setting it here on the bed."

They both knew she probably wouldn't be able to pick it up. Despite her mortification, she tackled her next problem. "It feels like I have leggings on. Do you have a knife?"

"I do."

He walked away, and she tossed away one idea after another. It was either her pride or her hands. She should have asked him sooner if she could remove the scarf and whatever he'd put over her eyes.

He stopped in front of her. "What would you like me to cut?"

She thought she could do it, have him slit her crotch, but she couldn't. She just wasn't that brave. She took a deep breath. "Can you put it in my hand?"

She sensed him pull back, or was it the floor that told her he'd shifted his weight? "What are you going to do? I will not let you harm yourself."

"Oh, don't worry about that. Believe me, I have no death wish. I'll be eternally grateful that you found me when you did and that you're taking such wonderful care of me."

He didn't put the knife in her hand, though she wasn't sure how she would grasp it with the bandages around it. "Can I have the knife?"

"I understand. Sometimes out here, we have to do things we never would in civilization, but the laws for survival here are different."

She could debate that to a point, but her bladder was quickly taking over all—

"I cut your leggings when you were asleep, so you wouldn't soil them, but left most of them on for warmth."

"How could you?" As he stepped back, she squeezed her legs together.

"It needed to be done. I will go outside now. Call me when you need to return to my bed."

Mortified, she felt her cheeks heat as she listened to the sound of the door to the cabin closing. Unless he just pretended to leave. She didn't move, waiting to hear a creak as he shifted his weight, but there was none.

He was an older man who'd probably seen his fair share of women's bodies. She just hoped he didn't get any ideas. Still, she waited, but she couldn't feel him in the room. No breathing or spruce scent wafted toward her.

Her bladder finally decided it didn't care, and she gave in, much to her relief.

He watched Angel sleep after he'd finally convinced her to drink more tea. When she'd called him to help her return to his bed, she'd been crying. He had no doubt some of it was due to the pain in her hands as she'd used the toilet paper she'd requested, but he sensed a self-loathing, an emotion he was overly familiar with. However, in her case, he doubted it went deeper than her own feelings of helplessness.

He would have to remind her she was lucky to be alive and her healing would take time. The skin affected by the frostbite on her hands could take months to return to normal. He wouldn't tell her that until she regained her strength. One hurdle at a time.

Tonight, he would suggest taking off the scarf. With only the lantern to light the cabin, it should allow her eyes to adjust easier. At the thought of how happy that might make her, his spirits rose.

He scanned the cabin. Everything was in its place and ready for her gaze. Even the blankets he used on the couch were folded and put away in his storage room. The only thing that needed to be set to rights was himself.

He quietly moved to the foot of the bed and opened his chest. Pulling out the linen shirt, he donned it. He would need to wear it or the wool one at all times while she remained with him, unless he went out for a midnight run. It was a sacrifice worth making.

In the back of his mind, he couldn't help hoping that by saving Angel, he somehow made up for the death of Elizabeth, Victor's wife. She too had been an angel, but he'd been too blinded by his own pain and thirst for revenge upon his creator to notice or care. Her horror at his appearance had sealed her fate in his infantile mind.

Before he'd completed his second year of life, before Victor's death, he'd known so little, discovering what he could after first being abandoned by the man who'd created him, his "father," then betrayed by that father when he destroyed his female.

It had been too much for him to understand at his age. He'd been so young, yet in the huge grown body given to him.

Reading through the notes on his own creation had shed a tainted light on Victor, but Elizabeth, Mrs. Frankenstein, though married to the doctor for just a few short hours, didn't deserve to lose her life. If only he'd understood his own actions then. If only he'd had the control over his impulses that he had now, she might have lived to an old age.

His gaze fell upon the angel resting in his bed. She, he would never harm. He would do whatever he must in order to bring her to full health. He swore to fate and whatever gods still existed that no matter what she did to him, he would keep her safe…even from himself.

At peace with his oath, he prepared for Angel to wake. She

would need more food, so he set to work preparing an evening meal. He pulled the venison he had soaking in a marinade from the cold storage box. Sniffing it, he set it down. A man in Greenland had taught him to make the marinade. All he had to do now is add a couple of shakes of thyme and return it to the cold until it was time to cook. He chose a winter squash to go with it that he would sweeten with his birch syrup.

He didn't dare let her eat too much. If her insides were irreparably harmed from her hypothermia, he had no way to help her. His gut tightened. He had to believe she would make a full recovery. At least tonight they would discover if her sight was undamaged.

After checking again to make sure she slept and her breathing was even, he slipped outside. The sun shone and would for at least three more hours. The long days of sunlight were already shortening. By mid-November they would have just a few hours of daylight. He usually spent from then until mid-January reading and consuming the fruits of his labors. When the days grew longer he used the daylight to do repairs and make improvements before collecting birch sap and heading to Savik for seeds, plants and anything else he might need.

What would it be like if he had a companion during those dark months? The idea titillated him, but he brushed it aside. She'd be long gone by then—she'd have to be or she'd be forced to stay the winter because there was no way to leave once the darkness and weather made it too dangerous for planes to fly into Savik.

He walked to the marten skins hanging high between two trees. Could he get her to stay the winter? Her hands wouldn't be healed. It was already the end of September. If he could keep her with him another four weeks, she'd have to stay.

The lonely part of him urged him to prolong her visit, but he knew too much now to give in to such a base need. His Inuit teacher's image seemed to float in the steam of his breath as he untied a skin, and Akiakook looked sternly at him.

He had to help Angel regain her health enough to travel before the winter darkness took over. It was the right thing to do. He was no longer the monster he'd been. He lived every day with the torture of guilt after what he'd done. He refused to add more to his conscience.

Releasing the last hide, he gathered them up. A breeze swept over the ridge and the cold penetrated his skin. Though uncomfortable, it made him feel alive, much like he had when he'd first been created. He entered the cabin with a smile in his heart if not on his visage.

Bringing the marten skins into his pantry in the cave behind the cabin, he laid them in a crate. After placing the lid on it, he strode back into the kitchen and washed his hands. He stepped around the counter to inspect his face before the large shard of mirror. His beard could use a trim and his hair was long, making him look too wild.

He removed his shirt and dropped it on the couch before going to his equipment corner. Choosing a knife from his hunting pack, he returned to the mirror. Carefully, he cut off most of his hair's length. A large slice took off the majority of his beard, which he shaped, leaving enough so it remained soft, but keeping it to the outline of his jaw.

He double checked the leather choker around his neck, thankful for the replica of Akiakook's wife's gift, the original long gone now, like his mentor. The talisman figures around the leather had made his life easier simply by hiding his worst scar.

He stared at his eyes as they looked back at him. He could wear the sunglasses he used when going to the outpost, but she would suspect he hid something if he wore them inside. He'd just have to avoid looking directly at her.

After sweeping up, he strode back to the couch. He perused his bookshelf, determined to find suitable entertainment until Angel awakened. Pulling out his copy of Sir Walter's Scott's *Lady of the Lake*, he sat down to read.

Just as the lady sang of her love, his Angel woke.

"Are you there?"

"I am." Quickly, he donned his shirt, anxious to see the color of her eyes.

"Oh, good. It's weird waking up to complete silence. I live in the city of San Francisco and night or day, there's always noise."

He strode to her and sat in his chair, the light outside now shadowed somewhat by the north mountain as the sun began its descent. "It's not quite silent. There's some movement still in the forest, but the temperature is below zero now, so many animals are settling in before the nocturnal ones take over."

"That makes me even happier to be inside. I'm so glad you found me before a bear did."

"I doubt a bear would have paid much attention, but the wolves would have."

Her throat worked as she swallowed hard. "I'm thirsty. I would love some water."

"Of course." He rose and poured cold water into his tin

cup then set it directly on the stove a few minutes before he brought it to her. "Would you like to sit up?"

"Not yet."

Happy to oblige, he lifted her head and helped her drink. When she'd had enough, he couldn't wait any longer to broach the subject. "I think it would be good to remove the scarf and jar lids from your eyes tonight. Would you like to do so before or after dinner?"

Her lips broke into a smile as far as her chapped lips would allow. To him, it was as if the sun had risen and light streamed over the pristine snow.

"I would love that. Are you sure it's okay? Has it been enough time? Will it hurt? Can we do it right now? I can't wait to see what you look like." Her last words sent a shiver over his skin.

"I'm not a pleasant sight, so please keep your expectations low."

The corner of her lip quirked up. "Considering my condition, I have a feeling I look a lot worse."

To him, she was beautiful, but she would never understand why that was, so he didn't bother to elaborate. "The cabin is in the shadows now, so the sunlight isn't as bright. Or you could wait until darkness and I could light the cabin with one lantern if you prefer."

Her tongue came out and licked her dry lips as she considered her options. "I can't wait. If you think it will be okay, then I'd like to do it now."

He snapped his mouth shut as he was about to respond. Did he want to say now was fine because he too was anxious or because the right time had passed based on what knowledge he had? He counted back the days since she'd arrived. It had been enough.

He scanned the cabin. The coverings he used over his windows in the winter were absent now, and it was easy to see the landscape outside. From the porch to the forest was in shadow. If he stood next to the window, he could see the bright snow to the south, but she wouldn't be moving about.

He nodded, though she couldn't see him. "I think it's time for your eyes to adjust to being open again. If it's too bright, simply close them and I can lay the scarf over them until it grows darker."

"That sounds like a good plan. It would be so nice to be able to see. Without sight, it's hard to keep my mind from focusing on my hands."

She didn't mention the pain, but he knew it was there. Her sight would give her other things to think about, which would be good for her, but what if she thought about him? Would that scare her more?

No matter his inclination, he had to help her and if that meant her staring at him in wariness, then it couldn't be helped. Though he'd lived with it his entire life, he'd never become immune to being the object of fear. He was perhaps more human-like in that regard. Acceptance by others was still a strong, unmet need of his. Akiakook had tried to help him overcome that, but he'd failed.

"I'm ready. What should I do?" At her voice, he pulled himself away from his thoughts and leaned over her.

"Keep your eyes closed until I tell you to open them."

"Okay." She sounded nervous.

As he untied the knot at the side of her head, he hoped

she hadn't done permanent damage to her eyes. She needed to stay positive if she was to heal. Gently, he lifted her head with one hand and pulled the scarf out from beneath it.

"I'm scared." Her words were barely audible, but intense.

"Don't be. Just remember that it may be blurry for a while and the light might hurt a little, but you can close your eyelids anytime and rest your eyes."

"Of course."

When she didn't say anything else, he used his fingers to grasp the two jar lids. "Do you have your eyes closed?"

"I do."

"Good. I'm removing the coverings now." He lifted the two jar lids and put them on the end table next to the bed. "Now, slowly open your eyes."

"I can already see it's lighter." Her eye lashes fluttered and rose.

He sucked in his breath at the bright green color revealed as she turned her head toward him.

CHAPTER FOUR

ngela's heart lodged in her throat as she looked at her caretaker. It was like trying to see through a waterfall. There was black hair and maybe a beard and a dark tan-colored face, but no details. She could see colors, but shapes were distorted and wouldn't come into focus. On his shoulders was something white and that hurt.

Oh God, she hoped this wasn't what she had to look forward to for the rest of her life. No more adventures. No more job. She barely kept her tears at bay. "It's all blurry." She heard the panic in her own voice.

"Close your eyes for a minute then open them again slowly. They need time to remember how to function."

His ever-calm voice helped her control her anxiety, and she closed her eyes, turning her head so she would be looking at the ceiling when she opened them again. She started to count. One thousand, two thousand, three thousand, four—

"Did you have any bright blotches as you tried to focus?"

She thought for a moment. "No. Is that good?"

"Blotches would be a bad sign, so that's good."

He remained silent after that. She liked it much better when he talked to her. "When I open my eyes, what will I see on the ceiling?"

At her question, she could picture him looking up. "You will see pine boards that rise to the peak. If you look across the ceiling, you will see a large log that bisects the area below it."

"Good. I have an idea in my mind. Let's see if I'm right." She slowly opened her eyes and stared at the wood above her. It was still slightly blurry, but better than before.

Excitement flew through her, and she scanned the area to find the supporting log bisecting the open area about ten feet above her, but it went the opposite way she'd envisioned. She smirked a little and turned her head.

Her exclamation died on her lips. Though he still wasn't in focus, her mountain man was not what she'd imagined, though he did appear huge. He was much younger, and if she was a good guesser, much handsomer than she expected. Her gaze moved to meet his, and he quickly looked away, but before he did, the intensity in his eyes struck her even without clear vision.

"You can see." His words were spoken with no emotion or inflection at all.

"I can, but it's still not clear. I'm going to close them again and see if it gets better." With new hope and more confidence, she closed her eyes.

"I'll cook dinner. I think you should try some meat." As he spoke, he moved away, his voice not as loud as he turned toward the area he used as a kitchen.

Was he shy? Just thinking of him as shy made her want to reassure him. Maybe that was why he lived so far north. Maybe he wasn't comfortable around people. For all she knew, he could have a form of autism. She didn't know much about it, but from what she'd heard, that could be it. He was clearly very smart.

She slowly opened her eyes again and he came into view, but the white back of his shirt hurt her eyes, so she scanned other areas of the room, only to feel a little queasy.

Closing her eyes, she let her stomach right itself. Her vision was definitely getting better as long as she didn't move her gaze too fast. She waited to open her eyes again, listening to the sound her caretaker made as he prepared the meal.

The second the meat hit the hot pan, she heard it sizzle. She kept her eyes closed until a savory scent filled the room, making her stomach growl. Careful this time, she turned her head toward the smell before opening her eyes.

The mountain man was in profile to her as he tended the meat. Still, his white shirt bothered her, so she focused on the wood stove he cooked on. It was not very big, probably because he lived alone.

Her vision still wasn't a hundred percent, so she moved her gaze past him to the table he said was next to a supporting post. There were no chairs next to it and the top had two legs on one side with the other side supported by the post.

As she moved her gaze past it, she found the couch he spoke about, just on the other side of the front door. It wasn't short at all. It had to be about eight feet long, but definitely homemade. She couldn't tell if the cushions were store-bought or not, but they weren't red. They were brown.

Over the couch was a window. From where she lay she could see outside, and it looked as if everything was coated in blue. There was blue snow and blue-green evergreen trees along with a few bluish boulders peeking through parts of the snow. It looked cold.

Closing her eyes again, she reviewed all she'd seen. On the

other side of the front door was various equipment, but even that seemed neat. For someone who lived alone, he was very organized, or he had cleaned up for her benefit. He did seem like such a gentleman.

"Your dinner is ready."

She'd been so focused on her thoughts, she hadn't heard him approach, or was she already depending on her sight again? She opened her eyes to look at him, but he wasn't on the chair beside the bed. He had walked to the couch.

The scent of the meat and something sweet had her turning her body toward it.

"Stop. Don't move."

She froze, having barely shifted her weight. He hadn't yelled, but the tone of his voice made it clear it was serious. Was there a spider hanging over her? Did Alaska have spiders?

He strode toward her with a couch cushion in his hand. "If you move, your hands will start stinging. Ease back."

Shoot, she'd totally forgotten about her hands in her excitement over her sight. Carefully, she relaxed into the bed.

He bent over her, and she closed her eyes, his white shirt still a problem. When he'd lifted her and set her up so she could eat, she spoke. "Could you change your shirt, or just take it off. The color hurts my eyes."

There was a pregnant silence. Had she offended him? Shoot, she hadn't meant to. Her stomach growled at the delay.

"I'll change after you eat. Nourishment is more important right now."

She couldn't very well argue with that. "Okay, but I think I'll keep my eyes closed."

"That's acceptable." The chair creaked as he settled into it, and she heard the fork against the plate.

When the sound stopped, she opened her mouth, and he set a piece of food on her tongue. She chewed tender meat with an odd flavor to it. It was good, but it didn't taste like anything she'd ever had. When she was done, she opened her mouth to ask what it was, but another piece of food was inserted.

She smiled inside. He was right. She should eat now and talk later. The next mouthful was sweet, and she easily identified the squash since it was a food she loved. She obediently ate everything he put in her mouth. This time she felt satisfied and not as if he hadn't fed her enough. As before, he wiped her face when she finished.

When he rose from the chair and walked away, she opened her eyes again. She stared at his jeans since they were dark. She'd been right, the man was big. He'd moved to the stove and scraped a pan. When he was done, he strode toward her, so she closed her eyes again to avoid looking at his shirt.

The chair next to the bed was moved and when she looked again, he was seated at the table. Since looking at only the bottom half of him was frustrating, she occupied herself with the bed she was in instead.

It was obviously hand-built with logs. At the foot was a log that connected the two short posts on either side. The quilt looked like a mix of old clothes sewn together. That made sense. On top of it lay both her hands wrapped in maroon flannel. It was as if she wore mittens. She resisted the urge to move them, the remembered pain a strong deterrent.

Her arms were bare, but they didn't look sunburned or anything, so that was good. If she remembered correctly, she had a tank top on, and he'd obviously been a gentleman to have removed only her outer clothing.

She needed to repay him somehow. Maybe a shipment of supplies, though he didn't seem to need anything. She'd have to get him talking to find out what he might want. Maybe they could discuss his cabin.

She looked at the log wall the bed was set against. There were no windows along it at all. There was one on the opposite wall and the two on either side of the door. That was odd. There had to be a reason.

She looked toward him to ask him why, but he rose and moved back to the kitchen. She could definitely hear running water. How could that be? She wanted to ask but had no name to call him. He had to have name.

Her vision still wasn't good enough to pick out details, but now that she could see what he did, it felt strange to just blurt out a question without gaining his attention first by calling his name. So, she waited.

She wasn't known for her patience, but this was a good lesson. She might be dependent on him for another week or more, so she'd just have to suck it up.

He finally finished in the kitchen area. Once he moved, she could see there was a counter and cabinets. She didn't see a refrigerator, but since everything still had a fuzzy outline, she couldn't be sure. Then again, with all the snow outside and no electricity, he probably had some kind of cold storage.

He stopped at the end of the bed and pulled something out of the chest he'd told her about the other day. It looked like another shirt. Finally, she'd be able to look at his face without her eyes feeling like they'd just been punched.

"I'll change now."

She squinted at the shirt in his hands. "Is that wool?"

"Yes. It's very warm. However, I have kept it warmer in here for you, which is why I donned this one." He turned toward the front door.

"Oh." Now she felt selfish. If he changed, he'd sweat up a storm. "Wait. You don't have to change. I'm sure once it gets dark, your white shirt won't bother me. Please. Leave it on."

"As you wish." He moved back to his chest and after folding the shirt neatly, put it away.

Afraid he would go outside anyway to do whatever chores he might have, she asked the first question that popped into her head. "How old are you?"

He stilled. "Is that important?"

She shrugged, then wished she hadn't as the movement caused her hands to start burning. Luckily, it had been a small move, and she was able to take deep breaths to keep from crying. She blinked a few times, now sure the blurriness was water in her eyes. "I guess not. I guess I just imagined you to be older." Okay, that wasn't exactly nice.

Since when did she stumble over making conversation? "What kind of meat was that?"

"Venison."

Shoot, she forgot he liked to give one-word answers. "I've never had such tender venison. How did you get it like that?"

He still remained at the end of the bed, but she couldn't look above his waist.

"I marinated it overnight before cooking it on the stove with water and a cover."

Now she wanted to know where he'd learned to cook. In

Switzerland? Germany? She didn't remember having deer meat while traveling in those countries. Before she could ask another question, he moved to the couch and picked something up only to place it on the bookshelves adjacent to it.

"What was that?" Now she sounded nosey. What was wrong with her?

"It's a book. Do you read?"

"I do." She actually liked to read, though usually it was about different countries' customs and histories. "What were you reading?"

He walked toward the kitchen again, but answered her. *"The Lady of the Lake."*

It sounded like a romance or something. "I've never heard of it. I don't read much fiction."

He opened a door in the wall. He'd never said anything about a back door. She hoped he wasn't going outside.

He disappeared through it but left it open, so she waited. Seemed she was doing that a lot.

When he came back through, he had what looked like a big piece of fur and a pillow. "Sir Walter Scott wrote the poem for entertainment, but it's based on fact if you know the history of the struggle between King James V and the Douglas Clan."

Walter Scott? Didn't he write about William Wallace? She'd seen a movie about him, even visited Stirling Castle in Scotland as part of her work travels, but she'd never heard of a lady and a lake. "Maybe I could read something when my eyes feel better."

He dropped the pile on the couch and moved toward her. She lowered her gaze, though she wanted to see his face in the worst way.

"Your eyes hurt?" He stopped beside the bed, the concern in his voice making her kick herself for worrying him.

"Only when I look at something bright. Things are just a little fuzzy."

"You'll find your vision will grow stronger every day."

Despite the pain, she forced her gaze to skim over his white shirt to look him in the eye. Again, he avoided her gaze, but that just gave her time to study him. "I can't thank you enough for helping me."

He still didn't look at her. "I had to."

She was too busy trying to bring the details of his features into focus to register his response. He had hair as black as midnight and a beard to match, but it was well trimmed, accentuating his jaw. His eyebrows were black, too, and it appeared he might have high cheek bones and a prominent nose, but she couldn't be sure.

He turned away. "Would you like anything else before retiring?"

What? She glanced out the windows. It wasn't dark yet. "Are you going to sleep?"

"Yes."

She wanted to ask him to stay awake and talk with her, but that would be selfish. He spent his day waiting on her whenever she woke up. "Do you have any wine?"

"No." He was in the kitchen now, filling a pot with water.

"Are you having tea?"

"Yes."

Again with the one-word responses. Maybe one more night of sleep inducing tea couldn't hurt. "I'll have some, too."

He didn't indicate that he'd heard her but he moved about the cabinetry with efficiency, his back to her.

At least she could get him talking while the water boiled. "Was it hard building this cabin by yourself?" As much as she wanted to watch him, it wasn't worth it if she couldn't see his face.

"No."

Okay, she'd walked right into that one. "How did you do it?"

"I chopped down the trees and put it together."

She raised her brows. "Chopped?"

"Yes. I arrived here late in the year and the cave behind this cabin served as a good place to live until I could build. Whenever there was a good day with no snow, I would chop trees. I knew of Savik but I also knew any outpost out this far wouldn't receive supplies until spring. The chances of finding a chainsaw were slim, so I used the axe I'd brought with me."

She was still processing the fact that there was a cave behind the cabin when he moved the chair from the table to next to the bed. Then he returned to the stove.

"How did you get the roof on without someone to help you? I would think you'd need at least two people to balance the main support." She watched as he poured the liquid into the tin cup.

"I nailed a few boards together then hoisted them into place. After that it was easy to build the rest. Have you built a cabin before?" He sounded hopeful.

She gave him a small smile, very aware of the limitations of her chapped lips. If only she'd brought lipstick or lip balm with her to the glacier. "No, I haven't. I'm just a curious person about how others live. When I was preparing for this vacation, I read a lot and watched documentaries on living in the arctic."

He sat in the chair, and she looked away. When he was this close, it was as if a white wall was in front of her. He seemed overly large, but it might be because of the size of the cabin. Everything was a matter of perspective.

When he didn't immediately lift her head, she glanced toward his hands. They dwarfed the cup. It looked small, so that must be why.

"I'm waiting for the tea to cool. I don't think you need more burns."

Wow, this man was too good to be true. Why wasn't he married? He was so thoughtful. "Thank you. I really appreciate that."

When he didn't respond, she filled in the silence. "You haven't told me how you found me. Was I far away from here? Were you out hunting and saw my red parka?"

"No. You were on the mountain across from this one. It was a narrow ledge, not like here, which is a large one. I had planned to catch fish and looked up at the sun to judge the time when I noticed a reflection of sun bouncing off the ledge. That has never happened before so I investigated."

"I wonder what it was. I bet you were hoping it was gold. I heard there's been gold discovered here in the past."

"I didn't expect it to be gold, nor did I want it to be. I expected it to be the sun's reflection off a gun, but it wasn't." He leaned in and lifted her head.

So much for conversation. She could keep her lips closed, but that seemed rude. After taking a sip, she pulled back. "So, what caused the reflection?"

"It was a small square device you'd dropped." He brought the cup to her lips and she drank.

"That was probably my phone. I knew there was no signal out here, but I used it as a camera. It's probably dead now."

He didn't immediately lift the cup. "Dead?"

"Yes. The battery is probably all used up. I can only recharge it if there's electricity."

"I don't have electricity." He brought the cup to her lips, stifling any response.

She swallowed the soothing tea, but it didn't keep her from noticing the tone of his voice. It sounded like he didn't like electricity for some reason. It may be why he lived like he did.

Instead of wondering, she took the opportunity to ask. "Why do you live out here away from civilization?"

He lifted the cup to her lips again. "I don't like civilization."

She drank, having no choice, but he had to know what her next question would be. Why? When he lowered the cup, she opened her mouth to ask, but he interjected.

"When I found you, your clothes were scattered everywhere. I brought you here immediately, but had to wait two days to gather your belongings because I didn't want to leave you alone. I don't know if anything is missing. An animal could have easily taken something, but the 'phone' is here."

He was good at changing the subject when he didn't want to talk about something. Okay, she'd drop it for now, but she'd come back to it another way. Besides, his thoughtfulness once again undermined her need to know.

It was one of her flaws, her need to learn everything. "Thank you for gathering my stuff. I appreciate that, but why were my clothes everywhere?" She had to admit, for the first time she doubted him. "I can't imagine I had taken them off considering how cold it was."

He brought the cup up again, and she drank the final amount.

"It's not uncommon for someone who is suffering from severe hypothermia to begin to lose rational thought and to think they are too hot. I'm not sure of the medical process, but I've been told this is usually the last act of a person who is about to freeze to death."

His matter of fact tone scared her. "So you're saying if you decided to wait until dinner time to go fishing that I would have died?" She turned her head to look at him and found it didn't hurt so much as his shirt was reflecting less light.

He didn't look at her, his gaze on the cup, his head down. "Actually, if I had walked outside a few minutes earlier or later, the sun wouldn't have been in the right position to reflect off your instrument."

She turned away as a shiver raced up her spine. The chances that she would wander close enough and drop her phone in just the right position for him to walk outside at just the right time had to be astronomical! Her debt to him was even deeper than she'd realized. "I don't know what to say."

He rose from the chair, and she turned to watch him walk away. Looking at him was easier, but she still couldn't see details. She wanted to see him and know him. He was her hero.

He spoke over his shoulder. "It was fate. You're meant to perform a special task."

It would be easy to agree with him, but she was no one extraordinary. It wasn't as if she would save the world or something. She was more inclined to believe she'd been extremely lucky and she owed her life…and whatever she made of it, to him.

Suddenly, her confidence in the way she lived her life eroded beneath her. It was time to reevaluate.

He washed the cup then used it to pour himself the rest of the tea. He hadn't planned on drinking the same mixture, but as images of Angel lying on the ledge flashed through his mind, he preferred a little help to find sleep.

It *had* been fate. He hadn't planned to fish that day. He'd planned to freeze the last of his vegetables, but the sky had been clear of all clouds and as blue as glacier ice when the sun lit it, so he'd changed his mind and headed out the door.

That he might have found her that evening because wolves had smelled dinner, pierced his soul. He chugged down the too hot liquid then rewashed the cup. He was confidant now that she was his redemption.

He strode over to the bed and found her already asleep. Gently, he lifted her and pulled the cushion out that allowed her to sit up. Unable to resist, he picked up a few strands of hair that lay on her forehead and moved them aside, their texture like nothing he'd ever touched before. She was beyond beautiful, and he was anxious to discover more of the beauty inside as well.

Her gratefulness proved she had a good heart. He wanted to learn about her life, what she'd done, others she'd influenced toward the good. Akiakook had predicted that one day an angel would find him and test him and here she was. His test was obvious. Save her and bring her back to health. This he could do.

He forced himself to return to the couch and set the cushion in place. Despite the tea, he was awake, the light outside having faded to dark twilight. He preferred last month when the days and nights had a more equal share, but the days grew shorter now.

Unable to resist, he slipped outside. Sitting on the edge of the porch with his feet on the steps below, he listened to the sounds of the night.

The moon had yet to rise and true darkness yet to descend, but already the Aurora Borealis danced cross the northern sky. The green and red shimmered, first one brighter than the other, as if each wanted to lead. As the green turned bright, his heart lurched. Angel's eyes were that color, he'd noticed when she first opened them.

He feared tomorrow when she discovered the one scar he couldn't cover. Would she avoid looking at him? Would she start to fear him? He rubbed his right wrist then froze. He'd forgotten the wrist bands!

Immediately, he took a deep breath as Akiakook had taught him over two hundred years earlier. Reaching for his center, he found calm waiting for him. With his emotions under control, his intellect became more efficient.

If Angel had seen his wrist scars, she would have said something. Amusement lightened his spirits. She would say something about everything eventually. Her curiosity was strong. Her interest in every little thing, including him, was entertaining, when not uncomfortable.

The thought of spending every day with her lifted his spirit in ways it hadn't been lifted since the day Victor Frankenstein agreed to create for him a mate. It made him want to find other ways to please her. She had no idea how much lightness she'd brought to his life already.

A noise inside the cabin had him jumping to his feet. He opened the door to the sound of her voice.

"—there? I need help."

He closed the door and strode across the dark room, urged on by the fear in her voice. "I'm here. What do you need?"

"Oh, good. It was so dark when I woke up, and I need to use the chair you made for me. I'm not used to being so dependent on someone. It's a little scary."

As he lit the lantern, he guessed she minimized her real feelings because what he'd heard in her tone was a lot more than a "little" fear.

"You know, I'm going to have to call you something. Surely, in your entire life someone has called you by some name."

Now it was uncomfortable again. "Yes, in every place I've lived I've been given a name." Monster. Abomination. Murderer. Freak. "But none of those are who I am now, nor something I would want to be called."

"We're going to have to come up with something."

He didn't look at her, not in a hurry to acquire yet another name. Instead of thinking about what she might call him, he brought her chair to the side of the bed and removed the quilt from her.

Lifting her from his fur coat, which was still beneath her, he set her gently on the chair. Then he moved the paper she needed from the end table to the bed near her.

Though his help was a necessity, he could see she was still embarrassed by the situation. "I need to go into my storage room. You won't have to yell for me to hear you. Just say you're ready."

"Okay."

When she didn't say anything else, an unusual occurrence, he quickly left through his pantry door, anxious to put on the leather bands that covered his wrists. Once inside, he had no light and moved about carefully to find his other lantern.

Though he knew exactly where everything was placed, it still took him three attempts to put his hand on it and in the process, he kicked over a shovel. Striking a match from the box he left next to the lantern, he understood better how Angel must have felt, not being able to see.

Over the years, his body had grown more impervious to injury. At first if cut, he would bleed, but eventually that stopped occurring and wounds healed up faster and faster, no blood in sight. It was the same with his sensitivity to hot and cold. The longer he existed, the less difference he could tell in the temperature. He would give up his immortality immediately if he could feel like she felt because that was part of what made her human.

With the muted light of the lantern, he opened a trunk he'd acquired in a swap and pulled out a small box he kept important items in. Lifting the lid, he removed the two leather bands that snapped around his wrists for a snug fit. He'd had them made only ten years ago to replace the last pair.

He shook his head. It had taken him years after Victor's death to realize that by hiding his scars, he could avoid immediate revulsion, but it had taken him decades to understand humans' reactions to his gaze. He had learned so many things the hard way with no guidance until he'd met Akiakook.

Closing the small box, he put it away and turned off the lantern, anxious to be ready to help Angel when she called. He walked to the door and waited. His hearing, like his other senses and abilities, far surpassed that of man. While an advantage in his choice of lifestyle, it was simply one more way in which Dr. Frankenstein had made him different and forced him to be alone.

"Ready." The voice on the other side of the door was pained, and he threw it open to rush to her side.

Tears streamed down her cheeks and his heart squeezed. In an instant, he took in the tableau. Her right hand's bandages were twisted, the paper she'd used was on the floor and one leg was out to the side. He wanted to hug her to him and take her pain away, but to touch her like that would hurt her more.

She looked up at him apologetically. "I'm sorry I took so long. It was h-hard." The last word was choked out.

"I wasn't in a rush. Let me place you back in bed and then I'll change your bandage."

"Will it hurt?" As she looked up at him through long light lashes, her green eyes bright with her pain, he quickly moved his gaze, swallowing the lump in his throat. "It will. We can wait until tomorrow after you've rested."

"I like that idea better."

He walked to the foot of the bed and pulled his fur coat off it. With the fire so high, she should be warm enough now without it. He returned to stand before her. Very carefully, he moved his arm behind her back and the other beneath her knees. Rising, he stepped around the chair and laid her on the sheet.

Her face was filled with tension, her eyes closed and her lips pursed tight. Despite how careful he was, she still hurt.

"I'm sorry." If he could have moved her without pain, he would have, but he was not so naïve as to believe that possible.

Her eyelashes fluttered open. "It's not your fault. I did this to myself. I was so stupid."

He wanted to take her chin and make her look at him, but he didn't dare have her gaze into his eyes, so he settled for a stern tone instead. "You weren't stupid. You were ignorant. There is a significant difference." He covered her with the quilt, leaving her hands beneath it.

She closed her eyes again. "I guess."

She obviously didn't believe him, but her need for sleep was more important than a debate, so he didn't respond. Instead, he pulled the bucket out from under the chair and headed outside.

CHAPTER FIVE

At the sound of a chickadee, Angela opened her eyes, only to shut them tight again. The brightness still hurt. Shoot. That *had* to be a chickadee, but she hadn't read anything about those birds being so far north. She had to be imagining things. How could she even hear a bird inside the snug cabin?

She kept her eyes closed and let her other senses take over. The chickadee-dee-dee chirp came again. It was followed by what sounded like a woodpecker and footsteps. Slowly, she opened her eyes just a smidge and focused on the quilt. The French florets on one piece of material were clear as was the paisley design on another. Both her hands rested on top of it now.

She could see! She smiled wide only to stop suddenly as her chapped lips split. She had to be in the worst shape of her entire life. Licking the corner of her mouth, she opened her eyes a little wider but the sunshine was too bright.

Squinting, she could see the door to the cabin was wide open. Taking a deep breath, she inhaled fresh air and closed her eyes as it filled her lungs. It was cool, but not cold, probably because it was warmed by the wood stove as it rushed in.

She opened her eyes just slightly and could see evergreen trees past the open space in front of the cabin, but only the tops of the trees were visible to the left, as if those were a bit below. She must be on a mountain. No surprise there since she'd become lost in the Brooks Range.

Bending her elbows slowly, so she didn't wake up her hands, she pressed them into the bed to help her lift her head up. Briefly, white snow with footprints and rocks came into view before her head dropped back. It appeared she was incredibly weak to boot. So much for all those morning work outs in hotel exercise rooms.

She rested for a few minutes before looking for her mountain man. He wasn't in the cabin, so the footsteps she heard outside had to be his. Instinct told her if she called, he'd come, but for once, she was fine with waiting. She wanted to see what he looked like up close and personal without him looking away. She'd yet to clearly see his features.

When she'd thought he was an old man, it wasn't such a burning need, but after last night, her impression of him was that he was young, maybe her age or a little older and she planned to peruse every detail of his face including his elusive eyes, no matter how shy he was.

She relaxed to the sound of the birds, not surprised they were happy with the mild day. They were probably preparing for a cold, dark winter. Would she be healed by then? How many days had it been now, three?

Her patience was rewarded by the sound of footsteps on stairs, followed by two steps across what must be a porch and then he filled the doorway. She kept her eyes barely open so she could observe her caretaker.

The man was built. Even if the doorway was small, he filled the entire thing, his shoulders as wide as the jambs. He looked very tall, as in over seven feet, but that couldn't be. It probably appeared that way because she was lying on the bed. The leather bands at his wrists and around his neck made him look like a gladiator. She still couldn't see his face with the light behind him.

As he stepped inside, he closed the door then turned around.

Holy sugar with a cherry on top! Her heart skipped a couple of beats as she stared, completely forgetting to keep her eyelids lowered.

He was gorgeous. He did have high cheek bones, and his nose was straight, perfect. Above that were deep set eyes and his high forehead was covered by his hair. It wasn't the individual aspects so much as the whole shape and configuration that had her belly doing a happy dance.

As he strode forward toward the stove, it looked as if a pine needle or something had fallen on his cheek below his right eye. If she told him about it, maybe he'd look at her and she'd finally get to see what color his eyes were. "I think you have something on your cheek."

He turned toward her at the sound of her voice, but he didn't look directly at her. Instead, he seemed to be staring at the floor. "Yes, I do."

When he didn't elaborate, she started to roll her eyes, but stopped at the discomfort of the movement. "What is it?"

He turned back to the stove and opened it before throwing two more logs in. "It's a scar."

Oh, great. Didn't she just put her foot in her mouth? Was that why he looked away all the time? "I have a couple of scars myself. One from not getting stitches when I needed them and one from stitches. I don't think anyone makes it through life without a few scars. I've always said it proves that I've really lived." She smiled slightly, hoping to put him at ease.

He didn't respond, instead moving to the counter to pick something up and lay it in a pan.

"Where did you learn to cook?"

He didn't pause in his movements as he returned to the counter. "Everywhere."

She should have seen that coming. Maybe he felt self-conscious about her interest in him, which had quadrupled since she could finally see what he looked like and she'd discovered his outside was as beautiful as the inside. "My dad actually taught me to cook. He wasn't a chef or anything, but he managed to put a decent meal on the table. I didn't know about fancy cooking until I started to travel. That really opened my eyes…and my palate."

He continued to mix something in the pan.

"Who did you learn from…the most?"

He added some spice to the hot mixture and the smells woke up her stomach.

"A friend."

She obviously would have to be more creative in her questions. "Was your friend a chef? It wouldn't surprise me because everything you've given me has tasted wonderful."

He shook his head. "He was an old Inuit wise man."

She hadn't expected that answer, but it made sense based on some of the places he'd lived. "It sounds like your friend was wise about many things."

He paused as he lifted the pan off the stove. "He was. I've met no one better than he." He turned to the counter and moved the food from the pan to a plate and a bowl.

It was so glorious to see again, that she didn't mind that he didn't elaborate further.

He filled the pan with water and began washing it. That made so much sense. If the water was cold and the pan hot, it probably made it the perfect temperature for washing.

Still, she watched the steam rising from the food, wishing she could simply get up and grab a plate, but she could barely lift her head for more than ten seconds and her hands were worthless.

As she started to despair, he walked over and her spirits rose again. She couldn't wait for him to sit down so she could look more closely at his face.

He finally lowered himself into the chair he'd placed there before she woke.

Her gaze immediately went to his face and she stilled, her smile of welcome frozen on her lips. The scar he'd referred to under his right eye actually ran from his sideburn, under his eye, up along the crease of his nose and just under his eyebrow. Did he have a glass eye after a surgery like that? She wanted to know, but he wouldn't look at her.

"Are you hungry?" His calm voice brought her attention back to the food.

Immediately, her stomach tightened in anticipation, but she still lay on her back. "I think it would be easier for me if I sat up."

He didn't move to help. "Are you sure? Last night when I moved you, it hurt you. I don't want to hurt you."

Her heart melted at his words. "I only hurt because of my own actions, not yours. I'd like to sit up if you could help me. It's less painful with your help."

Putting the plate and wet cloth on the end table next to the bed, he rose without a word and walked to the couch.

That's when she noticed the fur blanket and pillow were gone, and for that matter, so was the fur coat he'd left at the end of the bed last night. He came back with a cushion and helped her sit. She was too busy avoiding moving her hands to study him.

When he sat again, her interest was renewed, but he still didn't meet her eyes. Instead, he focused on her lips, which gave her a completely inappropriate tingle.

At least it was a lot easier being able to see when he scooped some food onto his fork for her to eat. She recognized potato slices with onions as well as another vegetable she was unfamiliar with.

Instantly, she opened her mouth. As the flavors rolled over her tongue, she hummed. Chewing the mixture, she swallowed and nodded. "This is good."

She only had two seconds to speak the words before he had another forkful ready. When she was blinded and couldn't see, this ritual of him feeding her was simply part of healing. But now that she could see him, it felt like so much more. It felt intimate.

For him, nothing had changed and she had to remember that. For her though, everything had. He was maybe a bit older than her, possibly thirty-seven, thirty-eight, was incredibly handsome, even with the scar, and his voice now seemed sexy instead of simply deep.

She opened her mouth again and resisted the urge to playfully hold the fork in her mouth with her teeth. Teasing him when she didn't know him yet, wouldn't be smart. Without him, she'd still die. The last thing she needed to do was scare him away and based on his lack of eye-contact, she was sure he was far too shy for her usual assertiveness.

Chewing, she watched his hands as he scooped up more food. They seemed very large. Was it because she'd been without sight for so many days, or was he particularly big? She opened her mouth and stared at the leather wrist bands. This close, she could see they were decorated with dyed designs she didn't recognize.

As he moved his hand away, she studied the leather choker around his neck. Normally, she wouldn't have cared much for a man wearing a choker, but this one was decorated with what looked like ivory, but it could have been bone, and it was dyed with symbols that must mean something. On him, it looked primitive and definitely masculine.

She swallowed another mouthful as he scraped the remainder of the food onto the fork. Opening her mouth, she tried to catch his gaze, but he wouldn't meet her eyes. As soon as she took the food and started chewing, he rose, almost as if he couldn't wait to get away.

Once she swallowed, she watched him put the plate in the sink and pick up the bowl. He always fed her first. After placing the bowl on the table, he came back to the bed and used the wet cloth to wipe her face, forcing her to close her eyes. When he thought her clean enough, he lifted the chair and headed back to the table.

"That was wonderful. Do you always eat vegetables for breakfast?"

Once again, he finished what he was doing before answering. "No."

She sighed heavily. Having a conversation with him was like surfing the internet with a modem. "I'm not trying to be nosey, it's just that there's nothing else I can do except talk."

He glanced at her briefly at that before taking a bite of food. It wasn't a long enough look for her to see the color of his eyes, but it was enough to see they were dark.

"Then perhaps you should talk about yourself. I'm as curious about your life as you are about mine."

Of course! What an idiot she was. "That's a great idea. I grew up in Palo Alto, California and now I live in San Francisco. My job takes me around the world, but when I'm not travelling I work from home. I work for a computer reservations company. I'm with the loyalty program for worldwide resorts. I get to visit the properties so I can suggest the best way to market them to our members. It's a great job."

She paused to swallow, even her throat was a bit rusty. "I'm a big believer in getting the most out of life, which is why I take opportunities to explore wherever I am. When a particular place really interests me, I plan a vacation there." It was her typical spiel when meeting someone new, but after her brush with death, which had been hastened by her life philosophy, her entire introduction rang hollow.

Did he find it superficial after the life he'd led, eking out an existence in a never-ending battle against nature? Was that why he didn't comment? "How about you?"

"Do you have family?"

That's right. He wanted to talk about her. "I do. I have a brother, Michael. Of course, I had a mother and father." She hesitated since she rarely talked about her parents, but if it didn't come up now, it was sure to come up later in the week.

"My mom died of cancer when I was only six, so I have very fuzzy memories of her, but my dad, I just lost him two years ago. He took care of me and my younger brother. He was a good father, but…"

"But what?"

She'd been looking down at the quilt, so when he asked his question, she lifted her gaze to find him focused on his breakfast. "But he was what they call a functioning alcoholic. You know, those people who meet all their responsibilities but drink themselves into a stupor once they have. I don't think he was before mom died. He loved her more than anything, even more than us."

He didn't respond to her revelation. Instead, he pushed back the chair, rose and walked to the kitchen.

Usually, that story would illicit some kind of sympathy, at least among those she'd told to date. "What about your parents?"

He didn't stop washing the dish, just spoke over his shoulder. "I was abandoned the second I took my first breath."

Stunned, she shut her mouth over her next question. No wonder he didn't find her story very compelling! She doubted he'd been adopted or he wouldn't be so shy. She'd put her money on foster care, or did they have that in Germany?

Shoot, she didn't know crap about the countries she'd visited, not really. To be fair, she probably knew a bit more than those who didn't travel to them, but she'd never lived anywhere but California.

Was he dropped off at a church? Why had he said his "first breath"? He didn't seem the type to exaggerate, especially when he spoke so little. Was he one of those babies dumped in a trash can?

Oh God, just the thought of that made her want to cry. "Who raised you? Was it your friend Akiakook?"

He paused for a moment as he dried the dish. "You said you have a brother. Will he be worried about you?"

Good question. "He will be, but not yet. My trip was supposed to last a month and there is limited service on the boat, so he knows not to expect to hear from me until I land in Seattle. I'm hoping I can give him a call by then and not tell him what an idiot I was."

"Won't your shipmates wonder what happened to you?"

She started to move her hand to wave away his concern, but stopped herself just in time. At least she was becoming more careful in regard to her limitations. Then again, pain was a good motivator. "It's not that kind of trip. It's for eco tourists. We are allowed to leave the tour any time we come to a place we wish to explore further. It's one of the advantages of not taking a typical tour. However, it was a lot of paperwork. I had to get approval from every country on the tour and I had to waive all kinds of rights if I decided to stay at a particular stop."

She watched him put away the few items he'd used. The white shirt didn't bother her eyes anymore. Actually, it accentuated his broadness without being tight at all. "I certainly didn't expect to leave the trip so soon. I played with the idea of staying for a while when we got to the North Pole, but the costs to get myself home at this time of year were prohibitive."

"That's a long journey." He walked to the opposite corner, diagonally from where she was and lifted an axe.

That must mean he planned to go outside. For some unexplainable reason, she wanted him to stay. "I know. I've wanted to see the North Pole ever since I learned that Santa Claus doesn't exist. It's a little weird, but I always wanted to verify that he isn't there. I guess I'll never know now. After my recent experience, I'm not sure how adventurous I'll feel about going to cold places in the future."

He unlatched the door, but didn't look back at her. "You may want to wait on that decision. The cold areas of Earth have the most magnificent beauty. They are the best spots for feeling alive."

Before she could respond, he'd stepped through the door and was gone.

She tried to stifle her panic by listening, but didn't hear anything. Closing her eyes, she tapped into her residual hearing capabilities. She waited what seemed like forever, but was probably no more than a minute before she heard something.

Keeping her eyes closed, she turned her head toward the kitchen area.

Thwap. A few seconds of silence followed then another definite sound.

Thwap. She listened harder, pleased when she could hear a softer sound after every loud one. She imagined him splitting wood, half the log falling to the side and hitting the ground. Then he'd pick it up, set it in place and down the axe would come.

Thwap. Thump. Thwap. Thump…

She must have drifted off because the sound of voices woke her. Voices? Excitement had her senses alert at the prospect of being able to talk to someone who might actually give her more than one-word answers.

She opened her eyes. Though she still sat up, thanks to the couch cushion behind her, no one was in view outside the windows. She watched the window on the wall with the equipment, what her caretaker had indicated was the south wall.

A laugh sounded outside. It was definitely male, but instinct told her it wasn't her mountain man. Then a gray ski cap moved past the window. Would both men come inside or was the gray cap just passing through. If only she could move without pain.

Loud footsteps walked up stairs and approached the door. She chuckled to herself at how excited she was. Was this how pioneer women felt two hundred years ago?

The door opened and a man walked in, quickly divesting himself of his cap. Behind him entered her caretaker who made the man look small in comparison.

As the door was shut, she could see their visitor looked old enough to be her father, but it could be the weather that caused such deep wrinkles. He had a gray bushy mustache and when he turned to hang his parka on a hook next to the door, she noticed his gray hair was in one long braid down his back. He had hair longer than hers!

As soon as he turned back around, his gaze searched her out and he smiled then strode forward. "You must be Angel. I'm Timber." He held out his hand, then retracted it as his gaze fell on her bandages. His smile faltered.

She gave him a warm smile. "It's okay. Consider your hand shaken in welcome."

He regained his composure and sat in the chair next to her bed.

"While I'm flattered, my name isn't Angel. It's—"

"Ah, I see, Sas has already given you a bush name."

She raised her brows. "Sas?"

Timber looked to where her caretaker worked in the kitchen. "You didn't tell her your name?"

"It's not my name." The words came out in resignation as if the two had had the same conversation multiple times.

Their guest returned his attention to her. "That's his bush name. We call him Sas. Most people up here don't go by their given names. Some because they don't want to be found, but most because you can't escape a nickname once christened." He chuckled, a light-hearted sound that raised her spirits.

"Why did you name him Sas? He doesn't seem like the sassy type to me."

A grunt from the kitchen area confirmed her assumption.

"Oh, I didn't name him. Sturge did, the first time this big fella strode into Savik. I didn't even know him then, but I'd heard about him. I just so happened to be hunting out this way one day and as soon as I saw him, I knew who he was. Sas is short for Sasquatch."

"Bigfoot?" She looked at her host. He did appear to be rather large and he was shy, but he didn't seem hairy. No, there was no way she was recuperating in the home of Bigfoot. She turned back to find Timber smiling widely, showing off two missing teeth near the corners of his mouth. "You're kidding."

He shook his head. "Nope. When Sas walked out of the forest and down the center of Savik, everyone was sure he was the one and only Sasquatch. He wore a fur coat of brown grizzly fur and his beard and hair were much longer than now.

Plus, the man stands at least a foot over most men and two feet taller than others."

She snapped her head around to look at "Sas." He couldn't be *that* big…could he? He did lift her pretty easily. She'd chalked that up to being super fit. If he was that tall and lived off the land, it was no wonder his strength was in proportion.

"Don't worry, though. He's not Bigfoot. It's just a nickname and out here, the first name tends to stick."

It did, did it? "You said he named me Angel."

Timber nodded. "Yes, he did, and it's obvious why. Not only are you beautiful like one, but—," the older man hooked a thumb in the direction of the kitchen, "he's far less grumpy and more talkative with you around."

Huh? More talkative? She'd hate to see what less was. "I appreciate the compliment, but I'm sure I'm quite a mess."

"Sweetheart, take a look at Sas and me? Do you really think you have competition?"

Personally, she found Sas the best-looking person in the room, but she looked at Timber from beneath her lashes. "Oh, I don't know. You're quite handsome in this wilderness setting."

Timber laughed, the sound filling the cabin. "You're definitely an angel."

She grinned, loving the warmth of the older man. "So where did your name come from?"

"He has an annoying habit of yelling 'timber' to scare any animals away when he's going to fell a tree." Sas set a plate of food on his table.

"Bah, there's nothing wrong with a little safety."

"When the tree is actually falling, but not the entire time you're cutting it." Sas moved back to the kitchen area.

She chuckled as Timber shrugged his shoulders.

He winked at her. "How was I supposed to know that? When I first moved up here, I was nineteen and as ignorant as a polar bear cub in a grocery store. Of course, once I had my nickname, I had to live up to it. I yell out 'timber' while cutting down a tree to this day."

"I love that." She was really enjoying herself. "So how did you meet Sas?"

"You said you were hungry." Sas' tone sounded like his patience was nearing its end.

She couldn't think of a single time she'd heard that from him before.

Timber sighed. "He's a demanding fellow." Rising, he pulled the chair away from the bed and brought it to the table. "Thank you. This is a feast. Are you sure you can spare it?"

Sas didn't bother to answer, but Timber didn't exactly hesitate to dig in.

"Would you like something?" Sas looked at her from the kitchen, but at her hands not her face.

She wasn't hungry, but definitely thirsty. "Just something to drink that isn't that tea that makes me sleep."

"You don't wish to sleep?"

"Not right now. The pain is bearable if I don't move, and I'm getting better at that."

Sas' gaze flicked to Timber, and he looked up. Something had just been communicated about her, but she had no clue what.

"I can make you a labrador tea. It's more likely to keep you awake."

"I highly recommend it." Timber winked at her. "Especially with a bit of Scotch for extra kick."

She couldn't see Sas' eyes, but she could tell his patience was tried by the older man. Maybe the whole not-talking-much issue was more specific to Sas because Timber certainly had no problem with chatting.

"I'd love to try it." Not sure if Sas was game to make the tea, she backpedaled. "But if it takes too long to make, I can just have water."

"No." Sas turned to one of the upper cabinets. "This water is too cold. You need warmth."

"But it's been three days already. Surely, that's long enough."

"It's been seven."

Seven? How did she lose four days? She looked over at Timber who was no longer smiling.

"He's right. You need to stay far from anything cold, especially inside your body. Hypothermia is nothing to take lightly. I've seen far too many lose their life to it."

It would have been one thing to hear Timber's words from a doctor, but from someone like him, and Sas who'd seen her condition occur in the wild, the information hit her hard.

She swallowed. "How long will it take me to fully recover?" Her voice barely made it out.

Timber grinned. "Oh, you're out of the danger zone if it's been a week, but you'll be sensitive to the cold for a while, and your frostbite could take months to heal."

"Months?" She turned toward Sas, who had opened the wood stove and crouched to add more wood. "It will take months? You didn't tell me that." Her voice rose as panic set it.

Sas looked over his shoulder at Timber, who quickly rose.

"I need to step out for a moment." He practically ran for the door, grabbing up his coat on the way out.

She returned her attention to Sas. "Months?" Her voice ended on a squeak.

He closed the stove door and rose slowly. Pulling the chair next to the bed, he sat, which just scared her that much more.

"Your feet will recover much sooner. Your boots were of good quality and it was only after you took them off that the damage was done, but your hands…"

Even as he trailed off, her hands seemed to burn again. Tears gathered in her eyes. "Will I lose my hands?" Her question was barely a whisper.

"I'm here to make sure that doesn't happen."

Oh God. Oh God. "But a hospital would be better, right? They have equipment and, and stuff that will save them, right?"

He still wouldn't look at her. Instead, he stared at her hand as it lay on the quilt. "They may be able to perform other procedures, but you wouldn't make it to the hospital in your condition."

Finally, her tears overflowed and trailed down her cheeks. "I don't want to lose my hands." She stared down at the quilt, unable to pull herself out of her own sorrow.

Sas lifted her chin with his finger.

She blinked at the blurriness in her eyes as she stared into his dark gaze. The intensity despite the lack of clarity, froze her. The whites of his eyes appeared slightly yellow through her tears.

"I will not let that happen. Do you understand?"

Whether it was his gaze or his tone of voice, something inside her believed him for a few seconds before doubt crept up again. "But what if you can—" His finger on her lips both surprised her and silenced her.

"I will find a way. If I must, I will make you healthy enough to travel and carry you to a town that has a plane that can bring you to a hospital."

Her tears slowed and as she nodded, he dropped his finger and looked away.

She wanted to force him to face her again, but she couldn't even lift her hand. Before she could say anything, he'd risen and moved to the wood stove.

He'd looked right at her, if only for a few seconds, which meant he had it in him to meet her gaze. Maybe she could help him in turn to conquer his shyness. His gaze had been so intense and so were his feelings.

Her heart finally slowed. He was determined to see her healthy again. She was one lucky lady. Only one question remained for her.

Why?

CHAPTER SIX

He strode outside and found Timber emerging from the woods.

"I'm sorry, Sas. I didn't realize you hadn't explained how bad her frostbite is. I assumed when you asked about pain killers that it was pretty bad."

"It is. She has reason to fear losing parts of her hands. I won't know how severe until blisters start breaking. I've changed the bandages twice, lightly washing her hands, but we both know gangrene can still occur and if the nerve damage is too great…"

Timber nodded. "That blistering is another hell she'll have to go through. Have you warned her about that?"

He moved farther away from the cabin. Though her hearing wasn't as good as his, having recently been blinded, he had no doubt hers had sharpened. "I'm waiting for her to be healthier in other ways, including mentally. She is still realizing the near miss she had with death. I planned to explain things a bit at a time. Emotional upheaval won't help her heal."

"Man, I'm sorry." Timber bowed his head.

He laid a hand on the older man's shoulder. "You didn't know. Your aid in procuring pain medicine will be compensation enough."

Timber looked at him and grinned. "Happy to help. I have some at my place which will help her now, after I retrieve it. I was going in to Savik one last time before winter and stopped over to see if you needed anything, but I can delay that." Timber looked at the sky and the thickening clouds. "I think."

"I'll fetch the pain medicine from your home." He could travel much faster than Timber.

"You really want to leave her alone for two days. I know you travel faster than me, but it takes me a full day to reach you."

He shook his head. "No. You'll have dinner with us and when she falls asleep, I'll run to your cabin and come back here while you stay with her."

Timber sat on a boulder that was only half covered in snow. "That's the best idea yet. You're a lot younger than I am, and I'll take good care of your Angel."

His heart warmed at Timber's phrase. "Good." He looked up at the sun, which was behind the clouds making it appear like twilight. "We have much time yet until our next meal. You can help me with the projects I need to finish."

Despite his age, Timber jumped to his feet. "Tell me where to start."

"I'll retrieve the tools we need." He strode back into the house to find Angel not only awake, but alert.

"Is Timber coming back in or did he leave? Are you done outside? I wish there was something I could do."

Though he dared not look at her face, her tone of voice made it clear she was already becoming bored. He hated to disappoint her. He could send Timber in to talk with her, but a part of him didn't like sharing her, even if she wasn't his mate. It was wrong and selfish, and he tried to overcome the emotion, but it wouldn't be tamped down.

He pulled out the items he needed from his tool corner, mainly the chainsaw and gas can. "Timber is going to help me take down a few trees. Since I'm keeping it warmer in here, I will need a few more cords of wood for winter and with two of us, it will minimize my time out of the cabin."

"Oh, that does make sense."

Though she understood, her disappointment bothered him. He turned around and his gaze fell on his bookshelves. "Would you like to read?"

"I would love to." Her excitement over his suggestion was reassuring.

He stepped up to his selection and looked for something more modern since she had mentioned her familiarity with the classics was limited. He pulled two books from the shelves, knowing exactly where each was located and what he wanted to offer. He brought them over to show them to her.

She read the covers. "*The Three Musketeers* and *Gone with the Wind*. I didn't realize these were such long books."

"I thought since you wished to occupy your time alone, a long book would be appropriate. This one," he held up *Gone with the Wind*, "is about overcoming adversity and this one is about adventure." He held up *The Three Musketeers*.

She moved her gaze from the books to his face, and he quickly looked at the books. "I've heard of both of these, but they were never explained in quite the way you did. I'll tackle *The Three Musketeers* first because I haven't seen a movie of that one, while the other comes on television a lot."

He had a little knowledge about television and movies,

but only from what Timber had told him. It didn't sound like it would be worth his time, so he didn't give her reasoning another thought. Instead, he gently lay the old, hard bound book open on her lap.

"Shoot, this won't work. I can't turn the pages." Her shoulders slumped in defeat and she closed her eyes.

He was in a quandary about what to do. "Let me bring this equipment outside so Timber can begin cutting. I'll be back." He turned, picked up the chainsaw and gas can and left.

Timber sat on the porch waiting. "I thought you'd changed your mind about working. I know I would if I had such pleasant company to talk to."

Irritation at Timber's remark hit him unexpectedly. He squelched the unreasonable emotion. "There will be time for that over the winter months." He grabbed up his axe from the side of the cabin and walked back to the porch.

"Right." Timber chuckled. "You'll have to tell me how that goes, you being such a talker and all."

He jerked his head toward the trees he wanted to cut. "We have work to do. I don't have to worry about talking. I can listen." Actually, he could listen to her voice all day, if she wouldn't ask him questions about himself.

"I get it. Shut up and help."

Timber's footsteps behind him assured him the man followed. He set down the chainsaw and gas on a patch of pine needles not covered by snow and strode into the grove. Without a word, he walked to each tree he wanted to fell and carved an X in it with the head of the axe.

"Whoa, you're feeling ambitious today."

Timber's observation didn't deter him as he continued to

mark the trees. Most were dead, others alive, all were evergreen. The live ones they'd stack on the side so he could choose a log to mix with those already dried if he had to. Brand new wood alone wouldn't heat the cabin and would cause problems with his vent pipe.

After marking at least a dozen trees, he retraced his steps.

Timber's eyes were wide. "You sure you need all this? I don't even think Sturge has as much cut wood as you will, and he has a wife and a little one to keep warm. And a bigger cabin."

"If I was alone this winter, I'd already have enough, but I'm taking no chances." He dropped the axe and picked up the gas can to fill the chainsaw. "Which would you like, the saw or the axe?"

"Is that a trick question? I know you plan to cut up the downed trees with that axe while I fell the next ones." The older man's feet came into sight next to the chainsaw. "They don't call me Timber for nothing."

He silently agreed, mildly amused by the older man. Lifting the chainsaw, he handed it to him. "You can begin. I need to create something for Angel, then I'll start on the trees you have downed."

"Whatever you say, Sas." Timber walked through the trees to the farthest from them and started up the chainsaw. "Timber!"

Shaking his head, he strode back toward the cabin. There had to be a way to help Angel turn the pages of the book. Animals who didn't have fingers were able to maneuver things so they could survive. Even bears were able to scoop honey with their giant paws. Honey.

As the idea formed, he headed for the closest birch tree.

After breaking off a switch about a foot long, he used his pocket knife to peel off the bark and trim it up. Then he strode to the northside of his cabin.

Between the cave wall and the side of his home, he crouched down and scraped away the moist dirt. Beneath, was a wet dark clay. He dug deeper with his knife until he found what he sought. Scooping the light gray clay up with his knife, he balled it onto the end of the switch.

It seemed very delicate, but so was Angel. Excited to see if it would work, he ran up the steps and walked inside.

Angel smiled tentatively at him. "I finished these two pages."

He kept his gaze lowered and sat in the chair near the bed. "Open your mouth."

"Huh? Why?"

"I've created a tool you can use to turn the pages, but you'll have to use your mouth."

She looked at the switch in his hand then opened her mouth hesitantly.

Carefully, he placed the clean end between her lips. "Bite down. It's just a bigger piece of birch then the ones I give you to chew on to clean your teeth." Once she had it firmly between her teeth, he gave her instructions. "At the end is a piece of clay which should enable you to move the page to the side, turning it over. Try it."

She stared at the book then widened her eyes, smiling around the stick. Bending her head forward, she set the clay end against the edge of page two and pushed toward page one. When she lifted the stick away, the page fell into place, allowing her to read page three.

Angel laughed. "I did it! Oh." Her excitement at her success was short lived as her exclamation sent the stick tumbling into her lap.

He found it amusing that while she read, she wouldn't be able to speak, but at her disappointed look, he took pity on her. "If you can use it this way while I'm working outside, then later I'll find a way to hook the tool around your ears, so you can talk and not lose it completely."

Her eyes shone with gratefulness before he averted his gaze. "Thank you. I feel so helpless and demanding. I'm not used to this."

"No one would be. You're coping very well. Now, I need to cut more wood before it grows dark. Is there anything else you'd like to say before I place the stick back in your mouth?"

"Yes, but it can wait until tonight. Go on and get your work done. I'll read about D'Artagnan."

He didn't respond, anxious to make progress on more wood. Setting the stick between her lips again, he noticed that they had already begun to heal. At least that would be one less place that caused her pain.

When she had a firm hold of the birch, he rose and left, not wanting to say anything in case she felt the need to answer him. Striding toward the grove of trees where he'd left Timber, he heard the man's telltale call just before the chainsaw started up again.

Angela woke at the sound of footsteps outside the door. For a moment, she was disoriented at the darkness around her. Reaching for the light beside her bed, she yelled. Crap, that hurt. She closed her eyes as burning pain engulfed her hand.

Unfortunately, it reminded her exactly of where she was and why. Squeezing her eyes against the onslaught of tears, she tried to think of the snow outside, the ice-cold waters of the ocean and the nippiness in the air.

Huh? She blinked her eyes open and sniffed. It was still twilight out, yet the cabin seemed cold. How could that be? Sas couldn't have been gone *that* long.

The door opened and he strode in. It was darker inside than outside, so she couldn't see his features, but by his pause then sudden race to the stove, she had the feeling she wasn't imagining the chill.

"Timber, light the lantern." Sas' husky voice was thrown over his shoulder as he opened the stove door and threw in a log. Light shone on his face as the wood caught.

She sucked in her breath as the scar around his eye was illuminated in high resolution by the flickering flames, the uneven stitch markings making it appear as if he'd lost his entire eye and had been given a new one. It looked like a butcher sewed him together. As far as she knew, the medical field hadn't figured out yet how to successfully transplant eyes, so that couldn't have been what happened.

Light from the lantern filled the cabin in a soft glow and Sas turned to grab another log.

"Uh, Sas. She's awake."

At Timber's observation, her mountain man rose and strode to the bed. Without a word, he felt her forehead, then her cheek. It took all her willpower not to turn her face into his palm. She was *that* glad to see him.

"I should have come back and added more wood."

She shook her head, and he pulled his hand away. "Were you gone that long? I fell asleep just as D'Artagnan fought with the three musketeers for the first time. I don't think I made it very far."

Sas turned away, strode back to the stove to add yet another log. "We were gone three hours."

Timber tapped Sas on the arm. "Hey, don't cook us. It's not that cold in here. Right, Angel?"

It took her a moment before she realized the older man spoke to her. "No, it's not that cold. It's just cool. I'm fine."

Sas shook his head, but didn't say anything.

Now why did she have the feeling he was beating himself up over the temperature in the room. "After all, how cold could it get in here? You two were out *there*."

Timber had just hung his coat on a hook when he turned and shook his head at her.

She clamped her mouth shut.

But it was too late. Her mountain man practically growled. "It's ten degrees outside."

Shoot. He'd been so good to her, she didn't want him to be upset. "Hey, it might be cool in here, but I'm toasty warm under this quilt. I'd say you came back at the perfect time. So how did the wood-cutting go?" She stared at Sas' back but he kept his focus on the fire in the stove.

"We made more progress than I expected." Timber sat on the couch. "I got all the trees down he wanted and even started cutting some up while he chopped. You two will be plenty warm this winter once he gets it all stacked."

Winter? She wouldn't be here all winter, but that was a discussion she'd have with her mountain man in private, preferably when he wasn't angry with himself. "It sounds like you got a lot more done than I did."

She looked to her right where the book had fallen when she fell asleep. A small scrap of very yellowed paper had slipped out from between the pages. It looked like it had the initials V.F. written on it. There were some other words, but they were too faded to read.

"Were you reading?" Timber picked up the book.

She looked up at the older man. "Yes, but I guess there weren't enough sword fights in the story to keep me awake."

He smiled fondly, as if she was his granddaughter or something, and laid the book on the end table. Then he motioned toward Sas who had just disappeared through his pantry. "He'll get over it. Don't worry."

She grimaced. Her brother could be like that, beating himself up over silly mistakes. He could sulk for days. "I hope so. I'm kind of dependent on him."

Timber walked to the couch and sat. He crossed one ankle onto his knee and lifted one arm to rest on the back of one of the two cushions still there. "Oh, he'll take great care of you. You should have seen him the day I got pinned under my own tree."

Her mood lightened immediately. "That sounds like a story I want to hear."

Timber wiggled his bushy gray eyebrows. "Then you're in luck. Everyone in a sixty-mile radius has already heard it, so I'm happy to oblige. I was taking down a bunch of trees near the stream by my cabin a few winters back. I thought I'd expand my garden in the spring. I figured the closer to the stream my plants were, the easier it would be to water them."

She nodded. "That makes sense."

"Exactly." He beamed. "I had started clearing the trees when one knotty old pine got hung up in a spruce tree. That's a particularly dangerous situation all 'round."

"Why?" She'd never heard the term "hung up" but she guessed it meant the top of the tree started to fall but tangled in another's branches.

The older man put his leg down and leaned both elbows on his knees. "Well, you see, when a tree is hung up, you have no idea what it will do and no control over it. It could kick out from the bottom, fall from the top, roll to the side, bounce off another tree and generally come crashing down at any moment."

Timber's voice rose with his story, adding a wonderful dramatic feel to it.

She widened her eyes in return, not wanting him to stop. Not only was he a good storyteller, but she was anxious to learn more about the man who cared for her so diligently.

"Of course, I knew all this, but it didn't stop me from doing something stupid." He paused.

She quickly responded. "Oh no, what did you do?"

"I grabbed up the rope I brought with me, which I sometimes use to give a tree a little nudge in the right direction, and I wrapped it around that knotty pine as far up as I could reach. Then I walked toward that stream and tugged on the rope. You know what happened?"

She shook her head, completely into the story now.

"Nothing. Not a damn thing, excuse my language. I walked on the other side of it and pushed, but that tree was as stubborn as me. Of course, that meant I had to show it who was more stubborn. I mean, if I'm going to be stubborn, I want to be the most stubborn. No half-ways about it."

"Of course."

He nodded. "I knew I liked you. Anyway, I walked back toward the stream and yanked on that rope again and that pine tree shimmied just a hair. Now I knew I had him. I got a good hold on that rope, jumped up and yanked with all my weight."

Timber sat back and crossed his legs at the ankles in front of him.

"What happened?"

"I'll tell you what happened. That damn pine came off the spruce branch in a shower of needles and fell right on top of me."

"Oh no!"

"That's what I thought." He shook his head. "I was in a bad way. You see, when that tree started falling towards me, I was off balance and as I tried to get my feet under me, they slipped and I fell onto my back. Next thing I know the top of that tree smacks me across the ribs and stays there. But I was lucky. You know why?"

"Because Sas was staying with you and he heard you yell?"

"Nope." Timber shook his head. "Sas wasn't staying with me. The reason I was lucky is the snow wasn't so old that it had turned hard as a rock and as that tree hit me, I sank. If it had been old snow beneath me, I wouldn't be talking to you today. But don't think it didn't hurt."

She shook her head, anxious to find out what happened next.

"In fact, as I found out later, that tree done broke three of my ribs and bruised two." He rubbed his side.

"Ow. That had to have hurt."

"Damn straight it hurt, and here I was lying in the snow with a pine tree pinning me in. I couldn't even see anything except the sky with the snow pack towering over me and the tree in front of me. I tried to move that old tree, but it was sunk in the snow too, and I had no leverage, never mind my broken ribs."

She could picture the entire scene. "What did you do?"

Timber's gaze moved toward the kitchen, and she looked over to find Sas shaking his head. "He screamed."

"I didn't scream." Timber scowled then returned his gaze to her. "I yelled for help like any normal human being. Not that I thought anyone would hear me. Sas is my closest neighbor and it's an all-day walk in the summer to travel to my place from here. I knew no one would hear me, but I had to try on the off chance someone was hunting in my neighborhood."

She grinned. "And Sas was, right?"

"Nope. Not a soul for miles."

"What happened?"

"I damn near died is what happened. I couldn't get out from under the tree and though I yelled my fool head off, no one came. Once it grew dark, I knew I was in trouble."

"Of course, hypothermia."

"Wolves."

"Wolves? Oh right, Sas told me wolves would have found me if he didn't." She shivered.

Timber nodded, sagely. "Yes. We have a number of packs in this area. As I lay there in the dark, I could hear them howling. I must have fallen asleep for a while because the next thing I knew I heard a howl right next to me."

She caught her breath. "They found you?"

Sas spoke from the kitchen. "It wasn't right next to him. It was at his cabin. They found his deer."

"Hey, Mr. Silent, are you telling this story, or am I?"

When Sas moved the pan to the wood stove, Timber continued. "The wolves were at my cabin. Luckily for me, I had strung up a deer I had shot that morning and field dressed it. I'd planned to finish cutting it up after felling a few trees, but that didn't happen. The wolves must have caught the scent and they enjoyed a midnight snack and didn't come looking for me."

Timber frowned. "I lost a lot of meat that night, but at least I'm still here to regret that. Anyway, I was now wide awake and afraid to go to sleep since I had no idea that the wolves had enjoyed dinner at my place without me. There I lay, looking up at the stars, the wet from the snow now causing me to shiver. I figured I would die right there." Timber paused as if deciding what to tell her next.

A heavy sigh from the stove filled in the silence, and she bit down on her lip to keep from smiling as Timber sent Sas an irritated look.

The older man returned his attention to her. "I figured it was getting on into the early morning hours, though I wasn't sure, when I hear a rhythmic thumping."

"Thumping?"

Timber nodded. "Yeah, that was what I wondered, too. I had no idea what it could be, but if it was rhythmic, it had to be human. Even a woodpecker has stops and starts and doesn't peck the same number of times over and over again."

Not something she'd known and interesting in relation to the story.

"I started to yell again, but I only got about three words out before my raw throat gave up. That's when I tried to find something I could knock on the tree trunk with. I was desperate and unbuckled my belt, hoping I could get it loosened enough to tap the tree with it when the thumping came closer. I tried to yell, afraid the thumping would pass right by me, but all that came out was a squeak. That gave me the idea to whistle."

The smell of meat caught Timber's attention and he looked at Sas. "What are you cooking?"

Ugh. Beyond frustrated, she snapped. "What happened?"

Timber looked at her and grinned, his ploy having worked too well. "Out of the darkness, this large figure emerged." He motioned with his hand toward Sas. "I was never so glad to see a Sasquatch in my life." Timbered winked at her. "He picked up that old pine tree like it was a toothpick, threw it aside then lifted me up and brought me to my cabin."

She gazed at Sas who had returned to the counter and was dishing out the meal. He was a real hero.

"And that's where Sas stayed for the next two weeks until I could fend for myself. He even ran into Savik for me to find painkillers for my ribs. When I was able to move about more, he stopped by every couple of days until I was healed."

"Wow. I guess we're lucky he's our friend." She couldn't help feeling a bit in awe over the story.

Timber chuckled. "Oh, Sas doesn't have friends. I'm just too stubborn to accept that, so I bother him every once in a while. It's not good to stay out here too long without some social interaction. And as you've seen, he's not much of a talker, but he makes a great listener."

"Come eat, old man." At Sas' grumpy announcement, Timber laughed.

Sas set what looked like a small cookie sheet on his table and pulled the chair over from the bedside for Timber. Then he disappeared into the pantry and came out with a barrel that looked like it may have been used for aging whiskey. He set it next to the bed before returning to the counter to retrieve the plate. He sat on the barrel and fed her.

She wanted to ask him a dozen questions about Timber's story, but true to form, the second she opened her mouth, he filled it with more delicious food, so she enjoyed that first, but she was determined to ask once they were alone again.

When they had all eaten, even Sas, who cleaned the plate he used for her before eating his own meal, he turned to Timber. "You can wash the dishes. I will go now."

Go? Her stomach tensed. "Where are you going?"

He looked at her but not at her face. "I'm going to Timber's cabin to retrieve the pain medicine he has for you. It will take me less time than if he goes."

Timber pushed back his chair. "See, he thinks I'm old and decrepit."

Sas ignored him.

There wasn't much she could do about him leaving in the condition she was in. "How long will you be gone?"

"I will be back tomorrow." He pulled his bear coat down from its hook.

"Tomorrow?" Oh shoot, this would be awkward. "Can you do something for me first?"

He immediately hung his coat back up. "Yes. What do you need?"

She glanced at Timber then back at Sas. "Um, can you come here?"

Sas strode toward her, but Timber turned away. "I'm going out for a minute." Within seconds, he'd grabbed his coat and exited.

The older man had a sixth sense. "I need to use the chair you made me. I don't think Timber is strong enough to lift me."

"Of course."

Was it her or did Sas seem to stand a little straighter? If she didn't know better, she'd say he was proud she preferred him over Timber. Did he have doubts?

She had a lot of doubts, but not about Sas.

When he brought the chair out, she licked her lips. "Sas, I like Timber, but is he, um, I mean, I'm pretty helpless here and…." Shoot.

He set the chair down. "Are you afraid of Timber?"

"Not exactly. It's just that I don't really know him and I'm pretty helpless here."

Sas looked toward the door as if he could see Timber waiting outside before returning his gaze to the bed. "I wouldn't trust him with you if I had *any* doubts at all about the man."

She trusted Sas, so if he trusted Timber, she'd have to, too. "Okay."

"If you want. I will stay here. Timber can retrieve the medicine. It will only take him an extra day."

At his offer, she relaxed a bit more. "No. If you trust Timber then I do, too."

"Are you sure?"

That he would stay if she asked, made her feel so much

better. For some reason, he was very protective of her and she doubted that he would let anyone or anything, even Mother Nature, harm her. "I'm sure." She grinned, thankful that her lips were feeling better.

Sas nodded before he pulled the quilt off her and lifted her into the chair. He moved the toilet paper next to her. "I will be outside and I won't let Timber back in until you agree he can enter."

"Thank you." Though she gave him a hesitant smile, he had already turned away and left, completely forgetting his coat.

She grinned at that. The big man seemed so ready to please her. She really needed to think of something to do for him after she returned home.

When she was finished, her hands burned so badly, despite their bandages, that she had to take a moment before she could speak. She called Sas by his nickname, hoping he wouldn't stubbornly refuse to answer. Her wait was less than a second before she heard his footsteps on the stairs.

He strode in, lifted her carefully and gently laid her back in bed. He returned the toilet paper to the end table and spoke as he tucked the quilt in around her. "I've given Timber instructions to bring in more wood, so he can keep it warm in here while I'm gone." He stepped back when he'd finished. "Is there anything else you need?"

Her hands still throbbed from using them, causing her to be emotional. She was so grateful to him. "Yes, can you bend over so I can whisper to you?"

He didn't ask why, just leaned in close.

"Thank you for being so good to me." She lifted her head and kissed him on the cheek.

He moved away slowly as if stupefied.

"Be careful of the wolves."

He nodded absently before turning to go. He opened the door, about to step outside without his coat again.

"Don't forget your bear skin!"

He stopped, reached his hand in to unhook it, then disappeared from sight.

CHAPTER SEVEN

Angela sniffed as her tears slowly dried up. Hopefully, Sas wouldn't forget to send Timber inside.

A few minutes later there was a knock and the door opened partially. "Can I come in? It's colder than a witch's—ahem, ice rink out here."

"Oh shoot, yes. I can't believe Sas didn't tell you to come in."

Timber walked inside and closed the door. Rubbing his bare hands together, he moved through the cabin. "Sas looked a little distracted. I think he was anxious to get you those painkillers."

When Timber reached the stove, he held his hands over it. "Now that feels good. The cold is fine if you're dressed for it." He looked at her. "But you already know that, don't you?"

She nodded. "I just wish I'd worn the right gloves. I had bought a great pair, but I left them on the boat because I thought I'd only be gone a few hours, not a few days."

Timber shrugged out of his coat. "Don't worry. If anyone can get your hands back to normal, it's Sas. For a man who prefers to be alone, he's always the first one to come to the rescue of a stranger." He hung his coat on the spare hook and pulled out the chair at the table.

"I wonder why that is? Do you think he gets lonely sometimes and by helping someone who's hurt, he can limit the conversation?"

Timber raised an eyebrow. "I think he limits conversation pretty well whether a person is hurt or not."

She smiled. Now that the pain in her hands was subsiding a bit, it was easier to concentrate. "Yes, he does that quite well. Then why do you think he's so willing to help?"

The older man looked at his thumb as if it was the most fascinating part of his body before digging beneath the nail. "I have a theory on that."

She wanted to laugh, already knowing Timber could keep her entertained for hours, but his unwillingness to look at her made her squelch it. "What's your theory?"

"I'm thinking Sas has something in his past that he feels the need to atone for. I'm not saying I know anything. It's just a hunch combined with a few things he's said that makes me think he wants to be absolved of past wrongdoings."

"I can't believe that." He was the kindest, sweetest, shyest man she'd ever met.

Timber looked her straight in the eye. "You need to understand there is a percentage of men who escape to Alaska to get away from serious misdeeds. Maybe it's something they did when they were young. Maybe it's something they regret, or even feel justified in doing, but they are here for a reason beyond the struggle for existence with Mother Nature."

She swallowed hard as Timber went back to cleaning his nails. "You think maybe Sas wants forgiveness?"

"I'm not sure about forgiveness. I think he wants to make fate happy."

She squinched her nose. "Fate? You think he believes in fate?"

He nodded. "I know he does. He believes it was fate that caused him to take a midnight stroll the night he found me. It's hard to argue with him. No one takes a stroll after midnight in the winter."

She'd like to say it was coincidence, but that pressed the boundaries of believability. But fate? Like some mystic force?

"I know he thinks fate made him decide to go fishing the day he found you and to head out at exactly the time of day when he would see the reflection off your phone. He also believes that you were meant to drop it right there, so he could find you. He firmly believes that you were meant to be here."

That was a lot of believing. She didn't agree. She'd been stupid and lucky. That was easier to accept than that she was meant to almost die and possibly lose her hands.

"Hey, you look like you're going to cry. It's just one man's belief." Timber grinned. "That's the great thing about living out here. We aren't on top of each other so we can more easily accept our differences and get along."

She nodded, though she couldn't quite manage to smile. "I need to keep looking at the bright side of what's happened, and Sas finding me was definitely a positive. What about you? How did you two meet?"

Timber had laid his hands on the table, but with her question, he leaned back in the chair, tipping it onto its back legs as he linked his hands behind his head. "I shot him."

"What?" Her heart rate actually sped up at his pronouncement. "You shot him? Why?"

He chuckled. "Not on purpose…and not exactly." His

gaze moved off as if recalling the events and he lost his smile. "I swore I shot him. Looked down my sight through the underbrush as I leaned against a spruce tree, aimed and pulled the trigger on what I thought was a grizzly."

"Wait. Did you or didn't you shoot him?"

He moved his gaze back to her. "He said I didn't. When I looked to see if the bear went down, Sas moved out of the thicket. I stood for a moment with my jaw flapping, but no sound came out. I ran down to him asking if he was okay. He said he was, but there was a hole in his coat. He claimed the hole had been there. I wouldn't believe him, so he took it off and there was a hole in his flannel shirt as well, but the man was standing there talking to me. I insisted he take off his shirt."

"And was he bleeding? Was it a flesh wound? Did you just graze him?" She could picture the encounter, which made her anxious to learn if Sas was okay.

Timber gave her his full attention. "You watch a lot of those crime shows on television, don't you?"

She looked away. "Not a lot."

"Well, it was none of those things, and he wouldn't take off his shirt completely, but he did let me look at the left side of his chest. There was a slight red mark there, but no hole."

"How could that be?" In her mind, Sas was bleeding to death.

Timber shrugged. "I don't know. I swore I hit him, but he said the bullet hit a branch that smacked him in the chest and fate saved him. I have to believe him, but I wouldn't be surprised if the man's own pectoral muscle made the bullet bounce off. He's inhumanly strong."

She tried to imagine what Sas looked like without his shirt

on, but she couldn't. Now that she thought about it, she'd never seen him unclothed in any way. "Was it too cold for him to take off his shirt?"

He looked at her oddly as if he missed something. "Not for Sas. He likes it cold. I think he didn't want to take off his shirt because of his scars. I noticed one that ran horizontal across his chest just above the red mark and I'm sure you've seen the one around his eye."

"I did. Was he in a car accident?"

This time, Timber shrugged. "I figured it was a motorcycle accident or even a human versus train scenario, but I don't ask. That's one of the unwritten rules of living up here. You don't pry into someone's past, but questions about a person's safety, like asking if he has enough cords piled up or plenty of meat stored for winter are fine."

"Oh." She'd been about to ask another personal question about Sas, so she swallowed it. "But *you* don't mind sharing. Is there anything else you can tell me about you and living out here in the wild?"

Timber grinned, set down his chair and rose. "Since you're such a good listener, I'll tell you about the time I came face to unpleasant face with a mama polar bear, but first I need to wet my whistle and I'm sure you wouldn't mind another cup of tea."

"Yes, please." She relaxed back into the cushion and stared at nothing as her mind raced with thoughts of Sas. Timber's story only made her that much more curious. Up until just then, she'd been secretly bemoaning the loss of her adventure trip, but what she was learning and experiencing here was far better than that ever could have been.

Now if her hands would just heal completely, she could consider her vacation a total success.

Having dropped his coat on a branch not far from his home, Sas ran south in the general direction of Timber's cabin, but his mind wasn't on where he headed. Instead, it was on the featherlight kiss Angel had given him. He hadn't expected it and now his thoughts tumbled over themselves like a giant snowball rolling down the mountain.

Her lips, almost healed now, were soft and moist. He could still feel their impression on his cheek, or rather his mind did. She kissed him below the eye with no scar because that was the one he'd turned toward her.

It had been a kiss of gratitude. He understood that, but it had been given freely. His heart swelled. In his long life, he'd only been kissed by two other women, Akiakook's *nuliaq* and a woman he'd saved from the icy waters of the Arctic Ocean.

Akiakook's wife had often kissed him on the cheek for keeping her husband busy, which allowed her to visit with her daughter's daughters. The woman he'd saved was a scientist studying frost flowers near the North Pole. He'd been camped nearby when he heard her yell before a telltale splash. Once he pulled her out, she'd kissed him with shivering lips before she was borne away by her team.

It wasn't difficult to remember each woman despite the century between them. Now he had a kiss for the twenty-first century. Would she give him more?

The memory of holding Angel's cold body close to his when he'd first brought her back to the cabin slowed his steps.

He had never been that close to a woman before. It felt good. Would Angel want that?

He came to a full stop at Two Beavers stream. He'd read about how man procreated as well as the dozens of mating rituals used to bind the opposing sexes together for life. Akiakook had answered many of his questions about the pleasure it gave, far more than the simple release he provided himself.

But without a mate, he was destined to never know the joy of coupling. He'd come close once, when men had flooded the Yukon in a race to find gold. Amongst the mining camps, outposts cropped up that included places of drink and women.

He'd come upon Rangely's End by accident as he traveled west across the northern most areas of Canada. It was night, and as he walked through a darkened alley, he found a woman pushing a drunk man out the back door of the saloon. The man made a grab for her, and she yelled.

He had to step in, so he pulled the man away by the collar of his shirt only to have the woman grab the half empty bottle from the drunk's hand and smash it over the man's head. He crumpled to the ground in a heap.

She'd been happy for the help and took him upstairs, saying she'd give him a discount for being so honorable. Having been alive for over sixty years, he was thrilled to have the opportunity to finally feel what coupling was.

She'd bared her breasts by pulling them above her corset and put his hands on them. They were large and the nipples painted red, but he never forgot how they felt. He'd grown hard, his need rising fast. She quickly unbuttoned his trousers and grasped his cock in her hands.

He closed his eyes at the remembered feel of her stroking his shaft. She'd exclaimed at the size and her brow furrowed. She'd even chuckled uncertainly, saying they might not fit. The need in him was too strong and his own experience too lacking for him to stay in control.

It was a mere second before he'd picked her up and set her on the dresser against the wall, spreading her legs with his hands. She'd laughed, calling him a randy one. Then she'd taken his cock in her hands again and stroked his tip against her opening.

The warm moistness of her womanhood had undone him. He spilled his seed before ever penetrating her body. She'd chuckled, telling him she was flattered and that he could have that one for free.

After that, everything changed. She'd placed his hands back on her breasts, distracting him from what she did. It wasn't until she'd pushed him away that he'd noticed his linsey-woolsey shirt was unbuttoned, and she was staring at his scars.

Her voice was filled with fear as she yelled at him. "What are you? Get away from me, you monster. Get out!"

He opened his eyes, focusing on the cold air and the sound of a wolf's howl miles away. Its lonely call echoed the one in his heart. Every experience he'd had in his existence, he'd learned from. The saloon woman taught him what to expect from intercourse, and it wasn't something he wanted to repeat.

Crossing the stream in two strides, he continued toward Timber's place, increasing his speed until he ran straight out. Angel needed the pain medicine so she wouldn't lose hope. That was his mission now, not to look for anything more from their growing friendship.

His body eased into his strides. That's what he had with her. Different from his friendship with Akiakook and even Timber, but a friendship, nonetheless. Akiakook was the father he'd never had and Timber was like a persistent squirrel. A nuisance at first, but when absent, missed simply because the norm was changed.

Angel was different. Her helplessness made him responsible for her, but her brightness and curiosity was a balm to his ravaged and shriveled soul. Soon he would have to tell her exactly how long it would take her hands to heal. Once he gave her Timber's medicine, he could change the bandages and have a better idea of how long that might be.

Would she want to leave? He begged fate that wouldn't be the case. He wanted to spend the winter with her. It would take at least that long to learn enough about her to keep him company for years.

The snap of a tree branch had him coming to a sudden stop. His mind had wandered and he forgot to be vigilant about his surroundings. Whirring around, he was just in time to face a black bear standing on his hind legs.

"I have no quarrel with you, bear."

The bear roared, obviously upset that the element of surprise was gone. Then he attacked anyway.

The sting of claws slashing through his sleeve forced him to defend himself, and he smacked the beast on the side of the head, sending it back onto all fours. That just made it angrier, and it roared before ramming into his legs, forcing him back but not down.

The bear swung its head back and forth grunting before it rose on its hind legs again and swiped at his face. He turned his head, spinning around to kick the bear in its stomach. The animal fell forward and rolled before slowly getting to its feet.

"Go!" He stepped toward the bear, raising his arms high. Finally, it decided he wasn't worth it and it loped off into the forest. His sleeve was ripped, but no blood stained it. The grooves left in his arm by the bear's claws were already healing, the brief pain forgotten.

Scanning the area to make sure no other predator had come to discover what had caused all the noise in the silent night, he finally resumed his run, more determined than ever to return home by morning.

The bears were gearing up for a long winter of hibernation, making them that much more dangerous. The sooner he returned to Angel, the better. Jumping over a log, he sprinted down a hill, snow muffling the sounds he made as he ran.

Angela was awakened by bright sun streaming in the front windows of the cabin. She'd fallen asleep while still propped up by the couch cushion, so now she could see Sas' face as he spoke outside. She recognized the cadence of Timber's speech and the tone of Sas' as they conversed though she couldn't see Timber. As entertaining and solicitous as Timber was, she wasn't just relieved Sas was back, but happy, too.

Without a doubt, she had a crush on her mountain man. Who wouldn't? He was handsome, intelligent, gentle, caring, strong, and shy. That combination had her heart tripping and her imagination going a little crazy. Last night, she'd even dreamed of introducing Sas to her brother.

She wanted to know so much more about him and the

places he lived, but it was hard to get him to talk about himself. She'd peppered Timber with questions about Sas, but the older man could only answer what he knew.

At the sound of footsteps on the stairs, she closed her eyes. Maybe if they thought she was still asleep, they would talk more freely. The door opened and one set of footsteps entered. She waited, hoping whoever was still outside would come in.

After a few minutes of only Sas' footsteps moving about the cabin, she resigned herself to learning nothing new. Opening her eyes, she froze.

Sas stood with his back to her, taking off his white shirt, parts of which were torn. Scars from stitches ran from the top of both shoulders, around his shoulder blades and underneath his arms, as well as straight across his upper back.

That the deltoids and biceps of those arms were huge didn't escape her notice, or that there was a scar around his left elbow and one around his right bicep, but it was sympathy that rushed through her at the trauma he must have undergone to need such extensive surgery.

The rest of his back was thick with muscle that she appreciated on a strictly feminine level, especially as he lifted his arms to pull off the last bit of his shirt. She barely noticed it was ripped, as his movement accentuated the broadness of his shoulders and the slenderness of his waist.

Her gaze travelled lower to find what might be more surgical scars near the top of his jeans, but the sight was covered too quickly by Sas pulling on another shirt.

What had happened to him? It seemed as soon as she learned a little more, it fueled more questions. Since he'd gone to great lengths to avoid her seeing him without a shirt, she closed her eyes and waited until she heard him in the kitchen area.

She yawned loudly and opened her eyes. "Good morning." She smiled at him, though he only gave her a quick glance. She wished she could get up and wrap her arms around him and tell him he was awesome. She had her doubts that he'd had that said to him nearly enough.

Since he didn't return her greeting, not that she was surprised, she started the day's conversation. "Have you ever been married?" Okay, maybe not the most subtle approach, but since he was so good at not answering when he didn't want to, she really wasn't risking anything by being blunt. Though she had to admit it was an odd topic for first thing in the morning. It was probably more suited to morning-*after* conversation.

At the thought of her and Sas talking in bed after a night of passionate lovemaking, her whole body heated, except her hands which already burned.

"No." He didn't miss a beat as he mixed something in a bowl.

No? Right, no wife. "Serious girlfriend?"

"No."

"Okay, how about a few casual girlfriends?" The word "serious" could throw a man off.

"No." He moved to the stove and placed his pan on it as if he hadn't just admitted he'd never been in a relationship of any kind.

Now that was concerning. He was such a nice guy. What was wrong with him that he had no girlfriends? Was he a sex only man? She wouldn't have thought that.

She opened her mouth to confirm her assumption and quickly shut it. Maybe the scars had something to do with it. If only she could get him to be comfortable around her. She could show him they didn't bother her.

As she searched for another topic, she recalled his interest in her own life. That had to be a sign that he cared about her as a person as well as a hypothermia victim. At least she hoped that was the case. "I've had two serious relationships."

He didn't actually show a reaction, but his hand hesitated for a second before he flipped the food in the pan.

"The first one I ended." She waited to see if he would reveal that he listened, but he didn't. "We were just in different places in our lives. The second one, he ended. I thought it was a perfect match because he liked to travel as much as I did. Unfortunately, we didn't always travel together due to our jobs, and he found someone better than me who could go with him *all* the time." At the time she'd been devastated, but looking back on it, she was glad the relationship had fallen apart.

"He was a fool." Sas' sudden entrance into her monologue surprised her.

"He wanted what he wanted." She started to shrug, but stopped herself in time. She was finally adapting to her limitations. "I was the fool for falling for him in the first place."

Sas shook his head, but didn't say anything.

She smiled. "I'm better off anyway…except for my hands, that is."

He finally looked at her, specifically at her hands. "They will be better, too."

She had no doubt that he would do everything in his power

to heal her. It was an odd confidence to have, especially when she didn't even have that with doctors when she'd been sick or the one time she'd broken her ankle. Yet here she was, pretty much helpless, and she had complete faith in Sas, a stranger who had saved her life.

He placed the chair next to the bed then brought a plate over.

One look at the pancakes with berries in them and all thoughts of doctors and boyfriends flew out of her mind. "I love pancakes!"

He cocked his head as if surprised by her excitement. He obviously had no idea that she rarely had pancakes for breakfast, and the ones on the plate were slathered in syrup.

She didn't say another word, wanting him to know how much she appreciated the treat. Instead, she opened her mouth in anticipation.

He focused on her mouth, but she'd swear he wanted to smile. As she began to chew, she closed her eyes. "Hmmm." They were better than good. The syrup he used was different, obviously not maple. She couldn't place the berries. Probably wild ones that grew in the area.

She swallowed and opened her eyes and mouth, not willing to delay the next bite with questions. The ensuing silence was comfortable, not awkward as she enjoyed every forkful.

"You liked those." He made the obvious statement as he placed the fork on the now empty plate and lifted the wet cloth he always had ready for after she ate.

She gave him a full smile since her lips had healed enough to do so without cracking them. "I did. You're spoiling me."

He shook his head before he wiped her face. Then he

moved his gaze to look at her hands. "I have to change your bandages."

By his reluctant tone of voice, she could tell it wouldn't be a pleasant experience. Her tummy constricted around the delicious meal she'd eaten. "Today?" Her voice came out pathetic, but the pain her hands gave her was excruciating. Only by not moving them was she able to bear it at all.

He rose and walked back to the kitchen. "I have the medicine from Timber. You should take it now before I start."

Her relief was tinged with anxiousness at the finality of Sas' statement. He wouldn't be delaying the inevitable at all. She swallowed hard. "Okay."

He returned with the tin cup and a pill.

She stared at his face like she always did in an effort to catch his gaze if he looked at her. This time she noticed sweat beading near his temple.

Frowning, she moved her gaze to the opening of his shirt. He'd switched out the white one for a cream one that looked like it was made of wool. Though it was dashing with its tie neckline and full sleeves, she could see a sheen of sweat at the base of his throat. This was the one he'd mentioned would be too warm. "Why don't you change your shirt? You're obviously sweating in that one."

He shook his head. "This is the only one I have left."

"What happened to the white one?"

As if he anticipated a long drawn out conversation, he leaned back in the chair. "I ripped it when traveling to Timber's cabin, and before you ask, no, I don't have another. I had to rip up my flannel one to cover the hot rocks I placed around you to warm you up when I first brought you here."

Once again, he'd sacrificed for her. "Then please, take that one off before you can't stand being in here any longer."

"No." He leaned forward as if that settled it.

If she could cross her arms, she would. "Unacceptable." She could be stubborn, too. This was a perfect opportunity to show him he had nothing to be ashamed of.

His eyebrows rose. "Unacceptable?"

"Yes. I won't have you over-heating because you're so busy taking care of me. You need to take care of yourself because if you get sick, I can't help myself yet."

He shook his head. "I won't get sick. Now take this pill, so it doesn't hurt as much when I change your bandages."

She clamped her lips together tightly. It was a big risk, but she wouldn't take the pill until he took off his shirt.

"What are you doing?" He held the pill before her mouth, thoroughly confused.

She shook her head.

He sat back again, so she dared open her mouth to speak. "I will take my pill after you take off your shirt. Believe me, I've seen plenty of men shirtless, and it's not a big deal. There is no reason for you to suffer from the warmth of your shirt."

He frowned, his black eyebrows lowering.

If she had to bet on an emotion, she'd say he was frustrated. She just hoped he didn't call her bluff and start changing her bandages.

He leaned in again, holding the pill. "Take the pill and then if I need to disrobe, I will."

She shook her head again, keeping her mouth shut. She didn't put it past him to sneak the pill in if she spoke.

When he sat back again, a myriad of emotions crossed his

face, but she couldn't tell what they were without seeing his eyes. "You won't like it."

"It has nothing to do with what I like or don't like. You need to be comfortable and wearing that shirt out of some kind of decorum is silly. You take it off and I'll take the pill."

His jaw clenched as he sat there, holding both the cup and pill.

Part of her wanted to relent at his struggle, but her gut told her this was important, and as much as she hated to put him through revealing his many scars, she wanted him to be comfortable enough around her to do so. She didn't have a clue as to why.

Finally, he rose and set the pill and cup on the chair.

Her stomach tingled in anticipation. She had an idea of what to expect. She just needed to control her facial expression in case his front was worse than his back.

He continued to stand there, obviously still not completely decided.

"This isn't a big deal. Just take your shirt off, be comfortable and I'll take my pill. I care about your health as much as you care about mine." She gave him a soft smile.

He shook his head so slightly that it was barely perceptible, but she caught it. As if stealing himself for rejection, his neck muscles tightened just before he lifted one hand up, grasped the back of his shirt and pulled it over his head, gripping it in one hand like a life line.

Since he continued to look down, it gave her the opportunity to view his entire torso. The scars weren't surprising since they all continued from the back, two that circled his shoulders, one across his chest and the uneven ones on his arms.

What did surprise her was the muscle beneath, bulging between the scars as if they were what held everything in place. His chest was massive and his abdominals like the ripples in the dunes of the Sahara. He even had the v-lines on either side of his hips that disappeared beneath his jeans. The leather around his wrists and neck made him look like a gladiator.

"Wow, you're ripped." Her exclamation came out before she could stop it. Shoot, she didn't mean as in ripped up. She needed to clarify that. "I've seen other men ripped with muscle, but you're by far the strongest." She probably didn't make it better, but her heart was pattering in her chest at an uneven rate and half the blood in her brain had just traveled south. "I'm so glad I don't have to share you."

She wanted more than anything to look at his face, but on the off chance he watched her, she let her gaze enjoy the view.

"You don't find me repulsive." His statement was said in a soft tone as if he was in shock.

Good. Beauty was more than skin deep and he had a beautiful soul, but even his body was more beauty than damage. "Of course, I don't. Why would I? In fact, I'm grateful to whoever sewed you back together because if you weren't alive and in the strong condition you're in, I would either be dead or in a lot more pain than I am."

At her mention of pain, he seemed to remember what he'd been about to do. Immediately, he threw the shirt to the couch, picked up the cup and medicine, and sat down.

The spruce scent she always noticed when he was nearby, heightened as if it came from his very pores. There was a wildness about it that spoke to her base female instinct.

He leaned in and she opened her mouth obediently. After

placing the pill on her tongue, he tipped the cup so she could swallow the cold water.

It was the first time he gave her water directly from the sink, and its chill surprised her. It was refreshing, helping to take the edge off her rising desire. "Thank you."

"It will be some time before it takes effect. I need to go outside and bring in more wood for the stove." He rose as he spoke, quickly depositing the cup in the sink as he made a beeline for the door.

She snapped her mouth shut as he opened it and headed out without his shirt. It had taken far too long to get him out of it. The last thing she wanted to do was encourage him to put it on again.

Relaxing back into the cushion, she smiled. That had been a very pleasant surprise. Not only did she help him out, but she discovered that her mountain man was hot. He was the kind of eye-candy that could give her a toothache…if it wasn't for those scars. She had to find out what had happened to him.

CHAPTER EIGHT

As the cold air hit his bare torso, he breathed deeply, his muscles finally loosening. He'd contemplated refusing Angel's request and changing her bandages anyway, but she would cry from the pain. He couldn't bear to be the one to cause her tears.

He strode down the steps, headed for the wood pile. He hadn't dared to look at her face, knowing she'd be shocked and upset by his scars. When she sounded as if she admired his body, he couldn't help glancing at her quickly, only to find her smile growing and her pupils dilating, taking over more of her green eyes.

That look had sent sexual need speeding strait to his groin so hard that he'd barely kept a groan from escaping. Now he was the one in shock. Never had a woman looked at him with such appreciation.

Never.

A tiny flame of hope sputtered to life deep in his chest. He tried to ignore it, but it refused to be snuffed. Was there a chance she would stay with him after she healed?

He let his imagination run. Images of them eating together, sleeping together, and working side by side to make her as comfortable as possible populated his head. Visuals from books he'd read on human mating swirled around in his mind, causing his cock to grow hard with need.

He stopped to pull it out of his pants, a release almost imminent. He wouldn't scare her with his desire. If all that he read was correct, she must find fulfillment first. Her pleasure would be his.

He stroked himself as he looked downward from his mountain ledge. The cold barely registered against his skin, but where it did, it added excitement to his already growing pleasure. He tried to picture what Angel would look like beneath him, but the image wouldn't come, his experience seeing an actual naked woman sorely lacking.

Instead, he closed his eyes and let memories of others having sex fill his mind. Sounds of couples moaning, women yelling and men panting as they reached the ultimate nirvana in each other's arms sent his heartbeat racing.

His body tensed, his balls tightened and his release spurted from his cock onto the white snow. He focused on his pleasure, pulling every last drop from his body. As he calmed, the image of his intended mate infiltrated his mind. Her body curved, her pubic hair black and her breasts pointy. Her jaw had been delicate, her hair abundant.

Then the image of her body being torn apart filled his mind. The despair of that night flooded him all over again, and despite his euphoria of seconds ago, he fell to his knees.

"No." The word ripped from his throat was barely a whisper, the very air to make it extinguishing the small flame of hope that had lit in his heart. Akiakook had said memories returned when they were needed. The destruction of his mate was a reminder that he was alone…forever. He had no right to hope for anything else.

Cleansing his cock and hands with snow, he rose, zipping himself in even as he turned and strode back to the woodpile. Peace, that elusive state, was all he had the right to hope for, though even that was a reach.

Loading his arms with split logs, he ignored the minor scratching against the bare skin of his chest and walked back into his home.

Angel's eyes were closed, so he kept quiet, loathe to waken her until he had everything ready. His focus had to be on making her well. That was all.

Pulling the supplies from his cabinet, he quietly set them on the end table next to the bed.

"I heard you come in. I'm not asleep. Just resting. This medicine is good stuff."

He glanced at her face to find her eyes still closed. "You can feel it then."

"Oh yeah. I feel like I'm floating." She smiled but still didn't open her eyes.

It would hurt, even with the medication, but at least it should dull the pain somewhat. Gently, he lifted her hand by the wrist and unwrapped it. As the last piece of material fell away, her wrist jerked in his grasp.

"What's that?" Her voice was strained.

He examined the skin on her hands. Bumps covered it, some milk white, others dark. "You have frostbite blisters." He picked up the knife he'd sterilized in the fire after he added more wood. "Some have broken. I need to remove the extra skin."

"Oh God. Will it hurt?"

"Yes." He hated that she would cry, but he'd promised to save her hands.

"I can't watch."

He didn't look at her, but was glad she wouldn't see what he did. It would look like he made the situation worse, though in fact it would be better. He'd first seen the same process while living in Greenland.

Steeling himself against the crying that was sure to occur, he carefully began removing the dead skin. When no sound issued from her after he'd finished half of them, he looked at her.

He was surprised to find her eyes open and quickly looked down. She'd been staring at him.

"Is it done?" Her voice was strained.

"No. I've only completed half."

"Okay."

When she didn't say anything more, he risked a glance at her. She continued to stare at him, water in her eyes. Quickly, he went back to work, his chest tight at the pain he inflicted.

It had to be done. He'd promised. He refused to disappoint her. Focusing again on the white blisters, he finished with the burst ones, ignoring the few red ones. When he'd finished, he wrapped her hand in moss then in a clean strip of his former flannel shirt.

When he'd completed that hand, he set it down and glanced at her. Her beautiful eyes were closed and tear tracks coated her cheeks, but she hadn't made a noise or tried to pull her hand away. "That hand is done."

Her eyelids fluttered open. "That didn't take too long. Have you done this before?"

He lowered his gaze. "I have."

"I thought so. I feel so lucky that you found me."

At the tone in her voice, he couldn't resist looking at her. Her green eyes were bright and their moisture reflected the fading light of the day. Her gaze held gratefulness and kindness.

He turned back to his task. Gently, he picked up her other hand and went to work. When he'd finished that one, he set it down and rose to throw out the old bandages.

"I'm so lucky to have a hot man tending to my every need. Must be a perk of getting lost in Alaska."

At her unusual statement, he looked over his shoulder to find a dazed smile curving her lips. She rolled her head back and forth then looked at him again. "Yup. The view is definitely a perk."

He steeled himself against the interest his body had at her words. She was on pain medication and didn't know what she said. Unfortunately, his control over his body's response was limited.

Quickly, he resituated the chair toward the end of the bed. Her feet were far from the very end. After rearranging the supplies, he would need to change the bandages on her feet, he lifted the bottom of the quilt. "This shouldn't hurt as much."

"I'm sure whatever you do will be wonderful." Her voice was soft and had taken on a sing-song quality.

Resisting the urge to look at her again, he unwrapped her feet. Relief swept through him at their condition. Just a few blisters and no red ones. Even better was the fact that no blisters had developed on the bottoms of her feet.

When he found her, her feet were facing the morning sun and since her socks had been black, what warmth there was had found its way to her feet. "You should be able to walk again soon. We can check again in a few days." He forgot to avoid her gaze and looked at her.

Her smile was bright and her eyes had changed to a deeper green like that found on a spruce tree. Desire shot through his body so suddenly that he jerked before returning his focus to taking care of her.

"I knew I could count on you. I'm going to have to find some way to repay you. Maybe we should start with a —ow!"

He gritted his teeth to keep himself from turning his face toward her. He'd done nothing different with the blister he worked on now than the ones on her hands, but obviously the medicine had lessened her own control.

"That hurts." She pulled on her leg.

He clamped down on her ankle. "Don't move. I could cut you."

"Feels like you're already doing that." Her voice was less irritated and more whiney, which relieved him.

Still, he didn't delay in ministering to her feet. When he cleaned them, he wrapped each loosely in the remaining flannel. He was glad he'd requested Timber purchase him another shirt…if there were any large enough.

Once again covering Angel's feet with the quilt, he rose and turned away without looking at her. The medicine was playing with her mind and he wouldn't take advantage of that.

He threw out the old bandages and cloths he used and washed his hands.

"Sas?"

He stilled. She sounded sleepy. Maybe she'd fall asleep.

"Sas, please come here."

He took a deep breath, steeling himself against the temptation she presented. Finally, he turned around and walked back to the bed. "Yes?"

"I need to whisper."

"Then perhaps you should wait until later when you feel stronger."

"Please." She sounded so helpless, he acquiesced. Bending, he moved his head closer.

"You're one of a kind."

He froze as the words chilled him to his core. But no sooner had she whispered them, then she lifted her head and her lips touched his.

Shock held him immobile until her tongue begged for entrance into his mouth. His lips parted of their own accord, and she pressed their mouths closer as her tongue swept inside to touch his.

Need flashed through his body like lightning and he jerked away. No! Spinning, he strode to the door, threw it open and left.

Angela grinned. Wasn't that the hottest kiss she'd ever had that wasn't returned? She surprised the hell out of him. She loved that! And he tasted so good. Tart and sweet all at the same time. She giggled. Of course, it had to be the berries and syrup.

Closing her eyes, she continued to smile. Sas was all man from his bulging biceps to his soft beard. What would his beard feel like if he were to kiss her everywhere? Oh, she liked that idea.

She could lie here helpless as he made love to her. She

could see it clearly. First, he'd strip off all her clothes, carefully because that was his way. She'd lie there stark naked as he looked at her with his intense dark eyes. She'd shiver with anticipation.

Then he'd take off his jeans, and she'd finally get to see his legs. His thigh muscles would be well-defined and hard, his calves larger than what she could grasp with two hands. His skin would be smooth and absent of the scars his torso had, making him more confident.

Then he'd take down his underwear and a very large cock would greet her. She'd lick her lips and he'd bring it to her. Her mind drifted in pleasure.

Sas stroked her lips with the tip of his cock, the smooth skin begging her to lick and suck, but as she darted her tongue out, he pulled it away.

She pouted.

He shook his head. "You're too anxious."

"Of course, I am. I've been drooling over you for weeks."

He took her face in both his hands and tilted her head back. "But we had sex yesterday."

Before she could answer him, he plunged his tongue into her mouth, and she wrapped her arms around his neck, grasping his hair in one hand.

He let go of her face and braced his arms on either side of her, never breaking their kiss as his body covered hers. He was huge, scary in his size, but he kept his weight from her even as his cock found the place between her legs that was moist and waiting for him.

She bent her knees, urging him to enter her, but he didn't. Instead, he rubbed his cock against her, his base stroking her clit up and down, spreading her own wetness between them.

She tore her mouth away. "I want you inside me."

He pulled back to kneel between her legs. "You are too hot."

Too hot? There was no such thing.

He raised his hand and showed a small snowball the size of a large marble.

Her sheath flooded with anticipation. "What are you going to do with that?"

As usual, he didn't say anything. He simply stroked the little snowball across her nipples.

The cold sent erotic spikes to her core as her nipples grew so hard it bordered on pain, but he kept circling them in turn then brushing them with the snow until it melted, leaving her breathless and wanting.

She grasped his hand and licked the water from his fingers, then sucked them each in turn. Anything to get him to push his cock inside her.

But he pulled his hand away from her and produced another small snowball. He held it for her to see once again. Spreading his own knees, he pushed her legs open wider.

The snowball lowered and pressed against her opening. Holy sugar, he was going to put it inside her. Even at her thought, the snowball pressed into her opening, sending paradoxical fire through her veins.

Another snowball appeared in his fingers and was pushed in to join the one melting inside her. The next came faster and was thrust inside just before a fourth followed. Her body felt on fire, even within her cold sheath, but he gave no respite as he moved his cock over her clit and stroked.

Her sheath tightened on the cold hardness inside and her body tensed. He replaced his cock with his fingers, playing with her clit as her sheath tightened on the hard melt until her hips came off the bed and her scream filled the air.

She floated in his arms in the warm waters of the Banjar hot springs, exhausted yet frustrated. Would he ever come with her? He had her nestled in front of him, so she couldn't see him. He did that a lot. But how did she know that? Didn't she just meet him on this trip?

Confused, she pulled out of his arms and turned to look at him, but *he was gone. She stood to call his name, but she couldn't remember what it was. The steam from the baths grew thicker until everything turned bright white.*

She covered her eyes with her hand and shivered. Quickly, she crouched down into the warm waters and they came up to her neck, helping her relax.

He stood in the snow, his body's heat rising from him as the below-zero air hit him. Unfortunately, it didn't take away the shock of Angel's kiss. His whole being centered on the remembered feel of her lips and the touch of her tongue. He wanted that and more with every fiber of his soul…if he had one.

He fisted his hands and closed his eyes, stealing himself against the hope trying to come to life. He didn't deserve her. He was a monster, other than human.

A voice rose inside him from his youth. *But you were ignorant in what was good and bad, abandoned by the very man who created you, who should have nurtured your interest in all that was virtuous. He is the villain and you merely his tool.*

"No." He shook his head in an attempt to dislodge the thoughts that always tried to rationalize his crimes.

He had read *Paradise Lost* in his first year of life. He'd watched the cottage family and learned about history, the villainy of man and the virtues of good people. Yet, he'd followed the path of revenge.

A justified revenge against your creator, who turned away from you. A man who destroyed your only possibility for happiness when he dismembered your mate, the only other being who could be your equal in strength and immortality. You tried to reason with him, but he failed you.

As if he could escape the immature reasoning of his past, he ran up his mountain, focusing on his steps, pushing his muscles, avoiding the slopes where a fall would be imminent.

But what would it matter? Victor had created a being of immortality. If he fell, he would continue to breathe and grow hungry and be tortured by his own conscience. Did the good doctor know that would happen, or did he, and only he, have the knowledge of what could destroy him?

If only Victor had.

If only he'd never been brought into existence.

Then Angel would be dead, frozen to the ground and buried beneath the winter snows or torn apart by wolves like your doomed mate.

He stopped, his breathing barely heavy despite the high altitude. Once again, a sense that Angel could be his salvation churned in his gut. Could she give him the forgiveness he needed? Could he save her, all of her, including her hands and then find the peace he sought?

And then watch her leave to return to her life.

Even as he caught his breath, he resisted the urge to fight against the fact she would desert him. It was part of the sacrifice he had to make. It was necessary.

But what if she didn't want to leave? Again, the feel of her tongue on his own pushed to the forefront of his mind and with it the remembered feel of her body against his own as he warmed her back to life, but he refused to follow that thought to a happy conclusion. Fate had decreed that he—

A scream from his cabin, too faint for a man to hear, caught his attention. Spinning around, he ran down the mountainside, his heart now beating faster than a woodpecker's peck. Images of a bear breaking in, or worse yet, entering because he'd left the door ajar, filled him with fear. Reaching the cabin without mishap, he bounded up the steps and pushed the door open.

Inside all was calm, Angel's breathing even. Relief surged through him, and he sat in the chair next to the bed before his legs could buckle beneath him. Gently, he pulled the quilt up.

Timber had said the medicine might cause bad dreams. A nightmare. That must have caused her yell, but it appeared to have passed. His own body relaxed as a direct result.

Whether either of them accepted it, they were connected. No one he'd saved in his long life of reparation had been under his care for so long. Circumstances and fate had intervened this time, and he wouldn't disrespect that.

Angel's kiss had been no more than a strong medicine acting upon her psyche. If she remembered the action, it would embarrass her. He would act as though it never happened.

He folded his arms across his bare chest. It felt good to move about without a constricting shirt. That she hadn't turned away in horror was a testament to her kindness.

Curious, he rose and stood before the shard of mirror on his wall. He glanced at her before lifting his hair and examining the scar that crossed his forehead.

Unlike the other stitches made by his creator, the one across his forehead was perfectly symmetrical, following the curve of his head exactly. It had faded so much over the years, almost blending in with his skin tone.

Part of his rage in his first years of life was due to his lack of understanding of why people thought him a horror. He'd lived up to his monstrous outward appearance, going to great lengths to meet people's expectations by committing monstrous acts. It hadn't been until the object of his revenge,

Victor, had died while chasing him down to kill him that he'd turned his thoughts inward.

Dropping his hair, he combed it with his fingers to cover the scar again. Those stitches were a reminder of the genius brain he'd been given, much like the ones along his body bordered exceptional muscles.

Even his hair had been chosen specifically, according to Victor's journals. He was to be bigger and better than human. The only thing not in the journals was whether Victor had expected him to be immortal. Was that an accident or purposeful? He'd combed through every drawer and chest in Victor's apartment where he'd been brought to life, but couldn't find the answer. If only Victor had written down how his life could be extinguished, he would do it as soon as he'd achieved peace.

After leaving the ship where his creator had finally succumbed to his own mortality, he'd planned to burn himself on a pyre. He'd even told the ship's captain he would do so, but coward that he was, the minute the fire hit his skin, he jumped from the burning woodpile.

His anguish over his failure had been the very worst moment of his existence. It had also set him on a new path. Somewhere deep inside him was the fear that he wouldn't find the peace he sought before he lost all feeling. Today, if he were to step upon a burning pyre, it may well take an hour before he felt the need to escape.

He turned to look at Angel in confusion. Her slightest touch, given of her own free will, never mind the influence of the medicine, had broken through the insensitivity of his lips and jolted him into a new awareness. Once again, fate was at work and it was further proof they were connected.

It could be no more than as healer and the injured. He understood that and would have to make that clear if there were any other overtures from her. Those would make it difficult for both of them. He was the stronger one, the healthy one, and the one with the most life experience. He *would* resist.

Walking toward the bed, he checked once more to be sure she breathed comfortably. Once assured of that, blindly he chose a book at random from his bookshelf and sat down. Opening the cover, he stared at the title page. *How to Make Love to a Woman.*

Angela enjoyed the sound of Sas' raspy voice as he read the musketeer tale to her. It was so much more enjoyable to listen to than to read it herself. Luckily, they had started a new routine. He tended to her immediate needs in the morning then spent until lunch getting ready for winter.

After feeding her lunch, he brought in enough wood for the rest of the day and night then settled in to read to her. The story was over five-hundred pages, so even though she read a little in the morning, it would take them forever to finish it.

At night, he fed her dinner then they talked as he worked inside the cabin. "Talked" being a relative term. She talked and he listened for the most part. She only called it a conversation because she'd broke him of the habit of not answering questions he didn't want to answer. Now he said "I decline to answer," which was him saying something at least. It also cut out the long pauses in their "talks," during one of which she'd actually fallen asleep.

It had been almost three days of this routine, and she

loved it, which surprised her. It was so simple compared to her normal life or even her vacations. It must have to do with Sas. He fascinated her. Strong and kind yet shy and sexy.

There was only one problem. She stank. She wrinkled her nose as she lowered her face and took a breath. The mint leaves he'd been thoughtful enough to provide her with in the mornings may have helped her breath, but the only thing that had been washed on her body was her hands, feet and face.

Her dilemma was that her hands were no closer to being useful than they were three days ago, which meant to get clean, he'd have to wash her…if he even would. She licked her lips at her problem. On one hand, she was much more than a little attracted to him and him washing her could be a very embarrassing experience for both of them. On the other hand, she had to bathe.

Then there was the bathing itself. He still went outside and showered in the cold. She'd swear the man had ice flowing through his veins if his touch wasn't so warm. She'd lost count of the number of times he'd gone out without his bearskin coat, some of those times without even a shirt.

There was no way she could handle that cold, never mind having to—

"What's troubling you?" His change in tone caught her attention.

She smirked. "It's kind of personal."

He set down the book. "If you don't care for the story, I can read you another." His gazed flicked over the bookshelves before he cleared his throat. "Or I don't have to read anything."

"Oh, no. The story is fine. It's something else entirely."

From across the room, he actually met her gaze, which

was a nice change, except for the fact that she was having a hard time not looking away. She caved and looked down at the quilt, which gave her another whiff of herself. There was just no way to get around it. She glanced up at him and grimaced. "I stink."

"You stink? I don't understand. Is that a figurative term?"

Great, now she had to spell it out. "Sometimes, yes, but in this case, no. I stink in as I smell like I haven't bathed in over a week, which is actually the case."

His eyebrows rose up beneath his hair before he looked away and nodded. "Of course. I should have thought of that." He rose and strode toward the kitchen.

"No, you shouldn't have. I should have, a lot sooner than this. You take excellent care of me." She didn't want him beating himself up over this like he had about the cabin cooling off.

He opened the door to the pantry, but stopped at her comment. "I didn't think of it sooner because your scent pleases me."

He disappeared through the door, which was good because she could feel herself blushing. Shoot, how would she get through some kind of bathing if all he had to do is tell her she smelled good?

If only she could wait until her hands healed, but from the way they looked last time he cleaned them, it would still be awhile. At least the burning had grown less intense when she moved them.

Noise coming from behind the cabin had her craning her neck. Sas' cave was his storage and pantry. He actually told her all about it just the day before. It stayed very cool but not freezing which was perfect for storing potatoes and onions as well as meats and fish. He said it was well ventilated as well, so nothing grew mold.

She couldn't wait until she could stand on her own two feet and move around a little. She wanted to explore everything in the cabin. It would tell her a lot more about Sas than he did. She enjoyed being around a man who wasn't always talking about himself for a change, but it would be a lot easier to know him if he was a little more communicative.

A large pale pink square with rust on it came through the pantry door first. More of it appeared followed by Sas who carried it.

She was too impatient to wait. "What's that?"

He set it on the floor facing her. "An old refrigerator."

An old refrigerator? She studied it before realizing it was missing the door. The sides were a pale pink with a good share of rust, but inside was white and smooth. It had to be from the nineteen-fifties or something. "What's that for?"

As usual, he didn't answer right away. Instead, he tilted the old appliance onto its back. "This is what I use to wash clothes in the winter."

Now that was ingenious. "Where did you get something like that out here?"

"I found it at the dump in Savik. Four-Point allowed me to place it on a sled and hook it to the back of his snow machine. I gave him a deer I'd killed in trade. He has to feed his wife as well as himself."

No wonder she enjoyed being with Sas. Life out in the wilderness was creative and the people who lived out here really worked together. It was a refreshing change from city life where people bashed windows over a simple parking space.

And why? Because they didn't want to walk so far. Just keeping warm out here was more effort than that.

Sas moved to the kitchen and pulled out two large pots, far bigger than anything he'd used to cook with. They were the size of large lobster pots she'd seen when she'd travelled on the east coast of Maine.

After filling them with water, he placed them on the wood stove and added wood to the fire. She watched him work, enjoying the movement of his muscles, especially when he lifted the heavy pots. When his biceps tensed, the veins on the inside of his arms stood out in stark relief. She was so happy his shirt tore on his way to Timber's because it improved her view one hundred percent. Sas' body made her want to sigh with desire.

Not that she could act on that feeling. Right now, she was ridiculously weak. Once her feet were healed enough, she planned on doing squats and crunches and anything else to help rebuild her strength. Sas was certainly feeding her well enough to aid her in that direction.

He disappeared into the pantry again and her curiosity grew. What did doing laundry have to do with—oh. She stared at the refrigerator then moved her gaze to the pots and back again. That would be her bathtub.

CHAPTER NINE

Angela swallowed hard. When she mentioned bathing, she'd thought maybe a wet cloth, some soap and exposing one body part at a time. Not this. As she studied the appliance, she had to admit it was just big enough to fit her, if she bent her knees. It looked a little deeper than a tub though.

There had to be a way of tackling this task without getting completely naked and letting Sas wash her. Maybe he could tie plastic bags around her hands really tight at the wrists, but even as she thought it, her gut told her he'd never allow that.

A part of her wanted him to feel as uncomfortable and turned-on as she would feel. She had no doubt he'd feel uncomfortable based on the way he walked out on her the other day when she'd kissed him, tongue and all, which she shouldn't have done and wouldn't have if she hadn't been high on pain killers.

The sad part was, she didn't regret the action in the least. She just wished he'd responded in kind. It was torture to be in such close proximity to a man, every day, alone with him, and not act on her inclinations. If she wasn't such an invalid, she'd have followed that kiss with another and then some.

And would she have been embarrassed by his rejection? Probably. He'd done her a favor by walking out. He'd made it clear he wasn't interested without actually saying anything. Typical Sas. She couldn't help smiling at that.

He strode back in from the pantry with a bundle in one hand, a small package in the other, and a bucket hanging from his wrist. He set everything down on the table where he usually ate.

"Are those my clothes?" The green colored woven yarn sandwiched between jean material and what looked like black sweats had to be her sweater.

"They are." Sas opened the brown paper-wrapped package. Inside was a square wrapped in plastic.

Feeling a little happier to see her clothes, she couldn't contain her curiosity. "What's that?"

"Soap."

"Oh." And how would that actually be applied to her body? She could feel the heat in her cheeks. She would die of embarrassment.

Sas picked up the bucket and set it in the sink. Moving the lever that allowed the mountain ice water to flow into his house, he began filling it. He'd explained to her how it all worked until the winter freeze stopped all water from the mountain. Before that happened, he said he filled plastic jugs with it and stored them in his cave pantry.

When the bucket was full, he emptied it into the old refrigerator. He paused, examining the appliance.

Maybe it leaked and they'd have to do something else. She could only hope. Then again "something else" might be more embarrassing.

He pushed the fridge closer to the woodstove then returned to the kitchen.

She licked at her lips, thankful that at least *they* had healed. Wishing her hands and feet were better wouldn't make it happen, at least not in the next half hour.

Despite her nervousness, she continued to enjoy the view of Sas emptying buckets of water into the makeshift tub. His naked torso, despite, or maybe because of the scars, was like the Aurora Borealis she witnessed her second night on the ship, sharp lines with waves of movement.

Sas filled one last bucket with cold water and set it aside. He moved back to the stove and with his bare hands, emptied the pots of boiling water into the tub then refilled them and set them back on the stove.

She'd gasped silently as he lifted the pots, but the handles were wood, so they must not have conducted the heat. Still, he must have very calloused hands to withstand the heat. She swallowed hard at the thought of his coarse skin touching hers.

He turned and strode back through his pantry door. When he returned, he held one large and one small towel.

She glanced toward the door where he always hung his towel and noticed it was there. It made sense he'd have more than one towel, but since he owned only one plate, one tin cup, and one chair, she hadn't thought he'd have another towel.

What was stranger still was her disappointment that she wouldn't be using Sas' spruce scented towel to dry off. Shoot, she was thinking like a high schooler. That ship had sailed almost fifteen years ago. She needed to get her act together. But as Sas set the towels down on the table then headed toward her, panic set in.

"You first." She blurted the half-thought at him as he moved the chair aside.

He pulled back the quilt. "What do you mean?"

She crossed her legs, something she'd just found she could do without pain. "I mean, we have to take my clothes off, right?"

His Adam's apple moved in his neck as he swallowed. "That's correct."

"Then you first."

His brows rose to hide beneath his hair once again. "Why do I need to take off my clothes for you to bathe?"

Good question. "Um, since I can't bathe myself because of my hands, then you will get wet."

He stepped farther down the bed to her feet and began unwrapping the bandages. "If my clothes become wet, I will change into other ones."

She couldn't counter that with anything logical. Shoot, she would have to admit how uncomfortable she was. "Listen, this may sound silly, but I feel really uncomfortable being naked when you're not. I'm sure there is some psychological reason for it having to do with a balance of power or some such mumbo jumbo, but I don't even care about that. I'm just trying to figure out how to get clean without being so embarrassed I start crying. I know how men don't like it when women cry and I think that would just make you uncomfortable as well."

Sas had stopped unwrapping her feet and stood there looking down at them.

Oh no, was something wrong with her feet? She stared at them, but didn't see anything bad. In fact, they looked a lot better. All thanks to him. She moved her gaze to his face.

He frowned, clearly unhappy, but he didn't say anything.

"The honest truth is, there isn't much I can do if you

refuse. After all, I can't walk and I can't use my hands, so I'm at your mercy. It would be absolutely terrifying if I was with anyone else."

His head snapped up. "It would?"

She nodded rapidly even as his gaze slid away. "Yes. I'd be mortified. But I trust you, so that helps."

"I will undress on one condition."

Only one? If the shoe was on the other foot, she'd be making a list of demands. "What?"

"If you find me repulsive, you tell me and allow me to dress."

Her mouth opened but no sound came out. He was worried about how *he* looked? Even with scars all over his legs, he was a damn sight better than most of the men she'd slept with. Now that he pointed it out, looking at him might help her take her mind off him washing her. Yeah, right. "I agree."

"Very well. Allow me to help you first."

She nodded, but her throat closed as he stepped toward her.

"Carefully, lift your arms."

It was painful, but not unbearable. What was unbearable was Sas pulling her tank top up her waist, past her breasts and over her head. Beneath it was an elastic sports bra. She'd dressed in layers on purpose in case she got hot on the helicopter ride to the glacier. That seemed like a year ago now.

Sas' roughened fingers took hold of the bottom of the bra and pulled it over her breasts and up her arms until it too was off. At the scrape of the material, her nipples hardened, as she'd feared.

She couldn't look at him. Luckily, she didn't have to. He

stepped down to grasp her leggings at the waist and hooked her panties as well. She lowered her hands, but kept her elbows bent to take her weight there as she lifted her hips.

Sas pulled her clothing over her butt and down her legs. When everything was at her ankles, he stopped.

By this time she had closed her eyes, but when she heard his footsteps walking away, she opened them.

Sas had gone over to the counter and pulled a knife from a drawer. He came back, but kept his gaze on her feet. "I cannot get these off without hurting your feet. I must cut them."

If only she could have waited until her feet were completely better, but since she was this far, she certainly wasn't going to have him redress her now, especially in her smelly clothes. She swallowed hard to find her voice. "Thank you."

As soon as she indicated it was okay, he sliced the leggings at the ankles and maneuvered them over her feet with no pain at all.

Once again, she counted herself lucky in having such an amazing caretaker even as she wished she could pull the quilt over herself.

Without another word, he lifted her into his arms.

As her body touched his naked torso, every nerve-ending came alive with awareness. His chest and abs were as hard as they looked as he held her against him to bring her to the water-filled fridge.

"You must keep your hands out of the water when I put you in it, but first I need to know if it's too hot for you."

Too hot? Nothing was hotter than he was. "But I can't touch it." She looked down at the water. Despite the unusual container it was in, it looked so inviting, she forgot her nakedness for a moment.

With her still in his arms, Sas knelt on one knee. "Move your foot into the water. It will be very sensitive as you have new skin forming. If the water is even slightly too hot, you will know."

"Okay." Carefully, she moved one leg over the edge and dipped her foot in. "Oh, it's perfect!" Now that she was so close, she couldn't wait to get in.

As if he sensed her eagerness, he lifted her up again and lowered her into the water.

As the warm liquid flowed over her, she sighed. It felt so good. Every muscle relaxed.

Sas grabbed her wrists. "Don't let your hands fall into the water."

Startled, she looked up to find him bending over her, but his gaze wasn't on her face or her wrists. She flushed. "Sorry, I forgot. I'll keep them on the edge. You can let go now and take off your clothes."

He was slow to release her, his gaze clearly on her breasts. Did that mean he *did* find her attractive? The man definitely sent mixed signals.

Finally, he let her go and stepped away. His jaw tensed and his brows lowered as he unbuttoned his jeans.

She should be ashamed of herself for ogling her caretaker, but she couldn't help it. When she'd first asked him to get naked, it had been pure instinct to level the playing field, though they weren't playing and she was still at a major disadvantage.

If she'd been healthy, this scenario would have been completely different…and if he was interested. It was that doubt coupled with her helplessness that kept her usually assertive nature under control.

She watched, breathless as he lowered the zipper on his jeans, the pleasure of the bath almost forgotten, her only thought for it, keeping her wrists resting on the sides. She licked her lips. Would he wear boxers or briefs?

Sas pushed the jeans from his hips, revealing the V that outlined his pelvic region only to expose a large, hard cock. No underwear at all.

Her entire body lit up like the fireworks over San Francisco Bay. Tingles raced from her chest to her groin at the sight. That he was hard had all her drug-induced dreams resurfacing. The warm water she sat in was nothing compared to the heat of her body.

He lowered his jeans, stepping out of one leg then the other and turning around to fold them and place them on the table.

That was when her heart took control over her body, which instantly cooled. Sas' legs weren't free from scars either. Two looped beneath his groin as if his legs had been reattached. His right leg had another scar around the knee while his left leg had a scar around his ankle. What had happened to him?

She opened her mouth to ask, but he turned around and looked at her. She immediately gave him a sheepish smile. The last thing she wanted him to think was that his body shocked her. It did, not because it was ugly, but because the scars and muscle combination attracted both her body and her heart. "Thank you. I feel a little better."

He nodded, but didn't say anything. Instead, he picked up the soap, a block of wood, and a small towel and walked toward her.

Her stomach tightened at his approach, but it wasn't

embarrassment or fear now. It was pure lust. The bottom of her breasts barely hit the water and were completely exposed. Her legs were bent as her feet were firmly on the bottom of the makeshift tub, her knees, which protruded above the water line, squeezed together to stop her from making a fool of herself. This was to get clean, not dirty.

Sas knelt next to the fridge. He set the soap down and ripped the small towel in half. "I will wash your hair first."

Her hair? Shoot, she hadn't even thought of that. "Do you have shampoo?"

He picked up the soap and moved behind her. "Sturge's wife makes this soap for both hair and body. Now, move forward and tip your head back.

She'd never heard of such a thing, but it was the wilderness and just getting clean was motivation enough to comply with his directions.

He cupped the water in his large hands and let it fall over her hair. She closed her eyes, just in case any ran the wrong way. After soaking her hair to his satisfaction, she inhaled the scent of mint. The soap he used tingled her scalp, making it feel cleaner than it had ever been. That was probably because her hair was used to the chemical concoctions of the local drugstore.

As he shampooed, he massaged her scalp, relaxing her. Then he rinsed her head with the leftover water in the pot that he hadn't poured in. It was warmer than her bath water, but perfect for getting the soap out.

When he was done, she opened her eyes to see him take half the small towel and wrap her hair, keeping it from hanging in the bath water. She'd love to see how her hair looked when it was dry. She glanced around the cabin, but didn't notice a mirror.

Sas returned to the side of the tub and dunked the other half towel into the water and began washing her neck.

She closed her eyes and bent her head to the side, allowing him all the access he needed. As he moved the cloth to her shoulders and across her collar bone, her breaths came faster as need swirled in her belly. Instead of moving lower, he soaped her arms from wrists to elbows and underneath where the cloth brushed her breasts, making her nipples react.

She dared to look at him from beneath her lashes. He reached next to him and picked up the soap again.

She closed her eyes tight, knowing what was next. As the cloth moved downward from her chest, his touch lightened and it brushed over one nipple, making it far harder than if he'd grasped it.

The cloth moved around, over and under her breast as if he'd never seen one before and was fascinated by the shape. That was silly. He was probably just being thorough and the last thing she wanted to do was interrupt him.

The cloth finally moved down to her rib cage and over her belly before being lifted from the water again.

She opened her eyes to watch his large hand soap the cloth again. Sasquatch. That's what they'd nick-named him and right now, she finally saw it for the compliment it was.

Her breasts were not small, but as his large hand moved to her other one, it completely covered it. He washed that one thoroughly as well, all around, under and this time, he took her nipple between his fingers and rubbed it back and forth within the cloth.

Spikes of pleasure shot straight to her core, and she glanced at him in question. Did he want to have sex?

As she watched his facial features, he looked completely absorbed, like she did when the helicopter had crested the first mountain and below them was the ice of the massive glacier. She'd been in awe. That was the same expression on his face.

Could it be he'd never had a woman like her? Maybe the women he'd been around were smaller. Maybe that was why he was so gentle with her. Oh shoot. Of course! He'd said he never had a girlfriend. He'd probably never given a woman a bath. That would account for his intense gaze and fascination.

His hand finally pulled away as he reached for the soap again.

She took a deep breath. Her whole body was primed for sex. Would he wash between her legs next?

He moved behind her and bent her forward, washing her back from the tops of her shoulder blades to the top of her ass. She'd thought a bath would be mortifying, but instead it was titillating. The mint scent of the soap filled her senses, making her…happy?

Sas was determined to be thorough. As he reached her ass, he pushed his hand beneath her. She allowed herself to float up to give him access, her heart racing as the cloth moved from one cheek to the other before burying itself between them.

Her breath caught as excitement sped from her anal hole to her sheath. His hand retreated, and she lowered herself, finally taking a deep breath as she tried to calm down.

Sas nudged her so she lay back against the side as he wrung out the cloth. He soon soaped it up again and moved down to her feet. Lifting her ankle, he washed the new skin on the top of her right foot before cleaning the bottom. When he was happy with that, he moved from her ankle to her shin and calf then to her knee.

He set her foot on the edge of the fridge which forced her knee to bend toward her. Without a word, he grasped the soap which had slipped uncomfortably close to the juncture of her thighs and he soaped the cloth.

Every movement was purposeful, slow and thorough. He rubbed the cloth up her thigh, around it and to the inside.

She held her breath as a part of the cloth brushed against her labia. When convinced that leg was clean, he lowered her foot into the water again, only to start with the other.

Despite sitting in a fridge full of water, her sheath moistened as Sas brought the cloth over her mons and past her clit. Slowly, as if determined to touch every inch of her skin, he ran his finger with the cloth between her folds.

She wanted to grab his hand, press it to her and rub against him, but her hands had to stay out of the water. Her only hope was that he was as turned on as she was and would take care of her once she was clean.

Her sheath tightened when he brought the cloth up to her clit to make sure every crease was attended to. She pressed her wrists against the top of the bath and lifted her hips, unable to resist any longer.

Sas dropped the cloth immediately and pulled the soap from the water. Without a word, he stood, his hard cock letting her know she wasn't the only one affected by his ministrations to her cleanliness. He dropped the soap on the counter and started to fill one of the buckets at the sink.

She stifled a moan. She'd never look at bathing again in

quite the same way. Why had he purposefully made her crave him? She watched his tight butt as he walked to the wood stove and poured the cold water into the pots of hot water. When he crouched to add more wood, his ball sac peeked from between his thighs.

She closed her eyes. A vision of her on all fours with him pumping into her from behind, that very sac slapping with his movements, filled her head and heated her body even more. Shoot. She snapped her eyelids open, but the reality was even better.

Sas stood next to the stove looking at her. Though the water was opaque from the soap, her breasts were clearly visible and that's exactly where his gaze was locked. She glanced down to see his cock stood straight out from his body, which gave her hope that they might both find some release.

He stepped up to the fridge and her breath caught. "Do you think you can stand?"

That wasn't exactly the question she'd expected. "I don't know."

"I'll lift you." Without waiting for her agreement, he bent over and lifted her entire wet body out of the water. As her skin touched his, she wasn't sure if the shiver that raced through her was from him or her.

Slowly, he lowered one of his arms, allowing her feet to touch the bottom of the fridge. The position had her standing sideways against him from his chest to his cock, which rested against her ass.

Despite the sexual current running through her, she focused on her balance as her feet took her full weight for the first time in over a week. It was like riding a bike and yet not.

Her body remembered what to do, but it was a little unsure how to do it.

She leaned her arm against his. "I think I have it now. Why do you want me like this?"

"I need to rinse you. Don't close your eyes."

"Okay." She already held one arm out to the side to keep her balance, so as he carefully moved away, she extended her other one out as well.

Sas only needed to take a step to grab the pot of freshly warmed water. He held it above her shoulder and let the water flow over her. When all the water had run out, he did the same on the other side with the second pot, quickly finishing with both arms before returning the pots to the counter.

Her knees started to shake when he grabbed up the clean towel and lifted her off her feet again. This time, she held one arm around his neck, though she was careful not to let her hand touch him.

She thought he would place her in the bed so they could have sex, but to her disappointment he lowered her into the chair. Instead of relief, she found herself on the receiving end of more stroking as he methodically dried her off, from her breasts to the folds of her pussy, which just caused more wetness to gather there.

She closed her thighs tight against further drying. "I'm good."

He shook his head though he didn't meet her gaze, focusing on her calves instead. "It's important you're dry. Wetness conducts the cold air."

At the moment, she couldn't believe she'd ever be cold again. "Believe me, I'm quite hot."

His brow furrowed and he lifted the back of his hand to her forehead.

She barely refrained from rolling her eyes. He couldn't be that clueless. He had to be joking, but as he took his hand away, there was no lightness in his features.

"You don't have a fever. You're warm from bathing." He moved behind the chair she sat in and undid the towel around her hair.

If he wasn't taking such great care of her, she'd give him a piece of her mind. Her body was ready for sex, but despite his erection, he seemed oblivious.

He towel-dried her hair then walked past her to a shelf on the wall between the kitchen counter and the equipment area. Above it was a triangular piece of a mirror maybe a foot in length that she hadn't noticed before.

Sas removed something from the shelf before heading toward her.

Did he not know how hot he was? He obviously thought his scars should be hidden, but his body was muscle in motion. People thought the statue of David in Florence was inspiring, but that had nothing on Sas.

Not only was Sas not a statue, but his movement was so smooth that he practically glided, the muscles in clear definition as he strode across the room. In seconds, he was behind her chair, and she hid her disappointment at not being able to see him.

When a comb started through her hair, she widened her eyes. The man thought of everything. As with her body, he combed every strand on her head and then did it again. Either he was a little anal or he liked her hair. Of course, that meant he liked her body and hadn't just washed every inch of her because he was someone who had to be thorough. She grinned.

"Your hair is almost dry. If you're still warm, I suggest not donning any clothes until tomorrow. It will be better for your circulation."

Now he was talking her language. He came around to her side, but before she could ask him what was next, he lifted her once again.

She got her arm around his neck and held on as he lowered her to the bed. As he bent over her, she lifted her face to his and kissed him again, confident from his constant erection that he was definitely interested.

For a split second, he opened his mouth and his tongue pushed inside hers. At its forceful entrance, pleasure swept over her, and she moaned.

He pulled away quickly, but ever careful of her hands, and stalked toward the door.

"Sas? Where are you going?"

He jerked the door open as if she'd angered him. "I decline to answer." The door slammed shut.

Shoot, now what had she done? He'd made her hotter than a cat in heat then walked out on her? For the first time, she was more than frustrated. She was pissed.

When he came back inside, she would lay it all out there. She wanted to have sex with him and since she couldn't do much about it, he better. She just had to hold on to her anger until he returned.

She smirked. That shouldn't take long. He'd just left the cabin stark naked with what had to be, at this point, a painful hard-on.

CHAPTER TEN

He stood on the porch, desperate to control the raging need inside him, but it was no use. He'd pushed himself to his limit while bathing Angel, and her kiss broke him.

Striding off the porch, he turned toward the incline of his mountain and lay down face first in the snow. The coolness of it was noticeable, but it did little to tamp down his need to release.

Rolling over, he brought his hand to his cock, stroking it quickly. Even as he stared at the clouds gathering in the sky, his body bowed as his seed flowed over his tip and into his moving hand.

It left him wanting.

He sat up and cleaned himself with the snow. Washing Angel had been ecstasy and torture all at once. Her body was so different from his and every erogenous zone written about in the books he'd read was far more pleasing to him than the last.

It was one thing to read and look at pictures, but to feel a woman's body, in particular Angel's, was a new experience. She was soft everywhere as if made to embrace his hard lines. If he were a man, he wouldn't hesitate to take what she offered.

If he were a man.

The age-old anger against Victor reared its ugly head, the one that sent him down the dark path of revenge. He must be strong against it. The ramifications of his crimes were too hard to live with even now. If he took Angel, all hope for redemption would be lost.

Unless…hope, that new and fragile concept, rose to spite him. Unless it was what she wanted. Her interest in him was obvious from her questions to her kisses. What if pleasing her was the way to peace. Is that not what he'd been doing?

No, he'd been healing her. Saving her from death's grasping hands. That is what fate wanted. Did fate also want him to please her? Make her happy?

And when she left? His chest tightened. When she left, it would cause a pain like none he'd ever experienced. He thought he'd hurt when his mate was destroyed, but it would be nothing compared to Angel's departure.

Would he then be trading one torture for another?

He spread his legs out and leaned back on his hands, trying to feel the cold of the snow, the chill of the air, even the moisture of the clouds. It was there, sensations, but only shadows of what they'd once been. In another hundred years, would he feel anything?

The thought sent panic racing through him. There was very little he feared now, but the inability to feel was one. This might be his only chance to know what it was like to be with a woman. As the thought took hold, it grew stronger by the second.

He jumped to his feet and strode to his outdoor shower. He *would* feel while he still could. Opening the lever, he washed quickly, then skipped the steps all together as he jumped onto the porch.

He opened the door with such force, it banged against the wall. "I want you."

Angel's eyes rounded in obvious surprise then a shy smile formed on her lips. "I want you, too."

A tightness around his chest eased, and he closed the door. Grabbing his towel from its hook, he dried himself as he stalked to the bed. He moved the chair out of the way and stared at her mouth.

Her tongue came out to lick her lips, and his cock jumped to attention.

His decision made, he was anxious now to fulfill it. Reaching down, he whipped the quilt from the bed and on to the floor.

"Oh." At her exclamation, he scanned her face, but saw no fear.

Moving to the end of the bed, he kicked his clothes chest out of the way. He stood there savoring the sight of his Angel. Her long legs, the patch of short blonde pubic hair that hid what he'd only touched through cloth. Her wide hips that tapered into her waist. Her plump breasts that fascinated him with their softness and even now, hard nipples. Her slender neck made his lips itch to kiss the skin there and her mouth called to his tongue.

The flush in her cheeks gave her a healthy glow she was now capable of, and he risked a quick look in her eyes, the green within them almost as dark as pine needles. Even her golden hair seemed to call out to him, asking him to touch it.

He couldn't resist. He climbed onto the bed and pushed her legs wide, careful not to touch her feet. Moving forward, he knelt between her knees.

She raised her arms. "I wish I could touch you."

"And I'm glad you can't. I want to enjoy every moment and your touch would require I rush."

She licked her lips. "I don't think you could go too fast for me right now."

He shook his head, but didn't answer. Running his hands over her ribs, he cupped her breasts. They were full and warm and round, a texture like nothing on his own body and far more beautiful than the whore's he'd held last century.

He let his thumb stroke across the nipples and watched in fascination as they hardened more, wrinkling the skin of the areolas. Her body responded so quickly to his touch. They were connected.

But for how long?

He pushed the thought aside. *Now* was what mattered. *She* was what mattered. Lowering his head, he held one breast up with his hand and flicked at the hard nub with his tongue. It grew even harder, like his cock felt. He circled the nipple, listening to Angel's breathing.

Gently, he scraped his teeth across either side of her nipple and her breath caught. She liked that. Taking it between his teeth again, he rolled it.

Angel's moan of pleasure, urged him on. He sucked on her breast, rolling the nub with his tongue as her body bowed in response. Slowly, he increased his sucking until small squeals came from the back of her throat.

Letting go of that breast, he sat back on his haunches, waiting for her to regain regular breathing.

"What are you waiting for?" She sounded anxious.

"You."

"Me? I'm ready whenever you are. Can't you tell?"

Actually, he could. Her nipples had lost a little of their hardness, so he grasped them both between his forefingers and thumbs and pinched them lightly. He let go to see his handy work. That was better. He liked them like that, as excited as she was.

He pinched them a little harder and was rewarded with another moan. He rolled each nub between his fingers, and yet another moan issued forth as her legs against him widened even farther and she bent her knees.

He looked down at the shadowed area. This is where they differed the most, and he wanted to see it.

Stepping back onto the floor, he grabbed the lantern and hooked it on a nail in the wall near the foot of the bed.

"What are you doing?" Angel lifted her head up to watch him.

"I want to see you."

"Oh."

He climbed back on the bed, pleased that she didn't shy away from being viewed. When he knelt between her legs again, he noticed her nipples had softened. Immediately, he rolled them again, loving her intake of breath and the look of her breasts with their hard points.

Leaning over, he gave one breast attention with his mouth, sucking it before biting lightly. When it was a good hardness, he pulled back and moved his gaze to between Angel's legs. Pink folds covered in a moist shine greeted him. He frowned. "You're still wet."

"Of course, I am. You made me wet."

But he had dried her. He'd been very careful about that.

He tried to remember all he had read on sexual intercourse, but his mind didn't seem to be functioning that well. Using his index fingers, he spread apart her folds to find her entrance. As her opening was revealed, he looked at his cock.

He was not human. They might not fit.

Disappointment brushed over him, and he swallowed hard. If that was the case, he needed to make sure she had her pleasure first, so *she* wouldn't be disappointed. Stroking along the wet folds, he pushed his large finger into her opening, pleased when it spread for him.

"Oh yes." Angel's words were barely a whisper.

He glanced up at her face and found her eyes closed, which gave him the chance to watch her reactions. He pulled his finger back out slowly, the suction on it causing his balls to tighten. It glistened in the lantern light.

Instinctually, he put it in his mouth and sucked off the wetness. He closed his eyes at the intimate taste of Angel, a primal urge to mate tightening his gut. When he withdrew his finger and opened his eyes, he found her staring at him, her mouth slightly open. Then she licked her lips, and he stifled a groan.

Breaking their eye contact, he slid his finger inside her again. Her tummy sucked in with her breath. When he retracted his finger this time, he spread the juices over her hard nub at the top of her folds, what he'd read was the clitoris. This was supposed to be of particular excitement for women and Angel's moan confirmed it.

Bringing his finger back to her opening, he added another to test the flexibility of her female sheath. As his two fingers slid inside with no resistance, his own breath caught. Angel's eyes were closed once again, a sign she enjoyed it. After pulling his fingers out, he repeated his attention to her apex nub.

When she started to pant, he ran his fingers back to her sheath. Holding his breath, this time, he slowly pushed three fingers inside, the moist canal fitting around them like a tight glove. Angel moaned loudly, and his entire groin caught fire.

Lowering his head, he left his fingers inside as he licked at the moisture he'd spread over her clit. Her moans increased and her hips rose against his face.

She was close to fulfillment. The knowledge gave him confidence, and he began to ease his fingers out then push them back in as he continued to lick.

Angel's raspy squeals of pleasure filled his ears and caused his cock to leak. He refused to yield to his own need until she was happy. He increased the rhythm of his fingers, pushing harder, gauging her reactions.

Her hips bucked as if she were close but it wasn't enough. Without thought, he took the clit inside his mouth and sucked.

"Yes!" Angel's yell filled the cabin.

Her legs tried to close against his, so he pushed his fingers deep and held them there while he continued his suction.

Her yell fell to a loud groan and finally pants, her hips not pulling away from his mouth. He let go of her nub, but didn't remove his fingers.

He sat up and watched as she came down from her pleasure, her tummy rising and falling in fewer beats, her hard nipples softening. Her cheeks were a deep red in the muted light making her even more desirable.

Finally, her eyelids fluttered open and a soft smile curved her lips. "That was wonderful."

He forced his gaze away, afraid she'd see the need in his eyes and fear it. "I'm glad you enjoyed that."

"But you need to enjoy, too."

At her invitation, he was thankful his fingers still filled her sheath because the urge to ram his cock deep into her body almost overwhelmed him. He gritted his teeth to keep himself immobile.

"Sas, kiss me?" The uncertainty in her voice helped him pull his thoughts from his body to her.

"Why?"

"I want to feel closer to you."

Her words burrowed into his heart. He dared to look in to her eyes, and the caring in them spoke to long-buried yearnings. Even as he stretched forward onto one elbow to do her bidding, he knew the risk he took, but ignored the warnings in his head.

As his lips touched hers, she opened her mouth in invitation. It was permission to take what he needed. He swept his tongue inside and tasted every part of her.

Her soft moan as her tongue tangled with his heightened his awareness. He curled his fingers inside her sheath and her body pressed upward against him, her soft breasts flattening into his chest.

The craving to be inside her grew stronger than his will. He slipped his fingers from her and her cry of disappointment almost broke what little control he had. He brought his other hand up and held her head steady as he plundered her mouth.

Her hips rose and undulated, pressing her mons against his cock. He may be stronger than any man, but at her urging, he caved. He let go of her mouth and lifted his hips. Burying his hands in her hair, he turned her head to the side and kissed her neck.

Pulling his body back, he rubbed his chest over her breasts and licked at her jaw. His cockhead found her opening and pressed at it. He lifted his head as he breathed in the minty scent and musk that surrounded him, his need to thrust forward freezing him.

"Please." She spoke to the wall as he still held her head to the side, but her request scraped away all but the vestiges of his control.

His body strained against his mind and his cockhead pressed into her sheath. It was tight. *So tight.*

As if she understood his need, she rolled her hips upward and wrapped her legs around him. Her sheath moved against him and he slipped farther in. Still, he held himself back because to let go would be to hurt her. He'd never hurt her.

Her legs pushed on his back, beckoning him inside. Slowly, painfully, he inched forward, his body straining at his control. Her legs squeezed harder, begging him to fill her. He slid deeper until he could go no farther.

Taking deep breaths, he tried to regulate his breathing, but it wouldn't slow. He moved her head to face him. Her eyes were open. She mouthed a single word as her lips quirked up on one side. *Enjoy.*

The permission in her eyes, the utter trust in him, and the offering of her body for his fulfillment broke his control.

As Sas bumped against her cervix, she felt her sheath flood with her juices. She was so ready for him. For the first time in her life, she released control over the lovemaking. Sas was a wild-man, elemental in his simplicity. Her instinct said allow him to have his way and let go. Let him be the primal man he was, and she would love being all woman.

The intensity in his eyes was almost hard to meet, but when she gave up that final control, it bored into her as if tying her to the bed. Then his mouth came down on hers and took what she gave willingly at the same time his hips lifted. Up and up and up.

His first thrust sent a jolt through her like an electric shock. It brought her to the very edge of an orgasm. His next thrust sent her over into intense bliss, but instead of bursting and fizzling out, his next thrust brought her higher, lighting up her insides like fire.

His tongue ravished her mouth as he held her head where he wanted it while his hips pumped into her hard, thrust after thrust, riding her as if he might never come.

But he did and as he flooded her with his ecstasy, he ripped his mouth away and shouted his joy, which was but an echo in her ears as her own yell burst from her core and into the evening air.

She'd closed her eyes at the power and length of her orgasm. Letting go obviously had its rewards. At the feel of Sas' forehead touching hers, she smiled. "That was amazing."

"I didn't hurt you?"

She shook her head, causing him to raise his own. Opening her eyes, she looked up at him, but he avoided her gaze and kissed her cheek.

She was fine with that. She'd even be fine with him sleeping with her, which was not her usual sentiment. She usually liked having the bed to herself so she could sleep and she definitely wanted to sleep after that, but she'd be happy if he joined her.

She hadn't expended that much energy in all the days she'd been in Alaska. As if on cue, her hands started to throb. She almost smiled at the reminder she wasn't herself yet…almost.

Sas pulled his hips back, and she dropped her legs, her weakness creeping in now that the adrenaline rush of sex was gone. He stepped off the bed and lifted the quilt to cover her. "Rest."

She nodded, closing her eyes at the same time, a feeling of contentment filling her.

A throbbing in her hand woke her. Angela opened her eyes to pitch black darkness in the cabin, but she could tell she'd rolled onto her side. She must be feeling better if she was returning to old habits. The only problem was the pressure on her hand made it burn like it had before.

Quickly, she readjusted herself, lying flat on her back. Her stomach growled to remind her she'd fallen asleep long before dinner. She didn't want to wake Sas after all he'd done for her.

Another rumble sounded only this one was outside. Were there thunderstorms in Alaska?

A bright flash of light lit the cabin followed by a loud boomer.

That answered that question. Maybe Sas was awake anyway. She lifted her head to look in the direction of the couch. Another flash of lightning hit, and her scream lodged in her throat.

Sas sat on the couch, his eyes wide and wild before blackness reigned again.

A sizzling crack made her jump before another roll of

loud thunder followed. Fear skittered up her spine. Was he sleepwalking? She waited for the rumble to die away. "Sas? Are you awake?"

No answer.

She didn't like the idea of him being asleep but with his eyes wide open. It was eerie. "Sas! Wake up."

"I am." She barely heard him, his voice so low it sounded as if it was dragged up from the depths of hell.

"Are you okay?"

Another flash of lightning hit, but Sas hadn't moved. The thunder that followed was so loud the sound vibrated the bed. He still didn't answer her.

"Sas, please come here." She didn't know what she'd do once he got there, but anything to keep him from looking like a poorly made horror movie.

Lightning flashed again, but he remained where he was. This time it took a couple of seconds before the thunder vibrated the bed, but Sas was frozen in place. "Sas! Come over here, right now!"

Despite the rain hitting the roof, she heard his footsteps as he approached. Okay, now what was she supposed to do?

Sas didn't pull the chair over or even stand next to the bed. Instead, he lifted the quilt, crawled in and pulled her against him, fitting her to his chest as he lay on his side. His warmth was welcome, and she smiled in the darkness. "Thank you."

Almost a minute went by before another flash lit the cabin. Sas' body jerked at the light, but other than that he didn't react. When the thunder rolled in almost ten seconds later, he remained stock still.

Was he afraid of lightning? That was a little hard to

believe. Then again, if he was closer to the Sasquatch he was named after than they realized…Would that man/animal also be afraid of lightning and thunder? Many domestic animals were.

She tossed the idea aside. Sas wasn't an animal, he was a well-traveled, intelligent, very large man and nothing more. The storm simply played with her imagination.

When another lightning strike flashed and Sas jerked again, she was back to believing the man holding her had a lightning phobia. On one hand it was a shock, but on the other hand, it made her feel useful. Maybe she could make *him* feel better for a change.

She couldn't touch him with her hands, so she carefully turned toward him and kissed his chest before snuggling her head against his shoulder. His arm tightened around her, and he buried his face in her hair.

Thunder sounded in the distance as the storm moved farther away. There was still more lightning to come, but each time he squeezed her tight before relaxing again.

She wanted to cry for him. To be such a huge, strong man and to be afraid of lightning had to be embarrassing for him. Maybe his fear wasn't unreasonable. Some childhood trauma could be associated with it, or—oh shoot, what if it had something to do with his scars?

Her eyes started to water at the thought of him going through so much surgery as a young boy then reliving that every time there was lightning in the sky. His scars were faded enough where that could very well be the case.

When another rumble sounded only this one inside her tummy, she grimaced. Maybe he didn't hear that.

Sas pulled his head away from hers. "You're hungry."

Shoot, guess he did. "Just a little. I think it was all that activity." Though she spoke to his chest, she sensed his disagreement even before he spoke.

"No. I didn't feed you dinner because you were asleep. I will rectify that now." He removed his arm from around her, and she immediately missed it.

She didn't want him to go, which made absolutely no sense. "Kiss me first? I'm hungry for that even more." Shoot, now she sounded needy.

He stilled as if unsure of how to respond. There was something so vulnerable about that, which made her feel a lot better about her own feelings. She lifted her face up to where she knew he was though she couldn't see him at all.

Somehow though, he found her lips on the first try and breached them. As his tongue took command of her mouth, every muscle in her body went lax. *Take me* was the only thought in her head.

But Sas had much stronger willpower than she did and he broke the kiss.

She stifled a moan of disappointment as he rose from the bed, careful to replace the quilt around her. Though he didn't say anything, she had a feeling he wanted her fed so they could have sex again without depleting her strength. She was all for that, so she didn't complain.

Once Sas lit the lantern, she had even less reason to complain as he set about making her dinner while completely naked.

He sliced the onion and threw it into the pan with the elk meat.

His thoughts swirled in his head. Half of him wanted to run to the top of his mountain and shout for joy while the other half urged him to simply run as far from Angel as possible.

She caused a maelstrom of emotions to fill him and with no one to guide him, he was swept up in them like a snowflake in a blizzard. Burying his cock inside her had been a bliss he didn't know existed, didn't know was possible. It felt like…like heaven?

He dumped the mushrooms on the counter and proceeded to chop them. Everything about Angel was soft. She was his opposite in every way as if fate decreed he could finally be whole, despite the difference in their lifespans.

His hand froze in midair. That's why he wanted to run. The thought of having a mate only to lose her in forty years while he continued to exist for another forty hundred caused a pain so sharp in his chest that he flinched.

Recalling himself to his task, he finished cutting the mushrooms and added them to the pan. He pulled a box from the cabinet and sprinkled four of his spices over the food. Putting them away, he moved to the cold box and scooped a hunk of butter from the bowl inside. Flicking that into the pan as well, he stared at the food.

Something was missing, but his mind didn't want to focus. This was for Angel. The woman who depended on him to survive. The woman who let him enjoy her body until he was fulfilled. The woman who comforted him in the storm.

A rumble in the distance echoed his thought, and he turned from the pan and strode into his pantry cave. The cooler air stopped the sudden panic in his chest that she knew his only weakness. His fear of lightning.

Akiakook had told him he needed to face his fear to conquer it, but no matter how many times he tried, he'd failed. Now the woman who could be his salvation knew of his weakness…and comforted him.

Comfort. No one had done that for him in all the years of his existence. It had been denied him for so long that he'd thought it impossible for a being like himself as if his lack of comfort was part of the price he paid for his immortality. Not that he'd ever been given the choice. If he could have a finite number of years and grow old like man, he'd embrace it with whole-hearted enthusiasm.

He stared at the crates and barrels in his cave, trying to remember why he'd entered, but instead, he kept seeing images of Angel's naked body and feeling her snuggle against him to offer comfort.

A new vision of life formed, one with joy and happiness. One where he lived like a man, had a mate and shared every day with someone who loved h—

He grabbed his head as if to block out the tempting picture.

No! It wasn't possible. He was *not* human and he didn't deserve love. He was a monstrosity, an abomination like Victor said. His acts of repentance were no more than pennies against the cost of his crimes.

But you didn't know. His younger voice crept up again to tempt him. *You acted on instinct, the same instinct man has if not tempered by nurturing and goodness and education.*

No, not true. He'd understood. He'd even set up one innocent to take the blame for his crime. He didn't deserve love. All he could hope for was peace. Akiakook had said peace was the ultimate state for those who had gone against their own nature.

But you acted according to your nature. It was all Victor left you. He didn't treat you like the son you should have been. He created you and left you to fend for yourself, to learn who you were on your own with no guidance. He never gave you a chance. He dismissed you as a monster from the moment of your first breath, before you even knew what breath and light and life was.

That may be true, but that only made him less worthy of love. If his nature was to be a monster then he didn't deserve to mate. Wasn't that what Victor had feared? Why he'd destroyed the one woman who could have been his exact match?

"Sas? Are you alright in there?" Angel's voice floated through the doorway.

He didn't want to answer. The truth was, he would never be *all right*. "I will return shortly." He pushed away any further thoughts on happiness and searched for the small bottle of juice he rarely used. Finding it where he expected, he walked back inside to the counter and sprinkled a small amount of lemon on the meat. Though lemon balm had the name of lemon, it tasted of mint which wasn't what he wanted for their dinner, but lemon juice was a rare commodity.

"What are you making?" Angel's voice helped him keep his dark thoughts at bay.

"I'll tell you after you taste it."

"Uh-oh. That sounds like it might be something I'd never eat if I had the choice."

He moved the pan to the wood stove then added more wood. "You don't have to try it."

"Of course, I'll try it. I love everything you feed me. In fact, I was hoping to have a little of you for dessert."

Confused, he glanced at her to find her staring at his bare cock. Immediately, blood rush to that spot, and he hardened as raw lust built in his groin. He turned his back on her and opened the cabinet.

The thought of her mouth enveloping his cock had him gripping the plate in his hand. Was this more punishment? To tempt him with sex, knowing he could have nothing more?

"By the way, I don't mind having dessert before dinner." She practically purred her words.

His cock jumped, hitting the side of the counter, and he tightened his ass in response. He'd never been a saint, far from it, so if she wanted to suck on his cock, he'd oblige, knowing full well he would be sorry later.

"Though I have to admit it's smelling really good in here."

At her words, he forced himself to let go of the plate, pick up a spatula and tend to their meal. She needed her energy if she wanted to…he quickly flipped the meat and dribbled the juices over it. He had to concentrate on dinner. Having a hard cock near the stove meant he might burn himself and he had no doubt he would feel every hot sensation of it.

Moving the pan over to the counter, his thoughts brought new conclusions. While inside Angel he'd felt every sweet sensation. Obviously, the lack of sensation over the years hadn't effected that piece of his anatomy. That was odd. Maybe because he'd never had the experience of being inside a woman before.

He loaded the plate with food, cutting the meat at the

counter. When he walked to the bed, he found Angel staring at him.

"I hope I'm not embarrassing you. I've never been with a man of your size before and, well, it's pretty exciting."

He swallowed hard as her gaze left his face to wander down his torso. Before it reached his hardening cock, he sat and used the fork to spear a mushroom, onion slice and a square of elk meat.

She chuckled. "Okay, I get the message. Shut up and eat." She opened her mouth and he placed the food inside. She took the mouthful and chewed while he gathered more food onto the fork.

When he looked up again, she was licking her lips. Fascinated by her tongue as it slid along her full lips, his cock grew harder, hitting the bottom of the plate.

She opened her mouth again for another bite, but his desire was too strong.

Within seconds he stood, placed the plate on the chair and climbed onto the bed. He straddled her chest, still careful of her hands despite the lust riding him hard. Looking down at her face, he caught her sly smile.

He gazed into her eyes. "I want this."

A shiver raced across her skin before she winked. "Of course you do, every man does."

He shook his head. "I've never had it."

Her eyes widened before her gaze fell to his cock. "Then you're long overdue. Just remember to let me determine how much of you to take because you're far too long for me to swallow all of you." She raised her head and licked at his tip then looked up at him.

His voice caught in his throat, so he nodded to let her know he understood.

"Good. Now bring your handsome-self closer, so I can taste more of you." She licked her lips again as if to entice him.

He hesitated a couple of seconds, unsure if he'd be able to stay in control with such a new experience. He tossed the idea aside. Keeping her safe was too strong an instinct. He was confident he wouldn't go too far.

Finally, he lowered his cock to her lips.

She began by licking the entire head before pulling just that amount into her mouth. When her teeth ran along the underside of his ridge, a slice of pleasure sped up his spine. Then she sucked at the head, spiking his rising need.

She pulled her mouth away and tongued the underside of his cock from the start of his balls to the tip of his head. Shocks sped from his groin to his brain and back. She repeated the stroke a number of times until he thought he would have to stop the whole process.

As if she knew exactly what his breaking point was, she paused. "I need you even closer now."

Just her words had his body tensing. "Are you sure?"

She grinned. "More than sure. I've only had a taste, now I want it all."

He took a deep breath to relax his muscles before moving his hips closer. He rested his hands on his thighs, watching her mouth.

She lifted her head and took him inside past his tip, past the ridge and halfway down his shaft. Then her lips closed over him and her tongue played.

He gripped his thighs hard to keep from moving his

hips, her warning the only logical thought in his head. When she pulled her mouth down to his tip and back up again, he thought he would release right then. Leaning over her, he put his hands on the wall, tilting his hips to give her more access to his rigid cock.

She moaned with pleasure and brought her mouth farther up his shaft. The vibration of sound had his control slipping. His fingers dug into the log above her head as he forced his hips to remain still.

Her arm came around his ass, and she pressed him toward her.

Slowly, he gave in to her pressure, careful to stop when she let up. Her throat worked on his head as her tongue laved at his shaft and her warm mouth enveloped him. He leaned his forehead against the wall trying to hold on, but the sweet torture was too much.

He locked his hips to keep from hurting her as his release ripped from his cock, spilling into her sweet mouth. He threw back his head and yelled as the pleasure erupted through him.

When he had spent all he had, he looked down at her. She licked him all over as if she wanted to taste every last drop of his release. When she was satisfied he was completely clean, she kissed his tip. "That didn't just make me horny, but hungry too."

His cocked jumped of its own accord at her words and she laughed, a sultry sound that had his body responding again.

"Tell you what, Sas. Feed me that dinner that smells so good, and I'll be happy to have you inside me again."

Again, his cock jumped at her words. He quickly moved

away, climbing off the bed, uncomfortable with how addicted he already felt to intercourse with her. "You don't have to feel you need to accept me in your bed. I know I'm not what you're used to."

He lifted the plate and sat in the chair.

"No, you're not what I'm used to. You're better."

At her words, he caught her gaze. "Better?" She was mistaken. He'd never had sex with a woman before. He didn't know the nuances of it.

She gave him a lopsided grin. "Are you fishing for a compliment?"

He almost forgot to look away, his level of comfort with her growing by the hour. "I don't know what you mean. I've never had intercourse before."

Her eyes widened and her mouth opened. She started to speak a couple of times before she finally found the words. "You were a virgin?"

"Yes." He didn't understand why she was shocked. He was marked by scars, had an intense gaze, the whites of his eyes were slightly yellow and he was larger than any man he'd ever met. Plus, he was immortal, not that he could tell her that.

She shook her head. "I can't believe some woman hasn't jumped you by now. Where have you been, in jail or something? Did you commit some kind of crime?" She paused.

His stomached tightened into a lump of rock. His crimes once again slapping him in the face.

"Oh." Now she seemed truly afraid. "Please don't tell me you were a monk or priest or something like that."

He lowered his brow in confusion and shook his head. How could she think religious men worse than murderers? "I wish I had been a man of religion, but my lack of experience stems from my body and my geography." *And my immortality.*

"But you travelled all over and your body is hot." She looked askance at him. "If you're so inexperienced, how did you know what to do? I can't see Timber explaining it all to you."

He didn't answer, hurt that she obviously thought he lied. That was one crime he'd never committed. Rising, he set the plate down again and strode to the bookcase. Pulling out the book he had reread again just the other night, he brought it to the bed and held it up.

"*How to Make Love to a Woman* by Dr. Lindsey Sterns." She looked at him then back at the book. "Oh."

He placed the book on the end table next to the bed before resuming his seat and gathering a forkful of the now cool food. "Are you ready to eat now or would you like me to warm it in the pan again?"

She appeared distracted, but she nodded and opened her mouth.

He didn't hesitate, anxious to feed her and himself on the chance that she was still interested in intercourse afterward.

CHAPTER ELEVEN

Angela lay in the darkness wide awake after her long nap before dinner, even despite another very satisfying session of sex with Sas. His breathing as he slept on the couch was reassuring as it gave her alone time that until now she hadn't wanted.

Having sex with Sas had been incredible and giving him oral sex had her feeling proud of herself for finding another way she could repay him even without the use of her hands. But after he dropped the bombshell about being a virgin, her heart started to wrestle with her brain.

No one ever forgot their first lover, and she was no exception. She'd had an emotional bond with the boy she'd slept with back in high school. They dated most of her senior year, and she thought she was in love.

She didn't doubt he thought so, too. When he dumped her, she'd cried so much she made herself sick. Her father didn't get it, but he didn't make her go to school the rest of the week. It was all teenage drama, but the feelings had been real.

Knowing Sas was a virgin their first time together meant she needed to figure out what she wanted from the relationship because the last thing she wanted to do was hurt the very man who had saved her life. She owed him so much.

Her problem was that she'd viewed sex with him from a purely selfish standpoint, much like when she traveled and had sex with a local if she hit it off with anyone. Luckily, as far as she knew, she didn't have any diseases to pass on to Sas, and if she counted her days correctly since last taking her pill, she wouldn't become pregnant at this time of the month.

She also viewed having sex with him as another way to thank him. But now, whether he admitted it or not, there were emotions involved. She just had to figure out how *she* felt.

If they continued strictly as sex partners, she'd need to make that clear. But if there was more to it...ugh, she couldn't seem to separate her feelings of gratefulness from her feelings for him as a man. And even if she felt more for him than a simple fling, there were long-term issues to contend with. It wasn't as if Sas lived anywhere near her. Shoot, he didn't live near civilization of any kind.

When was she supposed to have a relationship with him? In between business trips? That meant she should keep it to just sex, but she'd be kidding herself and lying to him if she told him that. She was way beyond the "just sex" relationship. She really, really liked him.

With her other two serious relationships, she'd decided to just see where they went, take it one day at a time, but that wasn't possible here, and Sas wasn't like any other man she'd ever been with.

First, he was by far the kindest and most considerate. Second, he was also the biggest and most muscular. Her serious relationships had been with more "intelligent" types, yet Sas was very smart and well-traveled.

That he lived deep in the Alaskan wilderness was another unique trait. There was something about a man who could take care of himself and live a fulfilling life on his own that really attracted her. Maybe it was a little caveman-like, but it spoke to that small part of her that loved the idea she would be, and was, taken care of if she couldn't do it herself.

Her heart sighed. It would be so easy to fall in love with him. She could see herself learning to cook the different game so it tasted wonderful, like the elk they had for dinner. Though she wasn't particularly domestic since she wasn't home a lot, when she was home she enjoyed cooking and lounging in her apartment. She may work hard and travel all over, but she'd perfected the art of relaxing.

The problem was Sas' chosen abode. Here they were isolated. For any type of relationship with him, she'd have to give up seeing the world, unless he came with her. She immediately squashed that fantasy. Sas was out here for a reason. Maybe the answer to her dilemma was to find out what that reason was.

Who was she kidding? It didn't matter if he was running from the law or just liked pitting himself against nature, she was falling for him. Shoot. How did that happen?

She licked her suddenly dry lips. What if he changed once she was able to help herself? Would he resent it or would he welcome it? And how would she feel when it was time to return home?

Her chest tightened so hard, she could barely breathe. The thought of not ever seeing him again told her more about her feelings than anything else.

But what a relationship with Sas would look like was a

complete blank, even though leaving him almost brought her to tears.

She needed to know what he felt and getting that out of him would be a challenge. He may not look at his first time in the same way she did. He was born in Germany and lived a European lifestyle before making his home in the far reaches of the north, so she had no idea if he looked at his experience like she did as an American.

Feeling more confused than ever, she closed her eyes. For the first time since landing in her predicament, she wished she could talk with her brother. Though he was younger and turned over-protective sometimes, they were close. Losing their mom at an early age had done that for them.

How much longer before he began to wonder where she was? She'd been with Sas for over a week already. Was it now two weeks? Did she only have two more weeks with him? She wanted much more. She could take sick days. After all, she did have frostbite on her hands…if they even healed.

Her dinner lay heavy in her belly as her stomach tightened with worry. She had to have faith in Sas. If anyone could save her hands, it was him.

She listened to the sound of his breathing, blocking out all her thoughts. The knowledge that he was near made her feel safe. The only way she'd feel safer was if he were sleeping in the bed next to her.

Envisioning him next to her, cuddling, she finally drifted to sleep.

Sas kissed her awake, and she opened her eyes to stare into brown irises so dark they looked black. She grinned. "Good morning."

He kissed her nose before throwing back the covers. "Good morning.

We have much to do today." He rose bare-ass naked and set water to boiling on the stove. In no time, he dressed and headed outside. "I'll be in for breakfast."

She swung her feet over the edge of the bed, shivering in the coolness of the cabin. "I'm going to need more wood if you want breakfast." She winked. "And I'm not talking about your cock."

He let his gaze rake over her naked body, heating her up quite well. "I can do both."

She laughed as he closed the door. After quickly dressing in her favorite jeans and sweater, she strode to the stove and threw the last logs into it. Pulling the now boiling water off, she poured it through the coffee strainer, the scent filling her nostrils and making her mouth water.

Within seconds, she poured two cups of coffee and took a sip of hers. It was as if she hadn't had any in months. Once her taste buds were satisfied, she quickly sliced the bread she made yesterday and buttered the pan, setting it to heat on the stove. She pulled out the salmon they'd caught a couple of days ago and the neighbor's homemade cheese.

While she waited for the pan to heat, she started to whip up a hollandaise sauce.

The door opened and Sas came in with an armful of split wood. He didn't say anything as he dropped it and strode back outside.

She shook her head. He was just too talkative. Filling the stove with more wood, she worked on breakfast.

A shout outside had her running to the door. Throwing it open she froze. Her brother, surrounded by a pack of snarling wolves, aimed a handgun at Sas. Sas held his arms to the side as if inviting the shot.

She ran onto the porch. "No!"

One of the wolves looked straight at her and howled.

The gun went off.

She jerked awake. It was pitch black and her heart pounded

in her chest. She moved her hand to hold it, but as she made contact pain shot up her arm. She gave a small cry before the howl of a wolf sounded just outside the cabin.

Her breathing calmed as the sound connected to her dream, explaining where part of it came from. She listened for Sas' breathing but it was missing. She closed her eyes again and tried to hear him, but she didn't sense him in the cabin. "Sas?"

When there was no answer, her fear returned. What if he was hurt? Maybe the howl was because the pack had taken him down. She had to know.

Sitting up, she swung her feet over the side of the bed and carefully put her weight on them. They didn't hurt, but her knees felt wobbly. She braced her forearm on the back of the chair next to the bed and took a step.

Yes, definitely wobbly, but her concern for Sas drove her on. Taking another step brought her close enough to the table to brace her other arm on that as she gave up the chair. Her eyes were slowly adjusting to the diffused light from the moon hitting the snow outside, and the expanse of space from the table to the door was intimidating.

She looked out the window from where she stood, but she couldn't see either Sas or the wolf. Slowly, she made her way around the table until the void between it and the door loomed before her.

Another howl broke the quiet of the night. It sounded as if it was on the kitchen side of the cabin. She listened for footsteps, breathing, anything to indicate that Sas was nearby, but only silence greeted her.

What if he were bleeding to death? What if even now the

wolfpack had him surrounded as he lay on the ground hurt and in pain?

And what the hell could she do about it? She froze as she'd been about to let go of the table. What would she do? She couldn't even throw anything at them with her hands as they were.

Frustrated, she cast about for an answer.

She could scream and stomp and scare them away. She could do that. Refusing to think about what she might have to do next, she took a step toward the door, holding both arms out for balance.

After five more steps, she took an extra-large one and fell against the wall next to the door. She did it!

Another howl split the air and this one sounded as if it was right outside the front door. She shuffled over to the window to look.

There it was. A lone wolf. Didn't they travel in packs? Was it hurt? Why was it just sitting there? She scanned the area for Sas, but there was no sign of him. Did that mean the wolf was calling the rest of its pack to attack Sas? Why hadn't she read up on wolves when she prepared for her trip instead of researching polar bears, seals and penguins?

Looking back at the door, she slowly slid toward it until it was within reach, except she couldn't open it with her hand. She tried pushing the latch up with her elbow, but it wouldn't budge. Shoot.

Seeing no other way, she bent her knees to get her shoulder under it, but they gave out beneath her and she slid to the floor. This was not good. She would have to shuffle over to the window so she could use the sill to prop her arms on it to pull herself up.

But if Sas was in trouble then she had to do it. With determination filling her gut, she started to move her ass along the wall. She'd just cleared the door when footsteps sounded on the steps.

Sas!

The door opened and he strode in. As soon as he closed the door, he stilled. "Angel?"

"I'm okay, I was just looking for you." She gave him a meek smile, but since it was dark, he probably couldn't tell.

He crouched next to her. "What happened?"

She raised one shoulder to her ear. "I heard the wolf and thought you might be hurt."

He brushed his finger across her cheek. "You feared for me?"

"Of course I did. I was worried. It's the middle of the night and you weren't here and there's a wolf howling out—Hey, how'd you get past the wolf? Didn't he attack you?"

"I'm too big for Granddad. He was more concerned with warning the other wolf from encroaching on his territory. Let me return you to bed."

She nodded, but he was already moving one arm under her knees and another behind her back. She looped one arm around his neck as he lifted her up. Now that was a squat deadlift if she'd ever seen one. "Is that the name you gave the wolf?"

He didn't answer right away. Instead, he placed her in the bed and pulled the quilt over her. "Yes."

She grinned. She'd asked for that one-word answer. "Why did you name him that?"

He sat in the chair next to the bed. "Because he's a grey

wolf and grey is the color of wisdom and wisdom comes with age. I don't know how old he is, but he's been in this area for a few years."

"I like that. I like that everyone here has names with stories behind them. How come you call me Angel?" Not that she was complaining. It was so close to her real name he may have looked at her license, but if he didn't, she wanted to know her own story.

"I decline to answer."

She stared at him even though he didn't meet her gaze. Why would he decline to answer about the very nickname he'd given her?

He stood. "You need to sleep now."

"Wait. Where did you go? Why weren't you sleeping?"

He didn't sigh, per se, but there was a relaxing of his shoulders as if he'd given up. "I had to relieve myself."

"Oh." She should have thought of that. Didn't she look like an idiot now? Though to be fair, she may have thought of that if it wasn't for the wolf howling right outside.

And the disturbing dream she had. What did it mean?

He finished field-dressing the deer he shot and packed it into his tarp. He'd been lucky to find one so close to the cabin. Ever since he found Angel, his life had changed for the better, even his hunting.

Her insistence on moving about the cabin to exercise had at first alarmed him, but as her strength returned, he felt better about leaving her alone for a few hours at a time the last couple of days as he supplemented his winter store of food.

She wanted to come outside, but it was too dangerous as her hands still had some concerning pockets of tissue that he couldn't be sure would drop off. Any cold exposure would worsen the condition. However, he understood her need to breathe fresh air. Tonight, he would work on a fur hand-wrap, so she could come outside for brief periods.

Tying up the deer meat, he slung it over his shoulder and headed back toward the cabin. The fresh snowfall had made it easy to track the buck and with only a few inches of powder on the ground, the path wasn't hard to follow.

He found his pace picking up as he drew closer. It was almost time for the midday meal, and he looked forward to their time together afterward. They'd replaced reading in the afternoons with intercourse, now his favorite time of the day. Angel's body was an addiction that he catered to whole-heartedly.

He shook his head as he strode up the incline to the ledge where his cabin sat. He never expected to have the experience of mating. Now that he had, he wanted it as much as possible. He didn't understand why she would want to have such intimate relations with him except that she didn't know all there was to know.

His step slowed as the cabin came into view.

He hadn't told her about his crimes. If she knew of them, she would turn away, maybe even runaway despite her condition. That he was immortal was of little concern. She would leave him long before that issue raised its torturous head.

He came to a stop, staring at the cabin, trying to swallow the sudden lump in his throat. He couldn't imagine his life without Angel. No one had given him so much, her kindness, her caring, her body. She'd never know how much she'd meant to him.

Every night she asked him to sleep with her, but he claimed that he feared hurting her hands inadvertently, which was true, but his bigger concern was becoming used to her sleeping at his side. He had no hope that she would stay past the winter, and if she asked to leave, he had no choice but to help her. It was all part of what he hoped would bring him peace. He had to keep that enticement before him. Peace.

He started for the cabin, anxious to see her. He'd been gone almost two hours and he wanted to enjoy every second with Angel that he could. Quickly, he hung up the meat. He'd take care of it later, after she rested. Already, his body was anxious to feel her against him again.

The sound of a twig snapping halted his step. He looked to the west where the sound came from. Within seconds, the sound of boots in the new snow floated through the quiet landscape like a shot among the bird sounds to his sense of hearing. Disappointment sent irritation burning through his gut. Whoever it was, wasn't welcome.

He waited. If he could, he'd keep them from coming inside, despite the hospitality requirement of the bush.

As Timber's silhouette came into view, he sighed. Timber was the one person he couldn't push aside. The man brought medicine for Angel and a shirt for himself and who knew what else as the man loved to "bargain" as he stated it. Timber would stay the night to rest before trudging home.

"Hey, Sas. You're a sight for sore eyes."

The man's antiquated greeting had him shaking his head.

"I can think of at least a thousand other sights of much more interest, including the pine trees you just walked by."

Timber chuckled. "You're too literal, my friend." The man walked up and hit him on the arm, looking at the tarp hanging from the nearby tree branch. "New meat?"

"Yes."

"I have perfect timing, don't I?"

"Yes." Perfect for interrupting an enjoyable afternoon with Angel.

"So, are you going to invite me in, or do I need to invite myself?"

Crushing his honest reaction, he opened his arm toward the steps.

"Thank you. How's your patient doing?"

He didn't answer. Timber would discover that soon enough.

Before the older man could lift the latch, he reached around him and knocked. Yesterday, when he'd entered, he'd found Angel naked and sitting on the table, her decision to have intercourse immediately a pleasant surprise.

Timber glanced up at him, but didn't open the door. "Is she moving around now?"

"Come in." Angel's voice from inside saved him from answering.

They entered to find her sitting on the couch, a book open on her lap. When she looked up and spotted Timber, she closed the book quickly, dropped her stick for turning pages, and jumped up to greet him.

He took the opportunity of Angel giving Timber a hug to see what she read. It was the book on making love to a woman he'd been re-reading again last night. He'd left it on the couch, anxious to head out before dawn. Just the thought of her reading it and looking at the photos had his cock growing hard inside his jeans. He re-shelved the book before turning around.

"It's so good to see you." Angel's excitement at having Timber visit cut his own disappointment in half. If she wanted to be entertained by Timber's stories, then he was a bit more pleased the man would stay.

"Look at you. You're up and walking around. How did that happen?"

Angel stepped back toward him and wrapped her arm around his back. "This guy right here." She looked up at him, happiness sparkling in her eyes before he moved his gaze to Timber.

"Well, I'll be a muskrat's mama. Who'd have thought the big man had it in him. Good job, Sas."

He nodded before disengaging himself from Angel's sweet embrace and moving to the older man. "I'll help you with that."

"Great." Timber turned his back at the offer and slipped his arms from the straps of the large backpack.

He caught the heavy bag and set it on the table.

Angel came over. "That's bulging. What do you have in there?"

Timber pulled out the chair and sat. "Uh-uh. Not until I wet my whistle. What do you say, Sas? Got anything for a thirsty man who's been trudging through new snow all day?"

He moved to the kitchen and filled the tin cup with cold water. When he turned back to bring it to Timber, he found

Angel had stacked the three back cushions from the couch on the floor and sat by the table.

Shaking his head, he brought Timber the cup then strode into his cave storage for the empty barrel and brought it back. Just as he set it down, she moved to get off the cushions and lost her balance.

He scooped her up before she could fall to the floor. "Careful."

She looked at Timber. "See now why I'm doing so much better?"

Timber laughed. "Yes, I do."

He set Angel on the barrel and returned the cushions to the couch.

"I brought you a special gift." Timber unzipped his backpack and buried his hand inside.

Angel looked over Timber's head at him and pushed out her lips as if she would kiss him. He frowned. There'd be no kissing with Timber around. Didn't she realize he would stay the night?

Timber caught her attention as he pulled something from his sack.

"Oh, you sweetheart! How'd you know I love wine?" The older man's cheeks turned pink at her words. She looked at him. "Look, we can have wine with dinner."

"I don't drink."

Timber turned his head. "I know that. It's all for her."

She scooted off the barrel and gave Timber a kiss on the cheek. "Thank you."

The older man grumbled something in return before burying his hands in his backpack again. "I almost forgot. I also picked this up for you." The man held out a plastic package with a toothbrush.

She smiled sheepishly. "My breath's that bad, huh?"

Timber vigorously shook his head. "Not at all. Actually, from your minty breath, I figured Sas had given you mint leaves and a twig."

She looked back at him. "Can you put this by the bed for me?"

He strode forward and picked up the toothbrush, thankful to Timber for his thoughtfulness.

"I brought this for you, Sas." Timber held up a blue and black plaid flannel shirt. "It was the largest size Grubber had."

He took the shirt and held it against himself.

"You'll look handsome in that. I think blue's your color." Angel's face shone with animation.

Forcing his gaze from her, he nodded at Timber. "Thank you." He folded the shirt and put it in his chest. "Were you able to find any pain medicine?"

Angel shook her head. "I don't need any pain medicine. I'm doing so much better."

He raised one eyebrow. "We need to change your bandages again tomorrow."

Her smile disappeared, and he kicked himself for having reminded her of the pain he would cause her.

"Don't worry." Timber patted her arm to get her attention. "I was able to purchase a few pills."

"Thank you. I appreciate that." She gave the man a half-hearted smile.

"I would have been here sooner, but Sturge and Ginny

asked me stay an extra day. Sturge needed some help with his roof."

"What was wrong with it?" Angel's interest was quickly diverted.

Timber shrugged. "Had a slight dent in it. A tree branch fell on it and we needed to repair it, otherwise ice might build up there and cause a leak come spring time. Usually, Ginny would help him, but with the newborn, she's pretty busy."

"She has a baby? Out here?" Angel glanced at him before returning her gaze to Timber.

Timber crinkled his nose. "Yes, and that boy has lungs on him. He woke up last night and wouldn't go back to sleep. Crying his head off. That's when I decided it was time to skedaddle, otherwise I wouldn't have been here until dinner. Speaking of food…" Timber turned toward him, "isn't it about time for lunch?"

"Yes." He strode into the kitchen area and began preparations, listening to Timber and Angel's conversation.

"Did she have her baby here?" Angel's voice was filled with concern.

"No. She flew to Fairbanks. That's the closest hospital. There's an Inuit midwife, Frankie, in Savik that advised her on all that pre-birth stuff. After the birth, Ginny flew back with the baby. Sturge has a dogsled and team so it takes him a lot less time to get back and forth to Savik. It's only half a day for them in the sled. They just bundled the tike up really well and got him home fast. That was in August, and it was probably in the low forties then anyway."

"I didn't realize there was another woman out here. Are there more besides Ginny and the midwife?"

"Oh, yeah. There's probably about nine women in or around Savik."

"Hmmm." From the sound of Angel's voice, she was thinking hard. "Are there any women there that you're interested in?"

"Hell, no!" Timber paused. "Sorry about swearing, but I had myself enough of women down in the lower forty-eight. I came up here for peace and quiet. I don't need no woman jabbering at me."

"Sas, do I jabber at you?"

He turned to face her and noticed the gleam in her eyes. He wouldn't say she jabbered, but she did talk a lot. "I decline to answer."

Timber's laughter filled the room. "Now that's a phrase I need to start using."

Angel grumbled. "Please don't. I only insisted he use it because when he doesn't want to answer me, he just doesn't, leaving me waiting forever for an answer that's not coming. To be honest, I prefer knowing there will be no answer so I can continue with the conversation."

He saw Timber roll his eyes before he turned back to completing the meal preparation.

"Angel, sweetie. You *do* jabber, but I'm thinking that both Sas and I enjoy it."

She sighed. "If I didn't jabber, as you put it, it would be as silent as a graveyard in here. I like to think I've improved the atmosphere a bit."

As far as he was concerned, she'd completely changed the entire feel of his cabin. He picked up the plate and the baking sheet and brought the sandwiches to the table. Handing one to

Timber, he lifted the heavy backpack off it and set the plate before Angel.

She smiled up at him like he'd given her a gold nugget. "Thank you."

Something in her eyes caught his attention and he forgot to look away.

"Sas, is something wrong?" As her brow lowered in concern, he recalled himself and moved his gaze to the food.

"No, just thinking." *About the look in your eyes.* There was a tenderness in her gaze that wasn't there before. When did that happen? Yesterday? The day before? Had their intercourse affected her as much as it had him?

His heart expanded within his chest. She cared about him even more than just being worried for his safety. They were connected now. Even as the idea formed, he was hesitant to accept it.

He picked up her sandwich and made her take a bite before she continued to chat with Timber. Her face, body and even arms moved with her conversation, her animation a refreshing change in his solitary life.

And he didn't want to go back to the way it was before. She now meant more than simple redemption and peace to him. He wanted more. He wanted companionship and… love.

A new fear skittered up his spine—fear of rejection. It was actually an old fear born after Victor rejected him and later when Felix and Agatha rejected him. The pain was so debilitating that he'd avoided the possibility after that.

The saloon whore's reaction to him had not hurt because it was expected and based on pure physical revulsion, but to have Angel react in a similar way—the constriction in his chest took his breath away.

She didn't mind his scars. He breathed easier, the thought calming. That was the biggest hurdle, and she'd not even recognized them as the horror they were. That meant if she felt as strongly for him as he did for her…

He tore his gaze away from her as his feelings overwhelmed him. He *loved* her. He leaned against the support pole, the revelation so strong he lost his balance. He loved Angel. Somewhere between thinking of her as redemption, caring for her and intercourse with her, he'd fallen in love with her.

He tried to squash the burgeoning joy bubbling up from the depths of his soul. He didn't deserve her. He was a monster inside and out. But his joy refused to be dampened.

He loved her. It was as if he'd lived beneath an unnatural solar eclipse for three hundred years, and finally the moon moved, revealing the true brightness of day to shine upon him. Never had he felt such happiness. This new feeling was more than hope. It was the realization of that hope. He wanted to run to the top of his mountain and shout out his elation.

CHAPTER TWELVE

"Hey Sas, where are you? Did you hear me?" Timber's voice broke into his musings.

"No, I didn't." He found both Angel and Timber studying him.

"I said you better be ready for company. Ginny told Sturge he has to come by and visit Angel. She wants to come too, but he told her it was getting too cold for the baby to travel by dogsled. My guess is he'll try to convince Angel to come back with him to meet Ginny."

He wouldn't let her go. "No."

Timber's eyes widened. "No? What do you mean 'no'? No, that Sturge can't come, or no that Angel can't visit."

He moved to stand behind Angel, resting his hands on her shoulders. "No, Angel can't leave without me."

She looked up at him, worry in her eyes before she addressed Timber. "We'd be happy to have a visit from Sturge, but I think any visiting will have to be done by the both of us." She gave Timber a weak smile.

Timber looked at him then at Angel. His eyes suddenly widened and a grin spread over his weathered face, his nose becoming buried in his bushy mustache. "Well, I'll be a beaver's bunion. You two are a couple."

He froze as Angel's shoulders tensed beneath his hands, but then they relaxed and she looked up at him. "I think so. What do you think?"

Happiness skittered through his heart like a frightened hare. Did that mean she loved him?

"And don't even think about declining to answer." Her brows lowered over her searching eyes which revealed her own uncertainty.

He looked at Timber. "Yes."

"This is cause for celebration!" Timber returned his gaze to Angel. "We don't have a lot of bush matchmaking going on out here, so this would be considered an occasion."

She laughed, the sound filling his heart. "And how do you celebrate here in the wilderness? I'm guessing we won't be hiring a disk jockey or hanging a disco ball in the trees."

Timber gave her a look of horror, his eyes wide as he held up his fingers in a cross as if to ward off evil spirits. "Hell, no. We roast marshmallows and watch the northern lights while getting drunker than a caribou on whiskey."

Angel shook her head. "But all we have is the wine you brought me, and I'm pretty sure Sas doesn't have any marshmallows."

A gleam came into Timber's eyes before he winked. "I must be psychic then. Sas, hand me my bag."

He let go of Angel reluctantly, still half in disbelief that she agreed they were together and that it might mean she loved him. Bending, he lifted the backpack and brought it around to Timber.

"Just hold it like that a minute." Timber unzipped a side compartment while looking at Angel. "Don't know if you noticed, but Sas is like the strong man in a carnival. I think he was born with little biceps already developed."

Angel chuckled. "Oh, believe me, I know exactly how strong he is."

Timber coughed before pulling out a bag of marshmallows. "Ta-dah. But wait, there's more."

He held the bag still as Timber rummaged through another compartment. Watching Angel's expressions of happiness made him want to strip her naked and take her right there on the table. He'd be more irritated with Timber if he wasn't making her smile so much.

"Hah, found it." Timber pulled out a plastic bag of broken graham crackers and a large chocolate bar.

"S'mores!" Angel's face lit up. "I love those. Haven't had them since I was a child. Wow, you're a sweetheart." She hopped off the barrel and gave Timber a hug, still careful not to use her hands.

He didn't like her hugging the man. "Is that all you need?" He lowered the backpack to the floor.

Timber's face was bright red as Angel released him. "No, as a matter of fact. I need one more thing right now."

Holding the backpack up again, he waited while Timber rummaged through another compartment. The older man pulled peach-colored material out and held it up with both hands. "I'm not sure of your size, but I thought you might like a woman's shirt to wear around here."

Angel looked at the blouse. "It might be a little big, but not nearly as big as anything Sas might have."

Timber looked up at him then nodded, so he moved the backpack to the couch where the older man would sleep.

"I'm not a small man." Timber grinned. "But even I'd be swimming in one of the Sasquatch's shirts."

"I'm glad this one is a little large because I can't even get my hands through the sleeves of my sweater as we discovered. I'm just glad I dressed in layers when I went to the glacier that day because I'd worn a t-shirt over my tank top, so at least I have this."

Angel took the new shirt in the crook of her arm and walked over to him. "I'd like to change into this. Could you open the pantry for me?"

He looked over at Timber. "You can use the cabin to change. Timber and I are heading outside now anyway."

She raised one eyebrow, but didn't ask any questions. "Perfect."

"Let me just get my coat. It's getting a lot colder out there. You can tell winter is knocking at the door." Timber rose and pulled his parker from one of the hooks by the door.

"I'll be right there." He turned his back on Timber. "Let me help you with your t-shirt."

The door closed behind Timber and they were alone again. As much as he wanted to strip her naked and take her, he held back.

She dropped the peach shirt on the table and lifted her arms without a word, an oddity in itself.

He pulled the bottom of the shirt up her body and over her head, carefully working the short sleeves around the bandages of her hands. Her tank top did nothing to hide the points of her hard nipples and he sucked in his breath.

She stared at him, her gaze searching.

His gut churned with longing, so he quickly grabbed

up the new blouse and lowered it over her raised arms. The sleeves were long but loose, larger at the wrist than the elbow. The color made her look even healthier.

"It's exactly what I needed. What a dear man."

He nodded absently, his gaze riveted to her lips.

When she licked them, he lowered his mouth and kissed her. He'd expected to show her his passion, but instead he revealed his heart, gently moving his lips over hers before pulling away.

"Don't be gone long. I'll get lonely." She smiled hesitantly, reaffirming his suspicion that something had changed for them. Something important.

Finally, he turned away and followed Timber outside. For the first time, he wanted to stay inside.

Timber had headed down the incline of his ledge toward a small valley and now sat on a log waiting. It didn't take the older man long to start talking. "People in Savik are going to want to meet her. You know if you don't bring her in, they'll all start traipsing out here to find you."

He strode the final yards to the spot where Timber sat. "It's almost winter. It can wait."

His companion shook his head. "I would hope so, but you know how curious people can get."

He didn't respond. He didn't want to share Angel with anyone, not even Timber, but he owed it to the man. "Thank you for purchasing a shirt for her. I can give you some of the venison from this morning's kill in return."

"Don't even think about it. You need it for the two of you. Besides, that would make it a gift from you and it wasn't." Timber grinned. "I thought of it all by myself. Just don't tell her that I completely forgot about her hands." He lost his smile. "How damaged are they."

He looked down at his own large hands as he remembered Angel's delicate ones. "There are a number of white blisters that are breaking, but there are some red ones, too. I've changed the bandages regularly, but I have nothing to treat them with. I think some of the tissue is permanently dead."

To voice out loud Angel's prognosis made him finally accept the inevitable.

"Have you told her yet?"

He shook his head.

"I'd wait, if I were you. Remember that teenager we found over by Elk Run Ledge?"

"Yes." He'd never heard what happened to the young man once he was flown out.

"Well, the rescuers I ran into later in the spring told me that it looked like the kid was going to lose both his feet, but the doctors made him wait two months before they did surgery. Turned out, he was able to keep at least half of each. I gotta believe that was a relief to him."

"Do you think Angel might be able to keep all the tissue in her hands if she waits to see a doctor?" He hated doctors, but if they could help her, he'd stifle his feelings about them.

Timber shook his head. "Not necessarily, but if you found her the last week of September that means you'll have to get her to a hospital in two months, that would be the end of November and Charlie doesn't fly into Savik past November first. It's not like you can wait for spring because then any dead flesh will cause infection."

"I could bring her to the hospital by way of Tavva." He would just have to coax Sturge to be his guide.

Timber shook his head. "You would risk her in the cold that long? It would take you at least two weeks to get to Tavva and to rent a car. You'd be better off getting her to Savik before the end of this month."

It wouldn't take him two weeks to reach Tavva, but with Angel along, it could. Timber was correct, he couldn't risk her health like that, but the idea of putting her on the bush plane to Fairbanks without him made him sick.

"You're going to have to fly her out soon anyway."

At Timber's statement, he scowled. "Why?"

"She'd bound to have family and friends looking for her. It's not like she can call from here."

His mind whirled at Timber's comment. What did she say when she first woke? Something about her brother. *My trip was supposed to last a month and there is limited service on the boat, so he knows not to expect to hear from me until I land in Seattle.* "Her trip was for a month. She said no one would miss her until then."

Timber looked at him shrewdly. "I know you want to keep her all to herself, but if she wants to stay, she's going to have to let her family know she's alive and okay."

"You mean like you did?"

Timber looked away but not before his eyes reflected the pain his departure to Alaska had caused. "I made my choices and I'll live with them, but Angel didn't have a choice. You have to make it available to her."

He fisted his hands in frustration. Timber was right, but that didn't make it any easier to accept. If she wanted to go, he would allow it, but he didn't want anyone else to influence her decision and her brother very well could. "I do want her to myself."

"I know you do, big guy. You deserve her, but you can't keep her against her will. To tell you the truth, I think she's as infatuated with you as you are with her."

His mind had started down the old groove, much like water carved into a glacier when Timber mentioned him deserving Angel. But at his friend's observation, he pulled himself out. "You think so? Why?"

Timber chuckled. "Oh, my friend, you have it bad. How can I tell? By the way she looks at you, even when you're not looking. Trust me, she wants to be here. She's never once asked me to help her leave. In fact, she asked me more questions about you than anything else."

"She did?" Hope grew in his chest.

This time Timber rolled his eyes. "What do you think we talked about the night you ran down to my place to fetch the pain meds? She wanted to know everything about you, not that I could tell her much. You don't exactly talk about yourself, but I'm guessing you've told her more than you told me."

Had he? She was persistent. People in the wilderness didn't ask so many questions and they definitely didn't try to get the same information by asking a different question hours later. He felt his heart lighten as her interest in him became clearer.

"Well, what are you going to do?"

He refocused on Timber. "About what?"

"About her hands and her need to get in touch with family. You said she has a brother, right?"

He nodded absently, his gut tightening as if on cue. Even more than her need to communicate with the outside world was his concern over her hands. "I will make sure to do what is right for her."

"Good. While you're thinking about her, be sure to tell her as much about you as possible. Don't hold back any secrets. I can tell you from experience that when those secrets come out, you could lose her."

He opened his mouth to respond, but Timber held up his hand. "You don't have to tell me. I respect the Alaskan code, but with a woman, the rules change. Just remember that. Now if you don't mind, my ass is getting cold, so I'm heading back up."

Timber started up the incline back to the cabin, his words chilling the very air.

Just minutes ago, he was happier than he'd ever been in his life and now he had to do what was right and in every instance, he chanced losing Angel. If he had years to make a decision, the panic in his gut would be a lot less, but now it felt as if he walked across an ice bridge over a bottomless cavern as it slowly gave way.

Shaking his head, he pushed the fear aside. Tonight, he would enjoy Angel's happiness as she was entertained by Timber. Tomorrow, after the man left, he would show her exactly how much she meant to him.

He started up the incline. The following day, he would show her again. He wanted this happy reprieve from his existence.

He deserved it.

~~*~~

Angela kissed Timber on the cheek. "Have a safe walk home. Don't stop to play with any wolves."

The old man smiled. "I promise."

"And thank you for the s'mores and the wine and the shirt and everything. You spoiled me."

He looked above her head. "No, I think Sas is the expert at that. I just wanted you to feel welcome here."

She smiled as Sas pulled her back against him. "You did a great job. I feel very welcome."

"Good. I'll see you two next month, I imagine. Don't get into too much trouble until then." Timber opened the door.

Sas moved around her to follow him out. "No more trouble than you."

Timber's laughter floated through the open door before Sas closed it.

"He's a nice man and a good friend to you. I like him." Sas didn't say anything, his eyes riveted on her new shirt. Or was it her breasts? "Sas?"

His dark gaze lifted to hers for a brief moment before it returned to her breasts. "I want you now."

Every nerve-ending in her body woke up at his declaration. That they hadn't had sex yesterday must have pushed him to his limit. Would her tear her clothes off? Her belly tightened in anticipation.

Sas moved his hand behind his head and pulled his shirt over it even as he took a step toward her.

She watched it hit the floor and wished she could do the same, but her hands were useless.

He unbuttoned his jeans as he took another step, only to stop and unzip.

What she wouldn't give to yank his pants down to his ankles and grasp his cock in her hands.

Luckily, he wasn't going to wait for that. He pushed his jeans over his hips and pulled one leg off then the other, his proud, hard cock reaching toward her.

His next step brought him to her.

"I can't undress myself or I would."

Something flickered in his gaze as if he'd almost forgotten her handicap.

"It doesn't matter." His voice had dropped another octave, sending shivers of excitement up her arms. "I'd undress you anyway." He grasped the hem of her new shirt and lifted it over her head.

That left her in her tank top, which had recently been washed by him while she slept. That and all her clothes.

After dropping her shirt on top of his own, he brushed his fingers across her already hardening nipples.

The sensation through her tank softened his callouses which gave his touch a completely different feel, almost too soft. Because looking up at him gave her a kink in her neck if she did it for too long, she looked at his hard abdominal muscles that tensed in different places as he shifted his weight.

Without the ability to remove her tank, she was at his mercy. For a man who seemed to be in a rush with his own clothes, he suddenly found the control to dally with hers.

Instead of removing her tank, he ran his hands down to her own jeans and one hand cupped her between the legs. "You're hot."

Her breath left her in a whoosh. "Of course I am. You make me that way."

"I thought I make you wet."

She looked up at him. "That heat causes my wetness."

His nostrils flared at her response, and she swallowed a groan. She'd found over the last few days that allowing Sas to do what he wanted, explore where he wanted, was much more satisfying than telling him what *she* wanted. The man had an uncanny knack for finding just the right spot, rhythm, and pressure to send her catapulting into space with every orgasm.

His other hand found its way to her ass, and he squeezed her cheek.

In this position, he towered over her, making her five-foot eleven-inch frame seem tiny next to his more than seven feet of man-muscle.

His abs tensed before he let go of her ass to cup her face. He looked into her eyes, a rarity in and of itself, and she felt pinned to the spot with the intensity of his gaze. This man did nothing half way.

It was on the tip of her tongue to tell him how she felt, when he moved his hand from her crotch and unbuttoned her jeans. He was very good at it since he both undressed and dressed her. After he unzipped her pants, he let his fingers run over her mons teasingly.

Pushing her jeans over her hips, he crouched down, allowing her to lean against him as he pulled them from each of her legs. He was quick to lift her feet, one at a time and divest her of her socks.

Then he hooked his fingers around the sides of her panties and pulled them down. When they were off, he took a deep breath as if the scent of her readiness was an aphrodisiac.

She expected him to taste her right then, but once again

he surprised her. Instead, he leaned in and took one nipple in his mouth, tank top and all. The moan in her throat escaped as he sucked hard, bringing her to her toes. His hand behind her back held her against his mouth.

When he finally released her breast, her sheath was wet and her nipple throbbed with excitement.

He caught the hard nub with his fingers and proceeded to roll it, wet material rubbing along her nipple, spiking her need. Then his mouth encompassed her other breast, and he sucked that one, holding her in place.

By time he finished, she wasn't sure her legs would hold her any longer. As if he sensed this, he stood and sat her on the table.

Her body responded to the memory of him taking her there the day before Timber arrived, a position that she'd instigated.

But he didn't take her there. He did lift her tank from her body, causing her areolas to pucker as the wet material slid off her and the cabin air hit them.

Then he sank to his knees, putting his face level with her pussy. He spread her legs wide and blew at the moisture that lined her labia. He leaned in and licked at her readiness, his tongue diving between her folds, up around her clit and back again, his beard brushing against her sensitive skin.

She wanted to hold his head to her, but her hands were useless. The best she could do was rest her arms on his shoulders.

Sas looked up at her, his eyes boring into her, his desire causing her to shudder, but she couldn't look away. When his two fingers pushed into her opening, her body caught fire. Still, she couldn't tear her gaze from his. He started to pump his fingers in and out as he watched her.

The sensations inside her built so strong, she closed her eyes and let her head fall back. At the touch of Sas' tongue on her clit, she snapped her head back up. "Oh yes."

He didn't even hesitate as if he knew exactly how amazing it felt to have his fingers thrusting and his tongue licking. She felt her orgasm creeping up, the pleasure growing quickly. She tensed, her body ready to let go.

Sas pulled his fingers out and stood.

She moaned in disappointment, her tingling body calming without his touch.

He tilted her head up and lowered his lips to hers in a kiss so tender it surprised her into opening her eyes. When he broke it off, he cupped her cheek. "I need you now."

His words sent a rush of moisture flooding her sheath. At the look in his eyes, she nodded, her throat too tight to say anything.

"Wrap your arms around my neck."

She did as he requested and as he straightened, she wrapped her legs around his waist, his cock touching her ass.

He moved to the supporting post in the middle of the cabin. One side held the table, but the opposite side was empty and it was that side that hit her back as Sas pushed her against it. He was forceful, yet careful, a summation of his entire character.

Her short time to think ended as he held her ass aloft with one hand and positioned his cock against her entrance with the other.

She knew what would happen next, and the anticipation sent signals to her body to open for him.

He didn't move, though she felt his whole body tensing, its hardness even harder. This wasn't the first time he asked silent permission to enter her, and it had only taken once for her to understand. When he let go, he wasn't in control. She liked to think she caused that.

She turned her face toward his neck. "Now Sas."

As if his cock was the arrow in a crossbow, it speared her to her cervix in one quick thrust, slamming her butt against the post and throwing her to the edge of climax. She locked her arms around his neck as his hips pulled back and he thrust again.

She responded in kind, her hips meeting him as he entered then pressing her ass against the post as he pulled away. One arm wrapped around her and the post as if he couldn't bear for a smidge of air to come between them while his other grasped her ass, directing their rhythm.

Her body tingled with excitement as his rhythm increased, his thrusts spearing her, pushing her butt against the post, his raw need for her fueling her ecstasy. Through the thrills of his love-making she sensed something different.

Desperation.

She barely had time to recognize the feeling before her body took all thought away as it splintered into a thousand pieces.

Sas' shout as he came inside her filled the cabin, his release spiking her own.

As usual, it took them a long time to come down. She wanted to hold him close, but without her hands all she could do was cross her arms behind his neck and press her face to his shoulder.

Concern began to worm its way into her consciousness.

She lifted her face to look at him, but his forehead rested against the post above her head. "What's wrong?"

He didn't move a muscle. It was as if he'd been frozen in time at the peak of his ultimate contentment.

Finally, he spoke to the post in a raspy whisper. "I decline to answer."

Hurt and frustration hit her, making her wish she'd never suggested that phrase, but determination soon followed. She'd find out, one way or another.

She kissed his collarbone, completely confident in his ability to hold her up.

He pulled his head from the post. "What are you doing?"

"I'm kissing you, what else? I'd kiss your nipple if I could reach it."

His cock, still buried deep inside her, moved.

She loved that she could make his body react so easily. Now if she could get his heart in sync with hers, she'd be totally happy. *Then what?* The question came, unwanted. She didn't want to think about that.

Sas stepped away from the post, keeping her tight against him as he walked toward the bed.

When he sat on the edge, she eyed his nipple. Now she could make good on her suggestion. Leaning forward, she circled his nipple with her tongue, something she'd been dying to do for days. Without her hands to entice him, all she could use was her mouth.

Beneath her ass, his thigh muscles tensed. She grazed her teeth over his hard nub before sucking it into her mouth. Pressure inside her sheath proved he enjoyed her mouth as much as she enjoyed his.

She moved to his other nipple and played it with her tongue.

Sas' hands roamed from her ass to her back. Suddenly, he pulled away from her mouth. "You're hurt."

"What? No, I'm not."

His large hand brushed down the right side of her spine. "You are."

She shook her head. "No, really I'm fine. That's just—oh." Sas started to massage her back muscles and it felt so soothing, his large hand covering so much skin at once.

He stopped his movements and began pushing her off him.

"Wait, I'm okay. Really." She groaned as she slid off him and he set her on her feet, her knees not really capable of holding her up, but she didn't have to worry about it. Within seconds, Sas had her lying on her tummy, her arms at her sides, palms up so they wouldn't get hurt.

He climbed onto the bed and straddled her thighs. "Your skin is red from the post. I was too rough."

She rolled her eyes even though he couldn't see her. The man was too hard on himself. "No, you weren't too rough. I loved it."

He didn't respond. No surprise there, but when he started to massage her entire back, she grinned. Maybe it was okay if he thought he was too rough.

Sas' hands were like magic, kneading her muscles from her shoulders to her back. As he continued lower, he moved back, straddling her knees as he focused on her ass. She could imagine the red marks went down that far since she'd been instrumental in pulling her hips back against the post.

As he massaged her cheeks, he spread them then moved

them together over and over. She had the feeling he was no longer soothing her and doing more of his own exploration. The man was nothing if not thorough.

When he squeezed one ass cheek but not the other, she had a feeling she knew what was coming and her sheath moistened all over again.

Sas ran is large finger down her crease, over her anal rose and almost to her sheath opening. The tingles of pleasure that skittered throughout her core surprised her. He hadn't done anything but touch her.

"I understand this is another place for intercourse, but not all women like it."

Her sheath tightened at his words. She grinned at his unspoken question. "Yes, but you need lube to fit in there."

His finger ran along the same line again only with a little more pressure. Shoot, the man was making her wetter than the Trevi Fountain.

Sas moved his hands to cup her ass and push it up.

Naturally, she tilted her hips, giving him a view of her moist entrance. That gave her an idea. Carefully, she moved her arms so she could get her elbows under her and pushed backwards, lifting her butt so she was in the doggy style position, only on her elbows instead of her hands.

At her initial movement, Sas shifted back across her calves, but she felt him move close again. When his cock brushed her tailbone, she smiled. The man could take a hint.

Unfortunately, he didn't seem to be in a hurry to enter her. His fingers found her moist folds and played around her clit. After winding her up, his hand disappeared to reach around her waist and lift her to a kneeling position. One arm

remained securely around her while the other hand played…
with everything.

He started with her breasts, squeezing one then the other
before rolling each nipple and giving it a pinch. Then he turned
her head toward him and kissed her until she couldn't breathe,
his tongue dominating her mouth.

When he was satisfied with that, he moved his hand down
over her mons and cupped her, deftly inserting his middle
finger inside. He pressed his palm against her clit as his finger
stroked in and out of her.

It was a good thing he held her because the sensations
racing through her made it impossible to keep herself upright.
Small squeals of delight escaped from her as her body readied
for another orgasm.

Sas pulled his hand away. He was becoming very proficient
at revving her up and then slowing things down. Though it
was frustrating, she knew from experience that the end result
would be worth it. He slowly let her bend forward again and
she braced herself on her elbows, careful to keep her hands
from pressing into the quilt.

Her mind quickly shifted to her opening where Sas now
stroked his cock.

The urge to push back onto it was strong, but she forced
herself to wait. It would be even better when he was ready.

When his hand grasped her hip and his cock stopped at
her entrance, she swallowed hard. "Yessss."

Her hissed word wasn't even completed before he grasped
her other hip and thrust his cock deep inside her. Sparks lit up
behind her closed eyes at the pleasure that ripped through her,
but she had no time to bask in it.

Sas pulled his hips back and rammed his cock home again, pulling her ass toward him at the same time. His moan told her he felt every spike of excitement that she did.

He pulled back again and thrust forward, setting off a string of fireworks throughout her pussy. She panted as he pulled away then buried himself deep once more.

She felt her orgasm barreling toward her as Sas grasped her hips hard and pumped into her again. Out. In. Out. In. Her sheath sucked at him as her orgasm hit and she let herself go, gliding on a wave of joy that suffused her whole body.

Sas didn't move, his own release filling her, bringing her joy to a level she'd never had before with anyone. He bent over her, grasping her against him as his hips pumped a few more times before they both finished their journey of bliss.

She couldn't keep her ass up any longer and slowly slid down to her stomach. Sas kept his weight off her, but didn't let her break their connection. Carefully, he rolled them over onto their side, his cock still deep inside.

She lay in his arms as her breathing slowed. This was what she wanted, to have him hold her and stay with her all night. Of course, it wasn't night yet. It wasn't even lunch time. Sas' need for her hadn't waited long enough for Timber to walk out of sight. That alone filled her heart with happiness.

"Sas?"

"Yes."

"Could you sleep with me tonight, all night?"

He didn't answer right away. If he declined to answer at all, she had a feeling she might do him bodily damage.

"Why?"

His question caught her off guard. "Because I like being next to you, not just for sex, but just to be close to you."

"If I sleep with you, there may be too much sex."

At his answer, her whole body lit up and her sheath squeezed him. "That's okay."

"But you need your rest."

She turned her head to look over her shoulder, but she couldn't see his expression. It felt like he was making excuses. "Will you? Look, if you don't want to be near me at night, just tell me." She bit her lip at the hurt sound in her voice. He'd probably pull away now.

He didn't. His arm tightened around her, and he buried his face in her hair. They lay like that in silence, her harsh retort hanging in the air. Had she been wrong? Did he not feel the same about her that she felt about him?

Sas lifted his head. "I would like to sleep with you."

Her whole body relaxed in relief. She hadn't realized exactly how much she cared about him until that very moment. "Good because I want to sleep with you. I mean at night, not now."

His hand wandered from her waist to her cheek. He stroked her there for a moment before he gave one of his silent sighs. "I need to finish readying the meat for storage."

She nodded. "I know."

His hand left her face and he braced it on the bed as his hips moved away from her. She missed him, but knowing they would sleep together gave her something to look forward to.

She rolled over to watch him walk out the door to shower, his ability to stand the cold mindboggling. That he would be back to wash her up had her smiling. There were definitely some advantages to not being able to use her hands. Sas was very thorough.

CHAPTER THIRTEEN

He removed the empty dish from the table and brought it to the counter. Angel's insistence that they eat at the table and he eat at the same time made their meals together more enjoyable.

Whenever she started to talk about something he didn't want to discuss, he simply lifted a forkful of food to her lips. He found it humorous even though she frowned at him. It didn't keep her from her topic. It was simply a delay.

He heard her push the chair back and walk to the book shelves. Their evenings were spent reading or making love, dependent on what they did in the afternoon. He would prefer to having her both times, but he didn't want to hurt her while she was still recovering her strength. Anticipating their time together and sleeping side by side made him the happiest he'd ever been.

"Sas, do you ever take off those leather wrist bands and choker?"

Her question related to nothing they'd talked about over dinner, so it made him curious why she'd bring them up. "No." His scars beneath the leather were uglier than the rest, the stitches uneven and large.

"Why not?"

He rinsed the tin plate and lifted a towel to dry it. "They are replicas of gifts I received long ago." To help him look more normal.

Her footsteps came closer. "From Akiakook?"

"Yes. His wife made me a set, and when they were worn, I had an identical set created." And then another and another.

Angel's arms came around his waist. "Do you ever see them?"

He held the plate aloft, not wanting to accidently brush her hands. "They're dead."

She stepped away only to lean against the counter to face him. "I'm sorry."

"They died a long time ago." Over two hundred years or so.

"I don't think it matters how long it's been. There's still that void in your heart." She looked down at the floor, almost like she was embarrassed by her grief.

He set the dry plate down and lifted her chin with his finger. "And fond memories in your mind."

She looked up at him. "That's true. I remember my dad washing the dishes while I dried. Michael and I took turns. One of us would set the table and one of us would dry the dishes. Dad didn't see the need for a dishwasher."

He let go of her face and picked up the pan. Drying it, he put both it and the plate back into the cabinet.

"I need to get a message to my brother soon."

He stilled at her statement.

"Is there a radio or some way to get him word that I'm okay?"

He faced her. "There is in Savik. Grubber has a radio

which can contact Tavva. I'm not sure how far theirs reaches. Where is your brother?"

"Oh, he's in Oakland. But I could give someone his phone number and then they could call him and tell him I'm okay. If I don't, he'll be going to every port looking for me."

His gut tightened. Would she leave? Would her brother take her away? He placed his hands on her shoulders. "If you send this message, will he come for you?"

"What? No. At least I don't think so." She looked away. "Maybe. Oh shoot, I also need to let my boss know I need more time off for my hands to heal."

You'll have to get her to a hospital by the end of November and Charlie usually doesn't fly into Savik past November first. Timber's words came back to haunt him. He had to tell her. "Remember last night when I pointed out the dark areas on your hands and told you they would take longer to heal?"

Her eyes widened and her shoulders tensed beneath his palms. "Yes."

He swallowed hard, already knowing the pain he would see in her eyes if he looked at her directly. "Those areas may need to be removed."

"What?" She pulled away. "You said my hands were looking better."

The desperation in her voice froze him in place. "They're much better than they were. I'm not saying all the dark areas will need to be removed. It will take another month to determine that, but…"

"But what? Sas, tell me. I need to know. Will I lose all function in my hands? Will I lose my left hand altogether? That one is worse."

"No. That's not an issue. You won't lose a hand. I promised you that and it's true."

She turned away, walking to the couch where she plopped down. "Okay, so tell me the bad news."

"You need to see a doctor who can operate by the end of November."

Her brow furrowed. "So? It's not like I'll be able to return to work by then."

He moved to her and knelt down at her feet. "Charlie doesn't fly in or out of Savik past the first week of November."

"Okay, so we fly out early."

He shook his head. "Not we. You. And once you get to Fairbanks, a good doctor will make you stay until the end of the month to be sure that all the tissue that will heal has done so." If she could find a *good* doctor. He pushed the thought away.

Understanding dawned, her green eyes lightening with her sorrow. "And then I won't be able to come back to you."

He nodded, the lump in his throat too big to swallow.

"But why can't you come with me? I've lived here with you for almost a month now. You could come live with me for the winter, and…" Even she could see that it wouldn't work.

He stared into her watering eyes, not caring if she noticed the yellow in his gaze.

She lifted her hand to touch his face, but he caught her wrist, not wanting her to do more damage.

"Sas, I don't want to leave you. I love you."

His heart filled with joy. It was far more than he'd hoped for…*more than he deserved.* "And I don't want you to go, but your hands will need medical attention that I can't provide."

Now he understood the new pain growing in his chest. Despite how much he didn't want her to leave, he wanted her to be cared for even more.

He loved her. The feeling, so new and bittersweet, was strange and wonderful at the same time.

"There has to be a way." Her lips pursed in concentration. "How do you get supplies in the winter? What if there's a medical emergency?"

He rubbed her wrist with his thumb, reluctant to let her go. "We spend all summer stocking up for winter. If someone is hurt, we do what we can. If it's life threatening, Grubber will call into Tavva for a rescue, but that still depends on the weather."

Her eyes lit up with hope. "What about Tavva? Could we fly into there?"

Her determination to find a solution warmed his heart. "Yes, but I don't know how to get there from here. I've never been there."

She smiled, excitement shinning in her eyes. "You don't have to know how to get there. You just need to know how to get *here* from there. Do you know where your cabin is on a map?"

He shook his head, sorry to see her lose her smile.

"Oh, I have it! All we need is directions from Tavva to Savik, then you could find the way back here."

"Directions? We don't have roads up here."

She shook her head. "I know that. But if we have a compass and good wilderness directions, we could do it. It has to be worth trying, right?"

Her whole body seemed to move with her excitement and

her pulse beneath his finger raced. It could be done, but then what? Would she stay the winter? After that, would she leave forever? His heart twisted. He wanted to ask, but he was a coward. He didn't want to know.

"Why do you live out here?" Her sudden change in subject caught him off guard.

"I like it."

"Is that it? I mean, if we were to live together for a while in Fairbanks, there wouldn't be a warrant out for your arrest or anything, would there? I know Timber said I'm not supposed to ask questions like that, but if we did go into civilization, would I need to worry about that?"

He let go of her wrist and rose. Three hundred years ago, he was hunted in three different countries, justifiably so, but now… "No. There is no one looking for me."

She tried to look into his eyes but he turned away.

"Good." She spoke to his back. "I'm glad. I didn't think you were running from the law. I can't imagine you doing something illegal. My guess is you don't feel comfortable around people. You strike me as a serious introvert. I'm more of an extrovert myself."

Her confidence in him was misplaced, but it still warmed his heart. She loved him. The knowledge, delicate and precious, was like a butterfly in his large hands. He didn't want to hurt it. "I think your plan has merit, especially if we can enlist the help of Sturge and his dogsled."

He heard her rise from the couch and her arms wrapped around him from behind. "I knew we could figure this out."

He grimaced, not sure they'd figured anything out yet, but there was hope, and that's what she'd brought to his long existence—hope and love. He closed his eyes at the euphoria filling him.

She let go, and he listened to her footsteps as she walked around to face him. "Sas, are you okay?"

He opened eyes. "Yes." He was better than that. He loved a mate and she loved him back. Nothing else mattered. He would wrest every drop of happiness he could from these moments and keep them safe to look back on when—"I love you." He cupped her face with one hand and kissed her to show her how much she meant to him.

When he broke away from her clinging lips, he continued to hold her face.

Her green eyes were bright and filled with tears.

"What is it?" Had he hurt her?

She blinked. "I'm just so happy." She wrapped her arms around him and squeezed him. "I'll never regret getting lost in the snow. Even if it means I lose parts of my hands because I found you, the most amazing man in the world."

As he embraced her, his chest tensed beneath her cheek. *But he wasn't a man.*

Angela sat outside on the small porch listening to the sound of Sas stacking logs around the corner of the cabin. A month ago, if someone had asked her if she could be happy in a one room cabin in the middle of nowhere, she would have replied with a resounding "no." But a lot had changed since she'd embarked on her trip.

In three days, they planned to leave on Charlie's last flight out of Savik. They'd fly down to Fairbanks via Tavva and Coldfoot. She'd see a doctor and get them a room at a hotel, preferably on the outskirts. She wasn't oblivious to Sas' concerns about being in a city. That he was willing to go with her told her exactly how much he cared, so she wanted it to be as painless as possible.

The first thing she'd do is call her brother. She was supposed to arrive home today, but knowing her brother, he had probably already started worrying. He always did when she went on trips, even business trips. He knew her too well. She tended to get even more adventurous on her vacations. It would probably relieve him to know she was in no hurry for another adventure any time soon, if ever, after this one.

Her next agenda item was to contact work. She licked her lips at that quandary. Sas was used to living without money, but that was a hard life change for her. If she could figure out some way to get internet service to the cabin, she could probably work part time, but Timber had told her there were no towers anywhere. Satellite?

She had time to figure that out. She had plenty of personal time coming to her and she'd take it for her hands. Sas said the doctors might make her wait another month and then she would need time to recover. She raised her hands wrapped in the warm fur mitts without thumbs that Sas had made for her so she could enjoy the fresh air. At least it didn't hurt anymore to move them as long as she didn't press against anything or try to move her fingers.

She sniffed as her nose ran because of the cold. It was a warm day according to Sas, almost ten degrees. Then again, it was probably warmer in the sun where he worked piling up the wood he and Timber had cut.

The noise of log hitting log stopped, leaving the air quiet except for a diligent woodpecker. His footsteps sounded on the packed snow before he came into view.

Her heart rate picked up as it did whenever he was around. She'd never been one for the strong silent type, but Sas completely won her over.

Seriously, the man was hot. His new flannel shirt enhanced how really large he was, from his broad shoulders to his big hands and mega-height. He was almost a giant. She definitely could see why the people in the area called him Sasquatch. And now he was her Sasquatch. She wasn't sure if she'd tamed the wild beast or if he was the hero of her dreams. Either way she was happier than she'd ever been.

"You need to go inside now." Sas stopped at the bottom of the steps, having obviously taken a break just to get her to go into the cabin.

"But I haven't been out here more than fifteen minutes." Her face was cold, but it was so beautiful outside.

He pointed to the shadow the cabin roof made on the snow, his way of telling time. "You've been outside more than an hour. Your body can't handle the cold yet."

Though there was no intonation in his voice, she noticed his furrowed brow. He was worried about her. How could she argue with that? "I'd like to come back outside later."

"After our visitor leaves."

"Visitor?" She scanned the trees behind him, but didn't see or hear anything.

He strode up the steps. "Yes. I believe it's Sturge."

She stood, knowing if she didn't, he'd just pick her up and bring her inside. The man not only had incredible hearing and vision, but he was stronger than an African elephant and she'd seen first-hand what they could do.

He opened the door and followed her in. She grinned at his protectiveness. What would he do when her hands were healed, and she didn't need so much help?

Once inside, he relieved her of her mitts, dropping them on the couch before taking off the bear-fur coat he'd made her wear.

"How do you know Sturge is coming?"

He pulled the cap from her head and hung it up with the coat. "The dogs."

She could ask how he knew there were dogs, but it didn't matter. Sas was better at this wilderness thing than she was. If he said Sturge was on his way then he was. "Sturge is the man who has a wife and new baby, right?"

"Yes." Sas moved into the kitchen area and began pulling things out of cabinets.

"I wish there was something I could do to help." She felt useless without her hands.

He turned to face her, although he didn't meet her gaze. They'd have to work on that. "You can. You can talk when he gets here."

There was something in Sas' tone that told her all this company was wearing on him. "I'll be happy to do that for you. I'm pretty good at talking."

She expected to get a smile from him over that, but he simply nodded and returned to putting lunch together. She'd noticed he never smiled. That would be another thing they would need to work on.

No time like the present. She walked over to where he worked and leaned against the counter. "Can you smile?"

There was the slightest pause as he cut up the leftover meat from their dinner the night before. "No."

"No? Why not? Did you have surgery on your face that keeps you from smiling?" She wasn't being sarcastic. She'd not only seen the scar around his right eye, but discovered the scar across his forehead one night when they made love. If the lantern hadn't been in just the right position, she would have missed it.

It was possible he physically couldn't smile. Then again, he did have a beard and since it was neatly trimmed and not long, it was unlikely he had a scar beneath it as the hair wouldn't grow where a scar was. At least she didn't think so, but she never knew with him.

He finally turned and looked at her. His lips moved as he smiled wide, showing all his white teeth. He looked liked a psychotic serial killer and a shiver raced up her spine. It took all she had not to turn away, including remembering what a kind soul he was. "Oh. I think I understand why you don't smile, but we can work on that." She tried to sound upbeat, though she was still shaken by how completely different he looked.

He made a short low sound in the back of his throat before picking up the pan and putting it on the stove.

Her heart still raced and she moved away, disturbed more by his smile than she wanted to admit. So, he had a scary smile. He couldn't be perfect. She certainly wasn't.

She walked to the front window by his supplies. She'd learned to open the door with her elbow so she could play hostess, even if she couldn't cook. Keeping her gaze on the tree line, she waited. She'd just started to doubt Sas when the faint sound of a barking dog seeped through the window.

The sound didn't continue, but she'd definitely heard it. Then to the right, there was movement between the tree branches and within a few seconds she made out the dogs and a sled. "He's here."

She watched as six dogs came into view and then a man, all bundled up, at the rear. She clearly heard him yell "whoa," before the animals came to a stop in front of the porch. "What beautiful dogs!" She had her nose almost pressing against the window as Sturge pulled bowls from the basket at the back and walked to the side of the cabin. He'd obviously been there before.

Some of the huskies stood wagging their tails while a few sat, all of them watching their owner. The sound of Sas walking to the table and setting down a plate pulled her attention back to him. "Sturge is an odd sounding name. I'm guessing it has a story behind it?"

"Yes." Sas returned to the kitchen.

She smirked. "And what's the story?"

He came back with the tin cup and a mason jar. "I suggest you ask him."

Of course. She hoped Sturge was as entertaining as Timber. She turned back to the window in time to see him petting a dog here and rubbing an ear there. They all had bowls of water. It must take a lot of time to care for them all.

From studying him, she'd say he was maybe thirty-three. Definitely older than her but younger than Sas, who still hadn't revealed his age. Sturge had a full bushy beard and she could just see a little of his hair underneath the ski cap on his head. He wore sunglasses, so she couldn't see his eyes but he had a large wide nose.

Finally, he headed for the porch.

She stepped over to the latch and lifted it with her elbow before he could knock. "Hello, Sturge."

The man's light gray eyes widened as he held his hand out. "And you must be Angel."

She held both her wrapped hands up in front of her. "Sorry, I can't shake your hand, but it's nice to meet you."

He dropped his arm. "My fault. Timber told me of your frostbite. Just habit."

"Of course. Come in. Sas almost has lunch ready."

"It's ready." Sas' voice behind her made her smile.

She stepped out of Sturge's way, so he could enter then closed the door with her hip as he shrugged off his parka. Maneuvering the latch back into place took her a bit longer, but she got it done.

"Appears I came right on time, Squatch, eh?" Sturge straddled the barrel as Sas served hot fish and potatoes onto the cookie sheet he used for a second plate.

She nodded toward Sas as she took her seat in the chair. "He heard you coming."

Sturge nodded. "I'm not surprised. The man's more than half Sasquatch."

"Is that why you called him Squatch? Timber said people call him Sas."

The man shrugged. "It's a Canadian thing. We call any long-haired, wild-looking man Squatch."

She frowned. Sas had a well-trimmed beard and his hair was cut at the nape of his neck, though not exactly even. "But he doesn't fit that description at all."

"You should have seen him the first time I did when he

walked into Savik. We thought for sure we would all be rich because we'd finally had proof of a real Sasquatch."

Sas grimaced. "Sorry to have disappointed you."

As Sturge laughed, Sas filled her plate with twice as much as she could eat since they ate from the same plate now. She had insisted on him eating with her and not after her. While he put the pan in the sink, she took the opportunity to do what she did best, talk. "I hear congratulations are in order. How old is your little boy?"

Sturge grinned wider than a Cheshire cat. "Jamison is two months now. Just wish he would sleep through the night. Having partial sleep makes for a long day, especially just before winter."

Sas piled the fork full of food.

She quickly asked another question before her first bite. "How is your wife feeling? Ginny, right?" She kept her mouth open, more than willing to start eating. The fresh air had made her hungry.

"She's doing better now. She was a little spoiled by everyone waiting on her hand and foot down at the hospital, but she's readjusted to being back home now and loving that she'll have the baby to keep her busy once winter hits full force."

Angela swallowed. "I bet the snow keeps everyone house-bound this far north."

Sturge shook his head. "Not the snow. The cold." He looked at Sas who just filled her mouth with luscious tasting fish. "This is great. What is it?"

"Lake trout from Redding Lake."

"Wow, no wonder it's so good. I've had no luck catching anything over there. You'll have to tell me your secret."

Sas didn't say anything, which didn't surprise her. He simply took a bite of their food.

She took the opportunity to address Sturge. "So why does everyone call you Sturge? Timber said there's a story behind every Alaskan bush name."

The man nodded as he swallowed. "There is. You just have to figure out how to get the story out of them."

"Oh, come on. You have to tell me. Please." Sas held a forkful of food in front of her and she opened her mouth, but never took her eyes from Sturge.

He glanced at Sas, a smirk on his lips. "Should I? It would be a shame if everyone was laughing at me except her."

Sas shrugged as he took a mouthful, and she quickly swallowed her food. "Oh, I promise not to laugh."

Sturge chuckled. "Don't do that or you'll take all the fun out of it."

Now she just had to hear his story, so she patiently waited, taking the last bite of food Sas fed her and not saying a word. It wasn't easy.

Sturge finally finished his lunch and sat back. "I didn't have the name when we moved here from British Columbia, but then Ginny had to go and tell Timber and well, once Timber knows about a thing then everyone knows, eh?"

Sas nodded in agreement as he picked up the empty plates and brought them to the kitchen.

She got a little sidetracked watching him walk, remembering how he did the same thing last night only he had no shirt on. She just loved the movement of the muscles in his back.

"Ginny and I were out fishing. Out there on the Columbia River. I was having a beauty of a day, hauling in trout left and right. Then I hook one that doesn't want to come in. I'm reeling and reeling and this fish actually pulls our boat over twenty meters, anchor and all."

She grinned. She'd bet that lengths grew with every telling. "What happened? Did it get away?" She winked.

Sturge looked up at the ceiling. "If only it did." He looked at her again, obviously getting into his story. "I pulled and yanked and let the line out and pulled and yanked until I thought my arms would fall off."

"I'm glad to see they didn't." She barely kept her chuckle in.

He gave her a fake scowl. "Oh, you think it's funny that I struggled with a fish, eh? Let me tell you, you wouldn't have been able to reel this baby in."

"I bet Sas could have." She looked fondly at her mountain man, who leaned against the pole that held the table up.

Sturge rolled his eyes. "Then we'd have no story to tell. Squatch would have hauled that sucker in, cut it up and eaten it for lunch."

She chuckled. "I'm sure he would have shared. So, if you were struggling so much, did someone help you with it?"

"My wife was the only person with me and she had the net, but I had a feeling the fish wasn't going to fit in our net... and I was right in the end."

He had her full attention now. How big could a lake trout get?

"So, I'm straining, standing in our little boat, reeling that fish in inch by inch. Ginny looks over the side and tells me she can't see anything yet, but she has that net ready. So I lean back, pulling it with all my weight when suddenly the tension disappears and I find myself flipping backwards over the side of my boat and into the frigid waters of the river."

She couldn't hold in her laugh at the image in her mind of Sturge going over the side. "Sounds to me like the fish did get away."

He shook his head, a gleam in his eye. Then he leaned forward. "Nope. That damn fish jumped out of the water and right into our boat."

This time she didn't even try not to laugh. "Oh my. That must have been a huge trout. Did you have it for dinner for days?"

Sturge shook his head. "We ate it for months."

She opened her mouth and stared at him. He had to be exaggerating. "Months? What did you do, eat a forkful a day? No trout is *that* big."

Sturge's smile grew wide. "Who said it was a trout?"

"What was it?"

"It was a White Sturgeon! I've been called Sturge ever since that story got out." He laughed heartily.

He had her so enthralled with the story, she'd forgotten it was to explain his name. "I think that's an excellent tale."

Sas squeezed her shoulder, and she looked up at him. He wasn't looking at her, but just having him touch her, like he wanted Sturge to know they were together, made her feel claimed. She never thought she'd enjoy that particular feeling, but the way Sas did it was so subtle, she loved it.

Sturge looked up at Sas. "I best get headed back, eh?"

"Already?" She really did like having someone around once in a while who talked a little more.

"Yeah, I need to get back in time for dinner, and it's half

a day's sled ride. Besides, Ginny will want a full report on you." He winked as he stood.

Sas dropped his hand as she rose from the chair. "Please tell her I said hello and hope to meet her eventually."

"I'll do that." Sturge walked to the hook by the door and pulled on his parka.

Sas stepped around her. "If you need any help this winter, tell me."

"Thanks, Squatch." Sturge slapped Sas on the arm before pulling the door open. "You two stay safe."

She leaned around the corner of the door. "Bye."

Sas nudged her back inside and followed Sturge out. She started to put her hands on her hips, but stopped just in time. It was a little irritating that he didn't want her outside all bundled up for more than an hour, but he could breeze out there with no coat.

Taking a deep breath, she calmed herself. He was never cold, and it was she who had suffered hypothermia. Maybe it was like heat exhaustion, once it happened, it was more likely to occur again with less exposure. She'd have to ask.

She stepped to the window and watched as Sas gave the closest dog an unconscious pat. The dog licked his hand to get his attention. He finally gave it a scratch behind its ear before stepping away and letting Sturge get his sled turned around.

After watching Sturge disappear through the trees, Sas came back inside. He walked right to her, pulled her into his arms and kissed her breathless.

When he finished, she sucked in air. "Whoa, that made my toes tingle."

He nodded as if that was his plan. "I need to finish stacking the wood, but then I'll be back in."

In other words, then he'd be back in for some lovemaking. It was as if he couldn't get enough of her, and honestly, she was flattered, not to mention excited at the prospect. Sas was an amazing lover.

"Do you have much left to do?" Did that sound too anxious? Because she was.

"Maybe an hour."

She could wait that long. "Okay, finish up."

He gave her another kiss, but this time it was one of those gentle ones that filled her heart. He was such a huge man yet could be so tender, her eyes watered.

He strode outside and around the corner before she remembered he said it would be okay to go outside after lunch. Shoot. If she still wanted to, she'd have to get herself bundled up without hurting her hands. She'd come such a long way, she didn't want to hurt them now.

With a new goal in mind, she set about getting dressed for outside. Luckily, she still had her boots on from earlier, so she pulled the chair over to the hooks by wrapping her arm around the back. She stood on it and easily slipped one arm through a sleeve of Sas' bear-fur. He insisted she wear it because it covered her legs as well.

Now came the hard part, slipping her other arm into the other sleeve while pushing the heavy coat against the wall and up. Her first attempt didn't work, so the second time she stood on her toes as she pushed her back with the fur against the wall and up. Looking behind her, she felt a moment of triumph that the fur cleared the hook. Now, she had to pull away fast.

She jumped from the chair and the coat landed on her shoulders. The thrill at having done something for herself lasted a whole minute, until she tried to hook the fur together. Shoot. She'd just have to hold it closed with her arms.

Looking up at the next hook, she eyed the wool cap Sas had given her to wear. Since it was big enough for him, it wasn't tight. She should be able to use her wrists to get it on, but the hook was again a problem.

Getting back on the chair, it took her three attempts to maneuver the hat onto her head and off the hook, but she did it. Now there was only one other very important piece of clothing to put on—the mitts. They lay on the couch where Sas had left them.

Sas' fur coat was heavy, but it was also thick, so when she knelt on the floor next to the couch, the wood floor didn't hurt her knees. Carefully, she moved the first mitt with her arm to turn the opening toward her. As she pushed her bandaged hand against the opening, it slid across the couch.

Shoot. If it was this hard just getting dressed to go outside, how would she function in Fairbanks?

With Sas.

She could call him, but she wanted to do this on her own. The coat and hat quickly made her hot and irritable. Taking a deep breath, she tried to find her patience. Moving the first mitt with her arm again, she turned it so the end was against the back of the couch. "Okay, let's do this."

She pushed her hand into the opening and the mitt slipped into place. "Yes!" Quickly, she moved the other mitt into position and pushed it on. Thrilled with the achievement, she stood, almost falling over as the weight of the bear-fur shifted. Her heart raced with her exertion. She didn't care. She'd done it.

Walking to the door, she lifted the latch with her elbow and stepped outside into the shade of the porch. Pulling the door closed behind her was a bit trickier, but she finally did it.

Since the cabin was in the shadows which were cooler, she strode down the steps and out into the sunshine. Though she held the coat closed, the cold air creeped in as she walked. She stopped and turned her face toward the sun. Despite the low temperature, the sun still felt good.

She definitely liked the outdoors in Alaska. The air smelled so fresh and the colors were particularly bright, probably because of the reflection of the snow. She'd have to buy some warm clothes in Fairbanks so she could be outside more often.

The sound of Sas stacking the wood carried over to her on the thin air. She took a few steps to peek around the corner. His movements were fluid like he'd made them a thousand times before. The number of large logs he carried at one time had her widening her eyes. She knew he was strong, but wow.

Not wanting to interrupt because that would just slow him down, she turned and walked past the other side of the cabin, curious about why Sas didn't add a window there. At first, she was perplexed until she walked along the side of it and it dawned on her.

The corner where the bed was located was completely in the cave. The rest of the wall was bookshelves so he had no room for a window. After living with him for a month, she'd also learned that the wall was on the northside of the cabin. It was probably colder.

She turned her back to the cabin and looked up at the mountains. It would be an amazing view from a window, but as she'd learned, survival was more important than beauty.

Besides, when they could take a few steps outside and see the snow-covered mountains set against the clear blue sky any time they wanted, there was really nothing to compare.

She wandered toward the tree-filled slope opposite the cabin where the land seemed to go on forever. The pine and spruce tops gave a dark green ambiance to the whole area. She was careful to keep the cabin in view, not in a hurry to repeat her last adventure with sound in the mountains.

On the ground, she discovered Sturge's sled tracks, still fresh in a few inches of soft snow, leading the way to his home. She turned around to look at the cabin. It was a welcoming sight, probably more so for Timber who walked everywhere.

A noise behind her caught her attention. Excitement rose as the possibility of seeing a deer or even a moose filled her. She turned slowly and froze.

A large brown grizzly bear looked at her and opened its mouth.

Fear kept her still. Her heart stopped as she stared at the bear's teeth before he closed his mouth and shook his head.

Adrenaline filled her and she ran for the cabin.

The bear huffed behind her and as she broke from the trees she looked over her shoulder, only to trip and fall to the ground. The pain in her hands took her breath away as the bear stopped in front of her and rose to its hind legs.

She screamed.

The animal growled and started to come down on her, the head larger than her oven back home. Suddenly, it was pushed over and rolling on the ground.

Flashes of blue amid the brown fur clenched her heart.

Sas! She pulled herself up as she watched the cloud of snow made by the bear and the man she loved.

He saved her life! Again!

She couldn't let him die. Running to the cabin, she jammed the latch up with her arm and stepped inside. To the side of the window was his rifle. She yanked the mitts off with her teeth and clenched her jaw as she pulled the rifle down.

On a shelf built into the wall were the cartridges. She quickly loaded the gun, fighting the pain in her hands as the snarling outside told her Sas still fought the grizzly.

Running back outside, she stood on the porch and looked through the site. Vomit rode up into her throat as she witnessed the bear's claws sink into Sas' stomach. No!

She'd never shot a rifle, only a hand gun and that was at a range with a stationary target and without her hands throbbing. The last thing she wanted was to shoot Sas.

Frustrated as the two stood facing each other, Sas holding his middle, the grizzly on his hind legs roaring, she tried to aim. Sas looked wild himself, his shirt, in tatters, hung on his torso, but his eyes bored into the bear.

The grizzly launched, grabbing Sas' shoulder in its mouth. The sound of cracking bone filled the air before Sas' shout of pain jolted her into action.

Giving up on aiming, she fired the gun into the air. When the grizzly refused to let go, she shot on the ground toward it, still afraid a ricochet would catch Sas. She'd read a grizzly's jaws could break a bowling ball.

The shot to the ground got the bear's attention. The grizzly let go and looked at her. She aimed for its chest, but its roar at her made her shake and she missed, the shot going wild. The bear dropped to its front paws and loped off into the trees.

She fired off another shot in the air to make sure it continued on its way then dropped the rifle and ran to Sas. "Oh, my God! Sas?"

He lay on his back, one hand on his stomach, the other on his shoulder and his eyes closed.

"Sas?" Tears rolled down her cheeks, her heart breaking. She couldn't let him die. "Please Sas, be alive. I'll take care of you."

He opened his eyes and looked at her, the irises as black as his pupils even in the bright sunlight. No one had black eyes. She pulled her gaze from his.

Was he really alive or did his eyelids open because of some weird physical phenomenon, like her undressing when she was freezing to death? Her heart filled with anguish, too afraid to hope.

"I will live." His deep raspy voice pulled her attention back to his face. She smiled in relief.

He may think he'd live, but not without some good medical care. "I'll take care of you. I'll get you help."

He lifted his hand from his stomach to touch her face.

She pulled away, recoiling from the blood on his hand, except when she looked there was none, only bear fur. Confused, she looked down at his bare stomach, expecting to see his gaping wound, but instead there were only five red marks from the bear's claws as if it had just grazed him.

She pulled back farther. She'd seen the claws go into his flesh through the gun sight.

He took his hand from his shoulder and braced it behind

him as he sat up. "Don't worry. I'll be fine." He reached for her arm, but she scooted back, out of his reach. His shoulder had teeth holes in it, but even as she stared, the skin closed, leaving no more than red marks.

"What are you?"

CHAPTER FOURTEEN

Angel's whispered words froze him, but it was the look in her wide, frightened eyes that sliced through his heart. She knew. She'd seen what he'd successfully hidden for the past nine years.

Still, he grasped at the happiness he'd experienced. "I love you."

She shook her head as she jumped to her feet. "No. You aren't human." She backed up farther as he rose to his feet. "You really are a Sasquatch."

He wanted to laugh at the absurdity, but the sound of Sturge's dogs intruded.

"Sas! Angel! Are you all right?" The huskies barreled through the trees followed by the basket with Sturge, who pulled it to a stop. He looked at Angel. "I heard a scream and immediately turned around." He turned to look at him. "Holy shit, Squatch! Did you tangle with a bear?"

Angel's hysterical laughter at Sturge's comment sent pain spasming through his chest. "Yeah, he did. And he won. Can you believe it?"

Sturge frowned at her. "There were shots."

She nodded, still with a strange smile on her face. "I fired at the bear, in the air, on the ground to get him away." She laughed again. "Silly me. I thought Sas would be killed."

Sturge looked at him in confusion.

He rose to his feet. "She's shaken."

"Shaken? Oh, I'm more than that. I'm furious. I thought you…we even…oh, my, God."

He took a step toward her.

"No! You stay away from me." She turned to Sturge. "Take me to Savik. I'll pay you whatever you want. Get you whatever you want."

Sturge's eyes rounded as he turned toward him.

In that moment, with her anger and disgust over all they'd shared spewing over him, he recognized the familiar burn of loathing deep inside his soul. He couldn't speak. Angel's horror too painful to allow words. He nodded to Sturge.

Angel hadn't waited for his approval. She ran into the cabin and came out with her own coat in her arms. She handed it to Sturge to help her don it.

He wanted to step forward and push Sturge out of the way. That was *his* responsibility. He used his willpower to stay where he was.

Sturge instructed Angel on where to stand then he came back to him. "Are you okay?"

The man looked him over as if he could see the wounds that plagued him. They were far too deep to be observed or healed, but he felt them like a knife slicing through flesh. He nodded again, his gaze on Angel.

She kept her gaze averted. She could have been his repentance, his peace, but he'd overreached what fate had offered. He'd been greedy. Now would come his true punishment.

Sturge stepped behind Angel and grasped the handles of the sled. He looked at him one more time.

He couldn't bear to see her taken away. He turned his back and walked toward the cabin.

"Mush!" One dog barked in reply and then the sound of the skates gliding over the snow filled the quiet mountainside.

He forced himself up the steps, the swishing of the sled already fading as it whisked through the trees, taking his heart with it.

As Sturge pulled the sled to a stop, Angela stared at the small outpost in shock, surprised by its condition. There were no more than six buildings, two of which looked in danger of falling down. The others were a mix of metal, wood and logs. The day was cloudy, making the settlement appear even more gloomy, which fit her just fine.

Sturge and Ginny had tried to make her comfortable on their couch overnight, but she'd tossed and turned, to the detriment of her hands. Her mind was restless, replaying the moments from the time she'd stumbled upon the bear to the moment when she'd discovered there was something otherworldly about Sas.

She should have known the perfect man couldn't be a man. She shivered. She'd never believed in aliens or mutants or Sasquatch. Whatever Sas was, it wasn't human and that freaked her out. That she had sex with him made her want to vomit.

But as soon as that feeling passed, her heart hurt. She'd loved him. Whatever he was, she'd fallen for him harder than any man she'd ever been with. His betrayal hurt far more because of that.

"Let's get you inside Grubber's. You aren't dressed for our weather." Sturge held his arm out toward what looked like a domed metal garage of some sort.

She nodded and started up the narrow path made by previous footsteps. Shoveling was probably a hopeless endeavor up here. Sturge opened the side door for her and she walked in.

Her first impression was it was warm and it was neat. Shelves upon shelves of food and supplies were set up in rows, stretching from where she stood to the other side of the structure.

To the left, the building went on forever and she could see a table and an empty chair near the end.

"This way." Sturge lead her down one of the aisles toward the table.

Everything was neat, but definitely not organized. There were canned vegetables piled next to hammers next to soap next to motor oil. It was a hodgepodge of merchandise, most of it dented or scraped in some way.

As they emerged from the aisle, the space opened up with tables, chairs, and a whole array of furniture, like a furniture store, including beds as well as snowplow blades and a couple of appliances.

"Angie!"

At the sound of her nickname she turned. "Mikey?" Her heart melted as her brother strode toward her.

Her eyes filled with tears, and she ran into his hug.

He held her tight as she sobbed against him, her scare and heartbreak too new to hold in.

"Shh, you're okay now. I'm here." Her brother's voice reminded her of normalcy, and she cried harder.

Would she ever know what normal was again?

When she'd finally spent all her tears, she wiped her nose with the sleeve of her parka and sniffed. "What are you doing here?"

"When you didn't return any of my calls on your trip, I started to worry. After the first three weeks, I finally decided to call the tour office. They looked you up and said you had disembarked in Alaska but didn't return. They weren't particularly worried until they had the staff look in your room and they discovered you hadn't taken anything with you."

"I hadn't planned to stay here."

"I didn't think so. I figured you more for a long North Pole visit, or at the least, Greenland."

She gave her brother a weak smile. "You know me well." Or at least the Angie she used to be. Right now, she wasn't sure about anything.

"Come, let me introduce you to a few people." Her brother turned her toward the Savik inhabitants gathered around a table.

As he made the introductions, she nodded and tried to smile, but she wasn't making a good impression, especially by keeping her arms crossed to avoid shaking hands. Besides, she was having a hard time concentrating.

Her brother turned her toward a man about her height with a receding hairline, lively hazel eyes and a substantial tummy. "And this is Grubber, the owner of this place, and my host for the last few days."

At that name, she found her focus. "It's nice to meet you.

You're the one with a radio." *And the one who had the blue flannel shirt Timber procured for Sas. The one in tatters though his skin wasn't.*

Grubber nodded. "I am." He held out his hand, ignoring her closed arms.

She gave him an apologetic smile. "I'm sorry. I can't shake your hand. I suffered severe frostbite."

As soon as she said the words, the entire atmosphere changed. Lenny, a tall, thin man who was responsible for the electricity in the outpost, immediately stood and gave her his seat. MJ, short for Mary Jo, a woman her own age with pitch black curly hair and a weathered looking face insisted she needed a coffee, while her husband, Four-Point, a stocky man with a long beard and hair to match, grabbed a blanket from one of the couches and put it on her lap.

Her brother took MJ's vacated chair. "I've never met such nice people. They'll do anything for you. When the pilot comes back in a couple of days, we'll get you to the closest hospital to have you checked out. In the meantime, you'll be in good hands."

I was in good hands. The thought came unbidden, and she pushed it away. "It's so good to see you."

Her brother smiled. His light brown hair had grown a bit longer since she'd seen him a few months ago, and he had a bit of scruff on his chin, but other than that he was the same. "You're going to have to tell me all about your adventure, but let's wait until we're alone."

"I have a feeling they're all wondering, too. I might as well entertain everyone. It's what's expected up here."

"Here you go." MJ put a cup of steaming coffee down in front of her.

At the aroma, she started to salivate. "Hmm, that smells really good."

MJ smiled. "I had a feeling you'd appreciate that. Sas doesn't drink coffee and Sturge said he was headed here to pick some up for Ginny, so I figured you haven't had any in a while."

She swallowed the lump in her throat at the mention of Sas then looked at her brother. "Could you hold it for me?"

His eyes widened as he realized the extent of her handicap. "Of course." He picked up the cup and brought it to her mouth.

The first sip burned her tongue as he wasn't sure how far to tip it, but she didn't say anything about that. "Hmmm, that's wonderful."

MJ waved her hand. "It's just generic coffee. We can't be too picky up here."

Lenny pulled over two more chairs from another table, and Grubber grabbed a third to rest his foot on.

An older Inuit woman, Frankie, sat directly across from her. She looked as strong as Grubber and she raised her eyebrow. "So, ya gonna tell us how ya got frostbite?"

"Of course." She smiled. Timber's and Sturge's storytelling had set the bar pretty high, so she had to make this one sound dramatic. She winked at her brother. "How about another sip of coffee before I start."

His face tensed slightly, a telltale sign he was concerned, but he lifted the cup and she took another sip. The coffee was hot but not burning.

She made eye contact with each person at the table like Timber would do and started her tale.

She covered everything, exaggerating a little from her surprise at being confused by the direction of the sound in the mountains, to waking up and not being able to see, to meeting Timber. She left out all the personal moments and her relationship with Sas.

MJ patted her arm. "Sounds like you were well taken care of. Why did you come into Savik?"

She glanced at Sturge, hoping he wouldn't say anything. She didn't know what Sas was, but it wasn't her place to expose him after all he had done for her. "Sas told me that the last flight before winter would be soon and that I need to have a doctor look over my hands."

She swallowed hard before turning to her brother. "He told me I wouldn't lose my hands, but parts might need to be removed."

"Don't worry. We'll get you the best doctor there is in Fairbanks." Her brother's support was reassuring, but his worry was written all over his forehead.

Sturge stood. "I best be leaving, eh? I've got to be getting home to Ginny and Jamison. You take care of yourself Angel."

She rose and gave him a hug. "Thank you for bringing me in. Tell Ginny I said thank you for the hospitality last night."

"I will. Any message for Squatch?"

Shoot, she didn't know what to say. "Yes, tell him to take care of himself and thank him again for all he did for me."

Her brother stood up next to her. "And tell him for me that we will find a way to repay him."

Sturge waved him off. "That's not how we do things here. We just look out for each other. No payment required."

Frankie slapped the table. "Not in paper dollars, but anything useful is certainly welcome."

Sturge said his goodbyes and left. That seemed to be the signal for everyone to tend to their daily labors and soon she and Michael were left alone. They strolled toward a corner of the building near the bed he'd been sleeping in.

He stopped and faced her. "You made your adventure sound fun and exciting, but you came in here and broke in to tears. What didn't you tell everyone?"

She should have known this was coming. "I didn't fully appreciate my experience until just now when I retold it. I was very lucky."

Michael shook his head. "That's not all it was."

"No, you're right, but I'm not ready to talk about it now." *I'm not sure I ever will be.*

Her brother nodded. "Okay, but once we're in Fairbanks, I'd like to know everything."

She didn't respond, unwilling to make a promise she couldn't keep. "If you don't mind, I'd like to rest for a while. Sturge's couch wasn't very comfortable."

Michael knew her well enough to recognize that she was avoiding the subject, but he also understood. "Grubber said I can have any bed, you just have to make it up. He keeps the spare sheets and blankets in his only armoire over there. You have to wonder how that huge piece of furniture got up here."

She grinned. "You know if you ask, there's bound to be a story."

"I'm sure you're right." He chuckled. "I guess I'll leave you to pick a bed. I can go down to Lenny's and see what he's working on. That man is a genius." He started to walk away.

"Uh, Mikey?"

He stopped. "Yeah."

She raised her wrapped hands. "Can you make my bed for me?"

His brows lowered in concern before he nodded.

As he made his way to the armoire, she chose a bed not far from her brother, but not right next to it. If she had another bad night, she didn't want to bother him. And something told her, it would be another bad night.

He watched from a stand of pine trees at the end of the outpost, his gaze on Grubber's place. Sturge would have brought Angel there.

He'd tried to stay in his cabin, but the need to be sure she was safe and cared for had been too strong. After stopping outside Sturge's last night and hearing the man tell his wife Angel was in Savik with her brother, he'd continued on.

Looking at the light shadows on the snow, he estimated the time to be close to nine in the morning, but the dark twilight wouldn't give way to daylight until almost noon.

Would she come out? Go to MJ's or Frankie's? He didn't want her to. The cold was too much. The temperatures hadn't risen to zero yet and with the day only a little over four hours long, if it reached five degrees, it would be a surprise.

Despite his wish that she not exit the building, he still scanned the area. If she *did* go outside, he didn't want to miss her. To see her one more time even if she didn't see him, to hear her speak again, was a craving inside he couldn't deny.

Through the long night, he had paced with his anguish,

his chest in so much pain he hoped it would end his existence, but he was doomed to suffer forever. He replayed the bear attack in his mind, trying to figure out what he could have done differently, but there was nothing.

At Angel's scream, he'd run, not caring what had caused it, only determined to protect her. He didn't even think as he rounded the corner and the grizzly stood before her. His burst of rage that the bear dared to threaten her filled him just like it had when Victor destroyed his female.

There had been no thought, only emotion and instinct—instinct to protect his new mate. That feeling remained.

He wanted to explain what happened, but every word combination fell flat in the view of her horrified expression when she realized his immortality. Once again, he wanted to shake his fist at fate, but it was a worthless gesture. His existence was one of punishment and pain.

He'd thought that before, but now he knew true torture.

The door to Grubber's opened and Grubber himself strode across the main road to Lenny's home on the other side. No one else had entered Grubber's since night gave way to dark twilight, which meant Angel was inside…with her brother.

Even though he shouldn't, he ran behind Four-Point's home, keeping to the darkest shadows. If he could hide closer to where she was, he'd be able to hear her, if not see her. He waited, every sense sharpened by the adrenaline rushing through him and the pounding need in his heart to hear Angel.

All was silent. He ran behind Frankie's home and crouched low. The woman's hearing wasn't perfect, but her eyes were sharp enough to hit a ten-point buck from two-hundred yards.

He could hear Grubber and Lenny talking in Lenny's

house, but he couldn't make out their words. His heart raced as he sprinted behind Grubber's building and inched his way along the back toward the corner where Grubber kept his beds.

Pressing his ear to the spot where the metal walls met, he listened.

At first all he heard were footsteps. Then a man's voice broke the silence. "Do you want to buy anything from Grubber to take with you?"

He held his breath, his entire focus on who would answer.

"No. MJ said the plane is small. You flew in it. Is there much room?"

He closed his eyes as Angel's voice came through clearly. It was like a soft snowfall on a crystal-clear ice ledge.

"Charlie has some storage space in the wings, but it's not much."

"I'll wait until I'm in Fairbanks. I won't even know what I'll need until after we consult with a doctor." Footsteps drew closer, far lighter than any man's.

He took a deep breath, wanting more than ever to smell the mint scent that mixed with her skin perfectly, but the metal wall kept that from happening.

"Angie, I think you should prepare for the worst. This is backwoods country. It's doubtful the care you received will save your hands."

"You're wrong." Her quick, adamant answer pleased him. "Sas gave me the best care. The fact that I'm walking proves it because I had frostbitten feet, too. And don't forget I'm alive despite hypothermia with no hospital in sight."

His heart warmed, hearing her defense of him. Did that mean she still cared?

"I know you have total confidence in this man, this Sasquatch, but you need to face the facts. You may have Stockholm syndrome and are seeing your experience through brainwashing on his part."

"Michael Jeremy Ellis. I do not have Stockholm Syndrome. I wasn't kidnapped and held prisoner."

"That's not what I meant. I mean the one where the patient falls for the doctor."

"I'm not having this conversation with you. Find another subject or I'm taking a walk."

He opened his eyes. Angel's tone of voice told him her brother had come too close to the truth. Was that what she felt for him, a false hero-worship? The term was erotomania. Their encounters had definitely been erotic.

Maybe she *hadn't* loved him. His chest pain started again. It was one thing to lose the woman he loved, but to discover she never truly loved him was another pain all together.

"Angie, I'm sorry. I didn't realize." Her brother's voice had softened. "You love him."

"I did. Past tense. It's a moot point anyway. After Fairbanks, I'm going home."

Her admission sent a shot of joy through him only to be crushed by her next words. She didn't want to see him again. She would leave and all he would have is the memory of her.

It wasn't enough! He wanted *her*. He wanted her love. He'd felt the happiness that could be. Why had fate been so cruel? How much more was he supposed to accept? He'd spent three hundred years atoning for his crimes. When was it enough?

Now. The whisper from his heart filled him. He was done being controlled by his past actions. He would walk inside and make her listen to him. Make her see they were meant to be together.

Make her see that he wasn't a monster.

Images of his past rose up before him. He was a monster and no matter how many lives he saved, he'd still be a monster. A monster who never died.

He fell to his knees as his eyes filled and he hung his head, defeated.

Michael's voice broke into his misery. "Have you thought about what you want to do to thank him and these people? If I know you, it will be something special."

"I have." Angel's voice sounded relieved to talk about something else. "I'm not sure how to make it happen though before spring, and I really don't want to wait that long. I'll figure it out."

Her brother chuckled. "You always do."

"You know, Mikey. You're much more fun when not connected to the outside world. Maybe you need to take more vacations in secluded places."

He could see her smile in his mind, a knowing gleam in her bright green eyes.

"Oh, no. Don't start on me. I'm not the adventurer you are. You had me worried sick. No, thank you. Flying up here to the middle of nowhere is enough for me."

Angel's laugh flew through the walls and filled his heart.

He leaned against the cold metal wall. If all he could have was her voice now, he would capture every nuance for his memories. He remained there listening the rest of the day and into the night, even after she'd gone to bed.

Hearing her talk with her brother and the other Savik

inhabitants reminded him of his first year of life, listening to Felix and Agatha and their family and friends, learning how to speak his first language and read his first words. Had his existence come full circle? Was there anything left to do?

He stood and placed his hand against the building, the frigid cold barely making an impression. Leaning his forehead against the metal, he whispered. "Goodbye, my Angel." Taking a deep breath, blinking at the tears that threatened, he turned away.

As he ran through the trees for his cabin, the sky lit with the green of Angel's eyes. In the darkness, he howled his anguish to the Northern Lights, but his soul knew no one cared.

~~*~~

The sound of a plane flying overhead woke him.

Angel!

Jumping to his feet from the couch, where he'd collapsed in the early morning hours, he ran to the door and threw it open. The plane flew westward toward Savik, toward Angel.

She would leave him forever today. She would step into that plane and leave his life. His entire body tensed at the knowledge.

He'd left Savik so he wouldn't be tempted to say goodbye to her. If he saw her, he'd never let her go, holding on to her despite her hate and horror. What he had to hold on to was the memory of her smiles, her body and her beautiful heart.

He would never make it to Savik in time to watch her leave, but he *had* to see her. Closing the door behind him, he didn't go west but turned northward as the reality of her leaving sank deep into his heart, stealing his breath.

Trying to escape the pain in his chest, he ran up his mountain. His anguish grew heavier even as the air became lighter. The snow was deep, but he pushed on, the need to see her one last time too strong to resist.

Crawling up a steep incline, he grasped at evergreen branches, pulling himself higher even when his feet slipped out from beneath him. Breaking through the tree line, the peak came into view.

His heart beat hard within his chest as if it wanted to escape his patchworked body and fly away with his Angel. The irony of her escape by plane wasn't lost, and he barked out a disgusted laugh even as he crawled on all fours toward the summit.

Finally, he reached the ledge just below it and stood upright, his breath releasing small clouds that looked like smoke signals though he was sure there were no words or symbols in any language that could describe the torment inside him.

His eyes stung as the wind buffeted him, but he didn't care. Just one last glimpse. He needed one more look at her face without the horror in her eyes. He took deep breaths, as much to slow his racing heart as to swallow the bile in his throat.

The sound of the airplane had him snapping his head westward. She would be flying by soon. He turned toward the final incline and scrambled up as fast as he could. When he reached the peak, he searched the horizon.

In the distance, he spotted the four-seater Cessna still ascending to flying altitude. Soon it would fly past him. She had to be on the northside of the aircraft. Seeing her face in the window would make it better. He had to believe that because to live the rest of eternity with such sharp pain would be pure agony. Far worse than anything he'd experienced in his entire existence.

He kept his gaze on the plane as it crept closer toward his mountain. It felt as if it flew slower than a salmon swimming upstream. He studied the windows, anxious for the sight of blonde hair and the face that had shown him what love was.

As it came closer and closer, he stared, on an emotional ledge that loomed before him, threatening to push him into an abyss he could never climb out of. The window came into clear focus. He watched, barely blinking.

She was there! His heart stumbled inside his chest at the view of her profile. *Angel. Salvation. Love.*

Suddenly, she snapped her face toward the window and one bandaged hand came up on the glass. She stared right at him.

Reaching up his arms, his soul screamed with pain at her forever-departure, destroying what was left of his heart.

Falling to his knees, he cried out one last time.

A-N-G-E-L!

As they took off from Savik, Angela ignored her brother's attempts to engage her in conversation. She didn't want to think. She didn't doubt what she'd seen during the bear attack, but her heart still hurt at leaving Sas. Everything was confused from her thoughts to her emotions. She didn't understand what had happened and pinned her hope for clarity on reaching home and returning to a normal life.

She had no idea what normal was anymore. Was there such a thing?

"What the hell?" The pilot's voice penetrated her thoughts. "There's a man on top of that mountain. He doesn't even have a coat on. I better call this in. He's got to have hypothermia."

She snapped her head around to look outside. Even before she found the lone figure, she knew who it was. Her gut tied itself into a tight ball as she stared at Sas. Pressing her bandaged hand against the glass, she watched as he sank to his knees.

Tears tracked down her cheeks as her heart went out to him. She followed him, looking back, unwilling to lose sight of him, even as the plane banked south and wiped him from her view.

"This is Charlie. We need a rescue. I've got a man on top of Najak mountain. He's suffering from extreme hypothermia. I don't know how long he has. Copy?"

She spoke into her head set. "Call off the rescue. He's just hot from climbing the mountain."

"You know him?" Her brother looked at her.

She nodded. "Yes. That's Sas. He does that a lot."

"How can you be sure that's Sas?" Charlie's doubt was obvious.

"Because he makes his home on that mountain." And he saved my life. Images of Sas feeding her, bathing her, making love to her, flitted across her mind.

"Rescue here. Where did you say the victim is?"

The pilot turned his head, moving the mouth piece away from his face. "Are you absolutely sure? Because if you're not, you just sentenced Sas to die."

But Sas couldn't die because he wasn't hu—"I'm absolutely sure."

As the pilot called off the rescue, she closed her eyes and rested her head back against the seat. She didn't want to think anymore. She just wanted to forget.

Thankfully, her brother didn't try to talk to her all the way to Tavva. After they boarded another plane, they flew to Coldfoot. Each landing and take-off took her farther from Sas and closer to her life, but her heart was still up north. By the time they landed in Fairbanks, she was exhausted.

Michael got them to a hotel and immediately pulled out his phone. He was still on it as he let her into her room. After dropping her room key on the nightstand, he walked out.

She needed to call work herself, but she just didn't care. Maybe after a nap, she'd feel better, back to her old self. She managed to take off the ski hat she'd bought at Grubber's, but the zipper on her coat was another matter.

She looked around the room for something she could use. What she wouldn't give for Sas' page-turner stick. Sas would have made sure she was comfortable before leaving her. It was just the way he was wired.

But what was he made of? His guts pierced, his shoulder bitten but no blood anywhere and his skin sealed up. What was that? She shivered. Had she been sleeping with an alien? Or had she completely lost her mind?

Frustrated, she took the edge of her sleeve in her mouth and pulled, maneuvering her arm out. Once she had both arms free, she lay on the bed and scooted out of the coat. Pushing the coat off the bed, she lay on the bedspread and tried to go to sleep.

A half-hour later there was a knock at her door. "Come in."

A key slid in the lock and the door opened. Michael strode in. "You're being admitted to the hospital tomorrow morning. I've made all the arrangements."

He was so proud of himself, so she didn't argue. "That was fast."

He sat on the corner of the bed. "Your condition is serious. They want to see you right away." Michael looked away, a sure sign he was hiding something.

She licked her lips. "What aren't you telling me?"

He stood again, walking to the window and opening the drapes. "You may have to stay there for a while."

"I knew that."

He turned and smiled. "Good, I wasn't sure you realized that. Now, what would you like for dinner? I bet you're just dying for something other than game meat."

The way Sas had cooked, she'd loved all the wild meat she had. Why did he eat if he didn't have to? Or did he?

"Angie?"

"What? Oh, dinner. I'd love some salmon."

Michael looked at her oddly than shrugged. "Okay. I thought you'd be craving a pizza or something, but we can do salmon. I'll call room service."

As her brother made the call, her thoughts swirled with questions. Would the doctors be able to save her hands like Sas had promised or would she lose them? Would she ever travel again after her fiasco or would she play it safe? Would she ever see Sas again?

CHAPTER FIFTEEN

Two weeks later.

Angela turned off the television in the private hospital room. Everything on there seemed so trivial. She would be leaving the hospital soon. Her brother would be relieved to get back to his job, but she didn't care about hers.

Her boss had been understanding, but anxious for her to work from home. She'd had to explain exactly how handicapped she was.

At least Sas had been right. The doctors had been impressed with the care she'd had in the bush and were able to save most of her hands. She would have all functionality back eventually after a lot of physical therapy. They would just look hideous unless she decided on plastic surgery, which could improve them, but not make them look completely normal again.

She didn't even care. She was alive and that was what mattered. If Sas hadn't found her, she wouldn't be worrying about her hands at all because she'd be dead.

And that's what bothered her. She'd never given him a chance to explain. She'd been so shocked, she just wanted to get away from him as quickly as possible. When she asked Michael if he could get a message to Sas, he'd declined.

That's when she realized there was another reason for her being in the hospital so long. Her brother had arranged for her to be watched in the psych ward. Luckily, she'd learned from her favorite nurse, Nancy, that she could check herself out since she'd been a voluntary check-in, but it had strained her relationship with her brother. His over-protectiveness went too far sometimes.

There was a knock at her door and then an older gentleman peeked his head in. "Excuse me, Miss. I have the library cart with me. Would you like to read a book?"

She hadn't read anything since leaving Sas and the idea appealed to her. "I think I might. Do you have any good ones?"

The white-haired stocky gentleman wheeled the cart in. "That depends on what you like. I have a lot of recent releases and a few classics. What's your preference?"

She'd never been in to old books, but Sas had given her a new appreciation for them. "Definitely a classic. I haven't read many of those. What would you recommend?"

The man bent to the lower shelf and pulled out three books. "I have *The Three Musketeers*, *Frankenstein*, and the *Complete Comedies of Shakespeare*."

"Ick, I'm definitely not a Shakespeare kind of girl." She gave him a small smile.

He nodded and put the rather large book back.

The Three Musketeers she and Sas had already read and from the looks of the book, so had many other people. "I'll try *Frankenstein*. It's not scary, is it?"

The older man chuckled. "I don't know. I've never read it. Just seen the movies."

She nodded as he lay the book on her lap. Her physical therapist wanted her to use her hands now that the surgery was over, so this would be a good exercise. Hopefully, the story would be exciting enough that she would want to use her hands to turn the pages.

"Enjoy your book." The man wheeled the cart to her door.

"Thank you."

After he was gone, she started reading. From what she'd seen in the movies, the monster came to life with electricity, had electrodes in his neck and walked around with his hands out in front of him.

It confused her to read the letter at the start of the story written by a man who was attempting to cross the Arctic Ocean, but when Victor Frankenstein appeared on an ice float, her interest was piqued.

Hours later, she placed a paper napkin in the book to hold her place and set it on her tray. She sniffed and wiped her eyes with her sleeve. She wanted to read more, but it was two in the morning and her eyes were tired.

She lowered the back of the bed. The story was far different from what she'd expected. Dr. Frankenstein described his creature as "beautiful" and bigger and better than man. Her heart went out to it when it awoke and Victor ran away. She shuddered when it killed Victor's brother and let the servant girl hang for the crime.

But when the monster told his own story to Victor, she sympathized with him all the more, especially when he begged for a mate. She loved the idea that he would have someone to spend his life with that was just like him.

When Victor literally tore apart the female mate in front

of his creature before bringing her to life, she broke down in tears, angry with the scientist and hurting for his invention. She wanted to find out what happened, but she'd have to wait until the morning.

Closing her eyes, she drifted off.

He crouched in the shallows of Redding Lake, his need for sustenance his only thought. Watching the chub swim near him, he grasped one in his hand and threw it to shore.

More darted by and he watched, waiting for the right time to strike. When another swam too close, he struck, grabbing it up and throwing it to the bank to join the others.

"Hey Sas!"

He whipped his head around at the interruption and growled, baring his teeth.

"Whoa there, it's just me, Timber. I'm not another grizzly you need to tangle with."

He ignored the man and went back to watching fish. He was hungry. He must eat.

"Listen, you've got a couple dozen of these beauties lying all over here. What do you say we gather them up, take them to my place and fry them for dinner?"

Yes, dinner. He stood and walked back to shore.

"Uh, Sas, where's your coat, shirt and, um, shoes? Aren't you cold?"

He started to gather up the fish, but he hadn't brought a bag.

"Here, use my bucket." Timber held it up. "I was going to do some fishing, but you did enough for both of us."

He took the bucket and threw the fish in. When he had them all, he looked at Timber. "Dinner."

"Right. This way."

He followed Timber to his cabin. It was small and smelled like wood smoke, not mint. He liked that. He brought the pail to Timber's counter and set it there.

Timber moved past him and grabbed a towel from a hook. "Here. Take off your pants and dry off. I'll hang your pants here to dry.

While Timber prepared some of the fish, he did as requested, not willing to think beyond immediate needs. Eating, sleeping, breathing, and staying cool were his main focus now. He didn't want interaction with anyone. He didn't want to think.

Timber threw some of the fish in the pan and the scent filled the cabin.

He walked to the table and sat, the towel around his waist.

"Here. You need this." Timber set down a steaming mug.

He lifted the cup and drank the warm tea. It was good.

Within minutes, Timber placed the food before him and he started to eat. The strong meat of the chub tasted of the wild. Timber piled more fish on his plate, so he continued to eat until he was full.

Timber was just sitting down to dig in, but he was done. Standing, he looked around the familiar space and found the couch. "I'm going to sleep."

"You do that, big guy."

Lying down, he closed his eyes. This was a safe place away from her. It was good. He welcomed sleep, the first he'd had in days.

~~*~~

Angela couldn't stop reading *Frankenstein*, her heart in her throat as the creature killed Frankenstein's best friend and wife. Despite the sun streaming in her hospital window, she shivered at the heinous acts.

Then she wanted to yell at Victor as he chased the creature through country after country until he finally died on the ship trying to find a path across the Arctic Ocean. Her eyes watered as the creature came onto the ship and felt the loss of his creator, admitting to the captain he'd gone down a bad path.

His final words had her crying again. "I shall quit your vessel on the ice-raft which brought me hither, and shall seek the most northern extremity of the globe; I shall collect my funeral pile, and consume to ashes this miserable frame, that its remains may afford no light to any curious and unhallowed wretch, who would create such another as I have been. I shall die. I shall no longer feel the agonies which now consume me, or be the prey of feelings unsatisfied, yet unquenched."

At the end of the story, the creature jumped off the ship and disappeared into the darkness of the arctic.

She let the book lie open on her lap. She'd hoped to be entertained, but instead she was sad, as if she had been a part of the story. She was just too emotional since leaving Sas, her own feelings tangling up in the tale.

Sas was no Victor Frankenstein. He was more like the creature than…she felt the blood drain from her face.

No.

Shelley's story was fictional. Sas was a real man, or rather something other than man.

Her mind conjured up the image of Sas standing naked at the end of the bed. He never *did* tell her where his scars came from, choosing to decline to answer. He looked like he'd been sewn together. He also said he'd been abandoned from his first breath, not from the day he was "born" as most people would state it.

She shook her head. It couldn't be.

She ran over everything she could remember about him, all of it fitting with the story from the country he came from to the others he'd lived in. They were all there in the story.

It just wasn't possible. Life wasn't a story, it was reality. The backwoods stories of Timber and Sturge came to mind.

Those were nothing more than dramatic interpretations of real life, not complete fiction. Not the story of an immortal, of which there was no such thing. Sas would have to be, what? Two hundred years old? Three?

She stiffened. Images of the bear attack and the skin healing before her eyes pushed their way forward. Quickly, she flipped back to the title page, causing the napkin she'd stuffed into the book to fall out. She picked it up, suddenly remembering the scrap of yellowed paper that fell from Sas' *Three Musketeers* book. It had the initials VF.

Victor Frankenstein.

"Oh, my God." She stared unseeing at the title page. Because he was born of the dead, was he immortal? Had the creature tried to kill himself only to discover he couldn't die? She focused on the date beneath Mary Shelley's name. 1818. Quickly, she flipped the pages to the first entry, the letter from the sea captain to his sister. It was dated 17__.

Had Mary Shelley actually written the "true" account as

the sea captain told it to her, thinking it was no more than an exaggerated story like the rest found in the cold wilderness? But what if it *was* true?

The ramifications of that thought stunned her. Sympathy flooded her and her heart ached as she meshed the creature from the story with Sas. Despite all he'd done, or maybe because of it, he'd saved her life, taken care of her…loved her.

She licked her lips. She had to see him. She had to find out the truth. No more declining to answer. And what if what she suspected was true? She shook her head. That wasn't important now. Right now, she needed to get out of the hospital and find transportation to Savik, preferably without her brother's knowledge.

For some reason, Michael had concerns about Sas' "influence" over her. She couldn't blame him. The first thing she'd done was cry all over his shoulder when they found each other. And she'd refused to talk anymore about her relationship with Sas once she'd discovered Michael had every intention of never letting Sas see her even if he showed up at the hospital.

She was thankful she hadn't divulged to anyone why she'd run away from the man who not only loved her but had saved her life…twice. Of course, she'd been in shock, trying to process what she'd seen.

She stared at the book in her lap as tears formed in her eyes. Maybe she could buy it from the hospital. It meant so much to her right now…if she was right. She had to confront Sas with it.

Wiping her eyes with the back of her wrist to avoid the stitches on her hand, she sniffed. Crying wouldn't help anything. She looked for the nurse call button then checked the clock. She grinned, Nancy would be her perfect partner in crime for getting away. Pressing the button, she waited.

~~*~~

Sas woke up to find the cabin empty. It wasn't his cabin. It was Timber's. Slowly, the memories of the day before came back to him. Or was it two days before? He felt groggy as if he'd been drugged.

He shrugged. It didn't matter. Nothing mattered. He had to keep his mind blank and focus on his bodily needs and right now, he had to urinate. He stood and swayed. The drugs Timber had given him must have been strong. He'd have to see if the old man had more, but first he had to go outside.

Walking across the floor in his bare feet, he noticed the texture of a new rug Timber had added to his home. His little cabin felt comfortable, safe.

Sas opened the door and walked out into the bright sunlight. He glanced down at the shadows. Late afternoon. No wonder he had to urinate. He walked over to a grove of trees behind Timber's house and relieved himself.

What happened to his shirt? Did he leave it back at his cabin? He shrugged. He was supposed to hide his scars, but he didn't care anymore. Wandering back into the cabin, he closed the door before heading for Timber's larder. Maybe there was more fish left from yesterday.

Opening the cold box, he took out a pile of wrapped food and set it on the table against the wall that Timber used as a counter. Lined up at the back of it was a row of bottles. Sas grabbed one and opened it. Ugh, it smelled of alcohol and cinnamon.

He looked at the label. It was whiskey. Timber said everyone drank it. He lifted the bottle to his lips and took a large swallow. Coughing, he set the bottle down. Why did people drink that?

He unwrapped the food as a warmth spread throughout his body. It felt good. He hadn't felt heat in a long time except with—he grabbed the bottle again and gulped down more of the burning liquid. *Don't think.*

Again, the heat warmed him from the inside out. Leaving the food on the table, he held onto the bottle, walked back to the couch and sat.

He took another swallow of the whiskey and focused on it flowing down his throat and into his gut before the warmth spread from there to the ends of his fingers and toes. He grinned. This was good. Tipping the bottle back again, he gulped.

The bottle was almost gone when the door opened and Timber walked in. "Hey Sas, good news, you're never—well, son of a biscuit eater, what have you gotten into?"

He held up the bottle. "Whithkey."

Timber rolled his eyes. "Boy, you just filled your gut with that on top of a bunch of drugs. You're going to be sicker than a seal in an oil spill."

He shook his head. He never got sick. He couldn't die. He had to stay alive and live his torture. Didn't Timber know that? He opened his mouth to tell him, but the man swiped the bottle out of his hand.

He scowled. "I need to finish that."

"No, you don't." Timber walked to his porcelain sink and emptied the bottle.

That was stupid. What a waste.

Timber picked up the food from the counter and dumped it into a skillet. "It's freezing in here. Why didn't you add wood to the fire?"

He leaned back, feeling lethargic. "I'm warm."

The old man shook his head as he crouched to stuff his stove with wood. "No doubt. That whiskey will burn a hole right through your stomach."

An image of the grizzly puncturing his stomach rose to fill his mind, and he pushed it away quickly before anything else followed. "Feels good."

Timber rose. "I bet it does." He placed the skillet on the stove along with a pot of water.

He let his head loll to the side so he could watch a chickadee on a branch outside. The bird's quick movements were far more interesting than Timber cooking. He let his eyes close, happy to drift off into oblivion.

"Sas. Sas! Wake up. You need to drink this."

He opened his eyes to find Timber's hand on his shoulder and a cup of steaming liquid in front of his face. "What?"

"Drink this."

Seeing no reason not to, he took the mug and sipped the chamomile tea. The scent of venison filled the cabin, and his senses came more alert. "Food?"

Timber, back at the stove, scraped the skillet. "Yeah, food, so that whiskey doesn't make you sick. You need to sober up, my friend." He brought a plate of hot venison and vegetables to him. "Here. Eat."

He set the mug on the end table next to the couch and took the plate. He picked up a hot carrot and stuck it in his mouth, sweet honey sauce flowed over his tongue.

"Uh, Sas? Use these so you don't get my furniture sticky."

He looked up to find Timber holding a knife and fork. He took them and set the plate on his lap as he cut into the venison steak. Everything had honey sauce on it.

When he finished, he set the plate on the end table and drank the tea.

"How do you feel?" Timber's voice from across the room, reminded him he wasn't alone anymore.

He preferred to be alone. He nodded.

"Good." Timber strode forward and pulled a chair from his table over and straddled it. "It's time for you to talk."

He looked away. Talking was useless.

"Sas, I have some very good news for you, but a lot of people went out of their way to help you, and we deserve some answers."

He snapped his head back to stare at Timber, hoping his gaze would stop him from continuing.

"Don't give me that scary stare of yours. I've known you too long. You wouldn't hurt a hair on my head."

He wanted to deny it, warn him of what he could do, but even as he opened his mouth, he knew in his gut he'd never hurt the older man.

"Now that I have your attention. I want to know why you have scars all over your body and how come you can walk around half naked in below zero temperatures and why you can wrestle with a grizzly and take a bullet to your chest and not have a scratch on you?" Timber raised one eyebrow. "Well?"

He looked away. It didn't matter anyway. He couldn't stay in Alaska any longer. It was time to move on, away from his memories. "I'm immortal."

Timber slapped his leg. "I knew it!"

He snapped his gaze back to find Timber smiling like a jackpot winner.

"Oh, don't worry." Timber waved his hand. "We'll keep your secret. It's not every day we have an honest to goodness Sasquatch living among us."

His brain focused on Timber's first word. "We?"

"Just me and Sturge. And Ginny. But we won't tell anyone else." Timber chuckled. "Actually, I'm honored to call you a friend."

He lowered his brows in confusion.

"If you'll live forever, how come you have so many scars? You look like you were torn apart and put back together? Were you abducted by aliens or something?"

He shook his head, still off balance from Timber's reaction. "You don't think I'm a monster?"

"Hell, no. Why would I think that?"

Angel does. The thought came unbidden to his mind and a wave of misery hit him so hard he closed his eyes, gritting his teeth against the howl that threatened.

Timber laid hand on his shoulder. "Listen, Sas, I know you've had a rough past. I don't need to know it all to see it in you. I know you're hurting since Angel left. That's why I went to Sturge to ask for help for you."

"Help?" There was no help for him. His existence stretched before him, miserable and tormented unless he could revert back to how he'd been his first few days of life. Primal.

"Yes. I was worried about you. You were going wild on me, and I didn't want to lose you, so I contacted Sturge and he made a run to Savik to make a radio call."

He still didn't understand what this had to do with helping him. If they wanted him to talk to a psychologist, they didn't know him at all.

Timber sighed. "Sas, Sturge went to call Angel."

Angel? "No."

"Yes, but guess what? He didn't have to. She had called Grubber and told him the first window in the weather and she would be flying in to Savik, with or without Charlie."

His heart skipped a beat. "Why?"

"She said she wants to talk to you. No surprise there considering how that woman likes to talk."

He frowned at Timber. "You talk more than she does."

Timber chuckled. "Well, there is that. I think maybe she wants to come live here."

His heart leapt, but he squashed it. "Did she say that?"

Timber looked down at his thumb, suddenly finding his fingernail very interesting. "No, but why else would she want to talk to you?"

He stared at the older man, anger simmering inside him. "To ask me questions like why I didn't die from a bear attack? To determine if I'm really the monster she thought I was? Just tell her I am and save her a trip." His heart twisted in pain. If she came, it would destroy him. But wasn't that what he wanted?

Timber picked at his nail, clearly uncomfortable. "I told her you would meet her in Savik."

Rage poured through him. This man, who claimed to be a friend, wanted him to lay his heart bare again? "No." He barely kept from shouting. Instead, he stood and strode toward the door.

Timber jumped up and followed him. "Listen, I'm only trying to help. Maybe if you could talk to her, she'd want to stay. You two are meant for each other."

He snarled at Timber and yanked the door open. "I'm meant for no one." He ran out of the cabin and through the trees, heading north toward his mountain.

Anger boiled inside him. He'd finally blocked all feeling, reverting to existing only, and now the woman he'd loved—he did love—would return to torture him anew. He couldn't see her. He needed to leave Alaska. Now.

When he reached his cabin, he stepped inside and the scent of mint filled his nostrils. It was like the claws of the grizzly tearing through his gut all over again. He slammed the door behind him and stared at his bed, a bed he hadn't slept in since Angel left. He would burn the place to the ground. It was the only way to escape her.

Moving to the stove, he stirred the ashes until the banked coals beneath glowed red. Throwing in pieces of kindling, he waited for them to catch before pulling one out. He walked to the bed and held the fire over it.

Memories filled his head of them making love, her body against his as she slept, her mouth opening as he fed her, her green eyes lighting with pleasure as he answered one of her innumerable questions.

She's coming back.

He would be gone.

And miss the chance to see her again?

The fire on the wood licked at his fingers as it burned down.

He couldn't do it. He couldn't kill the memories of the

happiest time of his life. They were all he had. He dropped the wood on top of the stove where it burnt out.

Moving back to the bed, he lay down, the scent of her enveloping him, making him remember everything. His memories were vivid, filling his heart and torturing his soul.

He would rest then pack a backpack of supplies and books. It was better to leave than let hope ignite again.

~~*~~

Angela zipped up her jeans and after three tries, she finally got them buttoned, too. Her hands were still sore and they looked awful, but that she could use them somewhat was exciting. Seeing Sas again was exciting, too.

Charlie had called her yesterday, finally agreeing to fly her in. He had been a little put out that she was willing to use another pilot. Who knew bush pilots were territorial? Or maybe it was just him. The people in Savik really liked him and that had to feel good.

A knock on her door had her looking up. "Nancy."

The woman's dark eyes twinkled. "So today's the day. About time."

She laughed, her spirits lighter than they had been since the grizzly attack. "Yes, it is."

"I'm so excited for you, going back to the man that took such great care of you."

She grinned. "If he'll have me and if he answers my questions." She turned away and added the last of her clothes to a small bag. Her brother had bought her a few more items after her surgery.

"Angela, did your brother tell you the results of *all* your tests and which ones we couldn't do?"

She turned. "What do you mean, couldn't do? He told me that all my tests came back good except for those that were taken just before the surgery. Was there something else?"

Nancy frowned. "How about something you might want to discuss with the man who took care of you?"

"Sas? Why would I need to talk to him about—oh. Do I have an STD? We didn't exactly have protection. Should he get tested?"

"Uh, no." Nancy patted the bed. "Sit down."

Oh, God, it was bad. She sat on the bed, a new fear growing in the back of her mind. "What is it? What didn't my brother want me to know? He's too protective. Tell me."

"Oh honey, it's not bad. It's just that you're pregnant."

"Pregnant? But how…"

At Nancy's knowing look, she blushed, memories of her and Sas making love flooding her mind. It made so much sense. "Wow."

Nancy lifted her eyebrows. "Wow? That's it?"

"It's such a shock. I didn't expect it. I probably should have, but I didn't think the timing was right and I had my pills up until, I mean, I almost died and…wow." She placed a stitched hand on her abdomen. The fact was, she'd lost track of time and now she was pregnant. She was going to be a mother!

"Are you going to tell him?" Nancy's smile had faded.

"I have to, but I don't want him to want me just because of a baby. Shoot, a baby? I never even thought about whether I wanted children."

Nancy's smile returned. "That's not something you have to think about now. It's a done deal."

It was. She would be a mommy. "I don't know how to be a mother. Mine died when I was six."

"All you have to do is love that little one with all your heart. The rest you figure out as you go."

She gave the nurse a half-hearted smile. "Thank you for telling me."

"I just wanted to make sure you were aware. That was the test I was worried Michael hadn't told you about. Your brother reminds me a lot of mine. He's very protective."

At the mention of Michael, she squinted her eyes. "I can't believe he didn't tell me!"

"Now there was a lot going on with you between the surgery and your emotional state. Trust me, what your brother did is nothing compared to mine."

Her curiosity piqued, she had to ask. "What did he do?"

Nancy chuckled as she pushed the monitor back towards the wall and rolled the tray away from the bed. "Let's just say that the last guy who broke up with me got a knock on his door and a gun in his face."

"Oh, my God. He didn't shoot him, did he?"

"No, more's the pity." Nancy laughed. "But he did scare the bejesus out of the asshole."

Angela felt her heart calm down. "Thank you for putting things into perspective for me."

"My pleasure. I'm going to miss you. I don't often get patients in this wing who aren't addicted to one thing or another. If you're ever in Fairbanks again, look me up and we can go shopping. Trust me, if you decide to live up past Savik, you'll be dying to go shopping."

Angela hopped off the bed and gave Nancy a hug. "Thank you for everything."

"You're welcome." Nancy wiped at her eyes, which were suspiciously watery.

Angela turned away, not wanting to cry, too. She picked up the letter she'd written for her brother. Yes, she was a coward to sneak away without telling him, but it was what she had to do, and he'd ask far too many questions, or worse, insist on going with her. "Could you give this to my brother when he comes in?"

"I'll be happy to." Nancy glanced at the clock. "He won't be here for another four hours. Will that give you enough time?"

She grinned. "Yes, I'll be halfway to Coldfoot by then."

"Good. Now get the rest of your stuff packed. The wheelchair will be here any moment."

"I had hand surgery. I don't need a wheelchair."

Nancy headed for the door. "Hospital policy." She opened it then turned and winked. "Nothing but the red-carpet treatment for my friends."

As the door closed, Angela grabbed up a tissue and wiped her own eyes. Hopefully, she'd be able to take Nancy up on her shopping offer. Of course, that depended on whether she ended up living in Alaska or back in San Francisco.

She licked her lips. Would Sas even be willing to see her after the way she'd left? Her heart tightened for the eightieth time in the last two days. Now that she knew his history, she viewed her last moment with him from his point of view, and it was heart-wrenching.

Then there was that sliver of doubt that she was completely wrong and he wasn't the creature Victor Frankenstein had created. Those doubts weren't strong though because of his scars.

There were only two other explanations she could think of for those. The first was that as a child he'd been purposefully scarred to look like Frankenstein's creature, but that didn't explain how his body healed instantly. The other explanation was that he was an alien and that was as hard to swallow as Sas being three hundred years-old. The only way she could discover the truth was to make him talk.

She straightened her shoulders. Getting Charlie to fly into Savik near the end of November was a cake walk compared to getting Sas to talk, but she had to…for their baby's sake.

Placing her hand on her abdomen, she took a deep breath. She could do this.

CHAPTER SIXTEEN

S as closed the door on his cabin for the last time. Someone else would come across it and move in or it would be a good shelter for a traveler. He hadn't realized how peaceful his life had been.

On one hand, he wished he'd never found Angel, but as soon as the thought crossed his mind, he tossed it away. Wherever she was, he wanted her to be happy. He'd saved her as fate decreed. It was time to move to a new place. He hadn't been to Russia yet.

He strode up the incline from his ledge and crossed over to the adjacent mountain, where he'd found Angel. When he reached the spot, he stopped. The vision of her as she'd lain there rose to meet him. Relief that he'd seen the reflection off her phone that day surged through him.

As much as he'd hoped for something else, her leaving was for the best. How could they have a life together with him hiding the atrocities he committed which she would never be able to forgive? Even worse would be explaining why he didn't grow old with her then watching her die in his arms after years of having her in his life.

He had to focus on that. If it hurt this much to have had her in his life for a month, what would it feel like to lose her after decades of happiness? The same reasons for not growing close to her in the first place were still in play. If he hadn't been so weak, he wouldn't hurt so much now.

But she loved you in return. She wanted your body in return.

He shoved the thoughts away. She didn't really know him. He'd never told her everything. And when she discovered his immortality, she did what any other human would do. She ran. He should have expected no less, but he'd been blind, weak, greedy.

Forcing himself to turn away from the spot that had changed his life, he continued up the mountain. He'd head north and take the arctic ice over to Russia, find an isolated spot and continue to exist. He was resigned to his fate. He had nothing left to fight it. Three hundred years had worn him down.

He focused on putting one foot in front of the other, the early afternoon sun and unusually warm weather making the climb uncomfortable. Stopping, he shrugged off his wool shirt and packed it up, then continued north.

Twice he discovered his steps headed west instead of north. He needed to keep what little shadow he had to his right and not leave it behind him. It was as if he was being drawn toward Savik.

Luckily, the sky was clear, though clouds were gathering in the west at a slow pace, not unusual for an evening dusting, though with the warmer temperatures, he wouldn't be surprised if he saw rain. Determinedly, he adjusted his course for a third time and trudged on.

The sound of a plane in the distance halted him. It couldn't be? Charlie didn't fly after the first week of November.

He turned toward the sound and scanned the sky to the east, blocking the sun with his hand. His heart raced as he searched the blue expanse. To the east, it was as clear as a shallow stream, but a tiny flash brought his eyes to a dot.

Without blinking, he kept his gaze on that spot until a white shape became visible. It could be any plane, bush pilots were a common sight in the Alaskan skies, but his gut said it was *her*.

When Timber said she would be back as soon as she could, he hadn't believed it, especially not now.

What did it matter? They were still far too different. How could she want to be with a monster? Why would she want to grow old while he stayed young? Had she even thought about that?

She must have. She knows and still she returns. The voice of his younger, more impulsive self, caught him off guard.

That was true. She knew exactly what he was, or close to it. She was aware of his body's ability to keep death away, if not always pain, and still she came.

She wants you.

He shook his head. She still didn't know everything and as Timber had warned him, secrets between them would ruin anything they had.

Then tell her.

Talk to her? See her again? He couldn't do it. Yet even as he made up his mind to turn away, his feet headed west, toward Savik, and Angel. Unable to resist the pull on his soul, he led his shadow down the mountain.

He checked the sky as he walked, the outline of the plane becoming clearer. Yet even as he moved westward, it would take him until dusk to arrive in Savik. Charlie would need to leave before then. He could be too late.

After checking the position of the sun and that his shadow was now behind him, he took off at a run.

"Angel. I can't wait any longer. There's a storm coming in. You need to make a decision." Charlie emerged from one of Grubber's aisles, having just come in from outside.

"But I thought you didn't have to leave until just before dusk." That Sas was nowhere in Savik worried her. Was he that angry with her? She hated the thought that she'd hurt him.

Charlie glanced at the ceiling as if looking for patience. "I need to fly while there's still light. With a storm coming in, I lose the light, so I have to leave in a few minutes. You'll have to make a decision."

She looked at MJ who sat next to her at the table. "What did Surge say exactly?"

The woman set down her cup. "He said that Timber promised to give Sas the message." MJ patted her arm. "Don't worry, if Sas is still here, Timber would have found him. According to Sturge, Timber was worried about him. He was acting more like an animal than a man. He's probably just not here yet. If he waited until he heard Charlie's plane, he won't be here until tomorrow without a dogsled."

Her heart skipped. "What do you mean *if* Sas is still here? Is there a chance he left?"

MJ looked away. "I heard that Sas wouldn't go back to his cabin."

"Why?"

MJ shrugged. "I don't know, but Timber had him at his home, last I knew."

Shoot, now what was she supposed to do? If she left, she might miss him and if she stayed and he didn't come, she wouldn't get out until spring.

As if the woman had read her thoughts, she smiled. "You can always stay here in Savik. Between all of us, we can put you up for the winter, I'm sure. That is, if Sas doesn't come to his senses."

Angela licked her lips. This isn't exactly how she'd expected this to go, but she should have. She was well aware that travel and messages took longer this far out in the wilderness.

Would she run back to civilization or have her last grand adventure? If it was just herself she had to be concerned about, she wouldn't think twice, but now she had a baby to think of.

And that baby's father was somewhere out here. "Charlie, I'm going to stay."

"You are?" His raised brows almost made her laugh, but it was no laughing matter.

She'd never been through winter this far north and this remote. But if Ginny could do it, so could she. Besides, the baby wasn't due for another eight months. "What's the earliest in the spring that you can get back here?"

He shrugged. "It all depends on the weather. May for sure."

Her baby wasn't due until July. She'd have no pre-natal appointments except with Frankie, but then again neither did Ginny. She'd follow whatever Ginny had done. "Then I'm staying."

Charlie's eyes widened. "Wow, you must really love him."

She did, if Sas was who she thought he was. And if he wasn't? She'd enjoy her adventure with the people of Savik. Her letter for her brother had detailed instructions for her apartment and her job, in addition to her explanation of why she'd left. Still, she wouldn't be surprised if he flew into Tavva and hired a sled dog team to bring him to Savik in the middle of winter.

Shoot, look at her. She really was going to stay. She would lay her heart on the line for Sas and hope he accepted it. Rising from the table, she turned to the pilot. "I'll walk you out, Charlie."

Hearing something in the distance over the sound of his footsteps, he came to a stop.

The plane!

The sound came at the ground level which meant it hadn't taken off yet. Angel!

He sprinted toward Savik, ignoring the snap of branches against his body and the conviction that he wouldn't get there in time.

The plane engines grew louder as he dodged trees to get to the outpost. He *had* to make it. He had to see her.

Suddenly, the engines revved and he could envision the plane racing down the runway west of the buildings. No! He pumped his legs harder, his lungs sucking air as he sped toward Savik.

He burst through the trees in time to see the plane lift off, the now misting rain making visibility minimal.

"Noooo!" He stood in the middle of the end of the outpost, unwilling to believe he'd missed her.

"Sas?"

He moved his gaze toward the sound of her voice. Was it in his head?

No. There she stood in the growing darkness, just outside Grubber's in her parka, her hands in new mittens and a tentative smile on her face.

"Angel?"

"Yes." Her smile widened.

He stalked toward her, all thoughts gone with the need to hold her in his arms and kiss her.

"I'm so relieved you came. I need to talk—"

He swept her into his arms and inhaled the minty scent of her before taking her mouth with his, coaxing her open and tasting her like a man starved. His body came alive as she melted into him, tangling her tongue with his. *Yes. Mine.*

The rumble of thunder in the distance brought him to his senses. He broke the kiss and stepped away from her, shaken by his loss of control. Nothing had changed.

Or had it?

She stood still, her rapid breaths creating tiny clouds of moisture in the damp air.

"Why did you come back?" The question tore from him unbidden, his voice scratchy from disuse.

"I had to. I know who you are. I know about Victor."

His blood chilled, freezing him to the spot despite the light rain now falling. How? Yet even as he asked the question, he knew. The book Mary had written after finding Captain Walton's letters in her ancestor's belongings. "You read the book."

"Yes." Her voice was soft.

Was she afraid? "I would never harm you."

She nodded solemnly. "I know that. You were so young with no parent to guide you. I understand what you did."

He shook his head. How could she? Even he didn't. "William, Clerval, Elizabeth. They were all innocent."

"I know. But in a way, so were you."

He snorted. "So innocent I framed Justine for a murder I committed? So innocent I led my father on a chase over the world until he dropped dead?"

"He wasn't your father." Angel's angry tone caught his attention. "He was your creator, your betrayer, and your executioner, if he'd had his way."

He shook his head. "I should have let him catch me. Only he knew how to end my miserable existence."

She stepped up to him, blinking away the rain from her eyelashes as she looked up at him, into his eyes. "No. If that had happened, I would have never met you."

At her observation, his anger cooled. To have never known her would have been to have died without living. Thunder rumbled closer, and he looked to the sky. The storm was upon them. "You need to go inside."

Her eyes widened. "Why? Where will you go?"

"Away."

She put her hands on her waist, wincing as she did so, and he ached for her pain. "Sas, I did not come all this way to hide from a storm while the man I love leaves me. No, I'm here because I want a future with you."

Stunned by her admission, he ignored the flash of lightning nearby. "My future is forever. How can we have a future? I cannot bear to have decades of happiness with you and then watch you die. Would you torture me more?"

"I don't want to torture you. I just want to be happy."

He shook his head, holding one hand out against the happiness she offered as he backed away. "No."

"Please, Sas." She took a step closer. "There's more at stake than just us."

He backed up again, confused and desperate. "What do you mean?"

Her hand moved to rest on her abdomen as she smiled through the downpour. "We're going to have a baby."

He stared. It wasn't possible! How could it be? Joy like he'd never experienced, never even imagined, pulsed through him just as a light flashed and pain swamped his body. His ears were deafened by the sound of a crackle and his nostrils filled with the smell of burning flesh.

"Sas!" Angel's scream penetrated his senses as he fell to the ground.

His body hurt, but he couldn't seem to move. He wanted to get to Angel but it felt as if he was being stabbed by the sharpest knife, deeper and deeper. Darkness encroached on his vision, but Angel's screaming made him force it back. He had to get to her.

He felt his head being lifted, the rain stinging his face as the pain in his body changed to a hard throbbing. "Sas, speak to me. Please be alive."

He stared at Angel, her eyes filled with water beyond the rain. He tried to work his jaw, but it was stuck. Forcing hair through his throat, he grunted.

"Oh, God. Don't do that to me ever again. I don't care how immortal you are. Being struck by lightning can't be fun, and it scared the daylights out of me."

The throbbing was slowly fading and his jaw finally moved. "Pain."

Her brow furrowed and her gaze swept him. "Shoot, Sas. You're bleeding. All the scars on your chest are bleeding, on your arms, everywhere."

Bleeding? "Can't bleed." No matter what he did, he never bled, unless…was that why he'd always feared lightning?

She shook her head. "You are now."

Excitement filled his soul. Had he lost his immortality? "Show me."

She lifted his hand up so he could see it. Blood dripped from beneath his leather band and at the crease in his arm where another scar was.

His stitches. They bled. Euphoria filled him despite the pain and numbness.

"What happened?" Four-Point stood over them, his wife right next to him.

Angel put his hand down. "He was struck by lightning. Help me get him inside."

He hadn't even heard their footsteps in the slushy snow. His extra-sensitive hearing was gone. If he'd had any doubt, it was washed away in that single moment.

He wasn't a monster anymore.

He was a man.

Angela lay next to Sas, still unsure about what had happened, but happy just to have him with her. He rested peacefully on one of Grubber's extra beds after getting quite a bit of first aid.

If the residents of Savik were surprised by Sas' many

bleeding sites, they didn't show it. It had been a group effort, not only to get him inside when he couldn't seem to move, but also to bandage up what looked like fresh stitches all over his body.

He hadn't moved much except his eyes and his mouth for a few words, though that was less of a surprise. She feared he'd been paralyzed by the lightning strike. Between that and the bleeding when he never bled, she was afraid. What if he had to live through eternity unable to move? Who would care for him when she was gone? Their child?

Tears started down her face. If she hadn't come back when she did, he wouldn't have been struck by lightning, his biggest fear.

His fingers on her chin lifted her face up as he lowered his lips to hers. That comfort helped her stop crying. The kiss was gentle, letting her know how much he loved her, and she gave him the same in return.

Shoot. She pulled her face away and looked at him. "You can move!"

He nodded. "It would appear so, though not without some pain. I think in time I will have all movement back. Is what you said true? Are you with child?"

She beamed. "I am. It's still very early. I only discovered it because the hospital did some tests. I really don't want to raise a child by myself."

"I would never allow that. I want to care for my child like I thought I should have been cared for." He paused, obviously still surprised by the news. "I didn't think it would be possible."

"Why not? We certainly worked at it quite a bit." She winked.

His eyebrows drew together in confusion. "I thought I needed another like me to produce offspring." He moved his gaze back to her. "It never occurred to me that I could beget a child on a human."

"Now that we know, I'll need to look into birth control or I'll end up with a child a year." She shuddered. She was ecstatic that she would have a child with Sas, but the living would be hard. "Of course, this does mean we'll need to add on to the cabin."

"I can do that."

She smiled, relieved and happy all at once. "I was so afraid you'd be paralyzed for eternity."

He shook his head. "I no longer have eternity. All I have is what I can have with you."

She frowned. "Why? Because of the lightning strike? I did notice your eyes are whiter around your irises and they don't look black anymore, more like a warm brown. Is that why you didn't like lightning? You were afraid you'd become mortal?" Did she inadvertently cut his life short by returning?

He chuckled, a sound she'd never heard before. She stared in shock.

"No, if I'd known that lightning would take away my immortality, I would have stood out in a storm hundreds of years ago. I'm glad I didn't know because then I would have died without ever meeting you."

"So, you're sure you aren't immortal anymore?"

He nodded. "I'm sure."

She grinned. "Then you need to officially adopt Sas as your name. That is the name these wonderful people gave you, and I love it because it's so different."

"Sas." He said it as if testing it for the first time. Had he really never contemplated it as his name?

"Angel and Sas. Yes, I like it." He nodded as if he'd just made his name official.

"So that means you have no more excuses not to marry me, right?"

He started to smile, but quickly frowned. "I have no surname to give you."

"I don't need a new last name. I'm not sure how much you've kept up with the times, but many women keep their own last names when tying the knot."

"But you would take mine if I had one." His frown made her swallow her chuckle at his high handedness.

How frustrating to want her to take his last name but not have one to give her. She'd say it served him right, but he'd paid far too long for his crimes and mistakes.

This was a new start. He was a man now. "I actually think you do have a name. Dr. Frankenstein *did* give you life, which by default means you carry his name. Wouldn't he just hate that?" She smirked, unable to help feeling a little vindictive toward the long-passed doctor. In her opinion, he was an ass.

"You would take the name Frankenstein?"

Hmm, now that was a good question. There was nothing wrong with Ellis, but for her to keep her own name would hurt Sas' feelings. There was no other name that she could associate with him, so she was stuck. Besides, in the Alaskan wilderness, no one bothered much with last names.

"Hmmm, Angela Frankenstein. That is a mouthful."

Sas' eyes grew wide. "Angela? What is that?"

"That's my real name. Didn't you know that? Isn't that why you gave me the bush name of Angel?"

He shook his head. "I didn't know." He stared at her for a moment before he glanced at the ceiling. "Fate."

She frowned. "If you didn't know my real name then why did you call me Angel, and don't you dare say you decline to answer."

His gaze filled with love. "When I first found you, you literally looked like a fallen angel. Then I discovered you were still alive and believed you could be my redemption if I saved your life. And you have been. You've saved my soul."

Tears filled her eyes at his profound explanation and she brushed them away, wetting the bandage on the back of her hand.

He caught it and kissed it. "You will always be my Angel, but would you take the name of Frankenstein's monster?"

"I would. I mean I will, if you're asking."

He looked at her blankly before understanding dawned. "Angel, will you be my wife?"

Her heart filled with love for the man who had saved her life and now made her happier than any woman alive. "Yes."

Sas' lips curved upward, and she held her breath, afraid of his smile, but it had changed. It lit his face and made him more handsome than he had a right to be. Shoot, the man was even hotter when he did that. Good thing they would live in the Alaskan wilderness because with that smile of his, she'd have to shoot any woman who came close to him. No one could resist that.

"I love you." His words broke his smile, but they also warmed her from the inside out.

They'd come full circle from the days of him warming her from the outside in. She was one lucky woman to have captured the heart of Frankenstein. "I love you and now I'm going to show you exactly how much." She wiggled her brows as she lifted the blanket. "After all, I heard you were a little stiff."

Sas' laugh filled her soul, giving her a pleasure far surpassing what she was about to give him. It was her turn to take care of him.

EPILOGUE

Sas set the lantern on the hook in the low ceiling and pushed aside the blanket as he walked through the doorway into the main cabin. He would build a door next, but he couldn't wait any longer to show Angel her new bathroom. He wanted the indoor bathing area as much as she did, now that he found it too cold outside for showers.

He was still adjusting to being human. Dropping the refrigerator-tub on his toe had left it blue and aching.

Thankfully, he wasn't wearing his bear-fur coat when he was struck by lightning or it would have burned up. Now it was a must-wear piece of clothing when he went outside.

He found Angel at the counter, busy stirring something in a bowl. Just having her in his cabin made it more of a home, but she'd added a few touches to it, so wherever he looked or smelled, she was there. It pleased him that she insisted on helping and wanted to learn more about survival life.

Wrapping his arms around her from behind, he kissed the top of her head. "It's ready." His hands rested on the very small bump of her belly. Every time he thought about being a father, his torture over the centuries faded more.

She immediately dropped the spoon and laid her hands on his. "I can't wait to use it. Will I still need to empty my bucket?"

He turned her around to face him. "No. I'll do that for you, at least until spring when I can dig into the ground and run a pipe to wash away the waste."

She laid her hands on his chest as she looked up at him. "That sounds great. So what was the hardest part of building my wedding gift?"

"The shower."

Her mouth opened but nothing came out.

He chuckled to have struck her speechless.

She closed her mouth and her eyes took on a dreamy quality that seemed to come over her whenever he laughed. That look always made him want to make love to her wherever they were, but he wanted her to see her new bathroom first.

Quickly, he bent and lifted her in his arms, thankful that his strength didn't disappear with his immortality. He stepped around the small addition to the counter that separated the cooking area from his equipment area and set her down in front of the blanket hanging over the doorway that led to the new room.

In the spring, he'd add another room on the north side of the cabin so they could have a bedroom, and during the winter he planned to build a loft and move all his equipment up there.

"Can I go in now?" Angel's excitement was palpable.

"Yes." He pulled the blanket aside.

She walked in. "Oh, Sas. This is perfect."

"I kept the ceiling low. Once I build a door, the smaller space will stay warmer longer."

She looked at the blanket. "You don't have to build a door."

"Yes, I do. It will make guests feel more comfortable."

"Guests?" She raised a brow at him before turning away, the bathroom taking her attention. "How do you get water in here?"

He moved next to the tub. "The cold water is from the water that flows down the mountain underneath the rock. I added three taps to access that. One for the toilet over here when I have the piping in, one for the sink and one for the shower and tub. We will get a real tub eventually, but this should do for now."

She inspected the piping and levers of the shower. "Okay, I see how we can have a cold shower, but what about a warm one?"

"That's more difficult. We still need to heat the water on the wood stove, but we pour it in this barrel up here, allow some cold to mix with it, then open the lever here. Without a generator, that's our only option right now."

She faced him. "I think it's brilliant."

He looked into her excited green eyes. She really was pleased. "I'm glad you like it. I even added a small sink over here."

She looked at the small porcelain basin with a crack along the rim. "Let me guess, you found this at the Savik dump."

He nodded. "I caulked it so it won't leak."

"I love it. I love the whole room. Thank you." She turned to him and pulled him down for a kiss.

In that moment, he knew he'd have to get a very big tub, because the refrigerator only fit one person and as her tongue slipped into his mouth, he could see them making love in it while cleaning each other.

Her hand moved to his crotch, and she began stroking his

growing cock. If he let her continue, she would burn dinner again, and he didn't want her to be that upset. Taking her hand from his hard-on, he kissed it. "I believe we need to take dinner off the stove if you want to continue what you've started."

"Oh shoot." She tore away from him and ran out of the room.

He smiled. Having her as his wife had far exceeded his expectations. Every day he learned more about her and himself.

Leaving their new bathroom, he walked into the kitchen area to find that she'd saved their dinner just in time.

"I'm so glad you reminded me. I'm trying a new recipe that Ginny gave me when we stopped there last month."

"I'm glad I am of some help." He was also getting used to her not needing him as much, at least for her basic needs. Luckily, she still needed him for her passionate ones.

She tossed down the towel she'd used to remove the pan from the stove and sauntered over to him. "I'll always need your help. We're a team now. We help each other."

"I like the sound of that."

She picked up his large hand in hers and put it against her chest. "I'm going to need a lot of help with this parenting thing. I have no idea how to be a mother."

"And I have no idea how to be a father, but we'll learn and grow."

She smiled. "I have a feeling this will be the greatest adventure of my life."

A tiny doubt he'd had since bringing her back to his cabin resurfaced. "You never did journey to the North Pole. If you like, I can bring you there when our child is older."

She looked off for a moment, obviously contemplating

his offer. He was well aware of how much she loved to travel, and it had been almost three months since she'd begun her fateful trip.

Her green gaze returned to him. "I'm not sure how much that interests me anymore. I think I'm done with adventures since none of them can turn out as wonderfully as my last one did." She winked. "I think I've seen enough of the world. You're my world now."

His heart filled with love for this woman who had saved him. He raised her hand to his lips and kissed it, the scars on his wrist, slightly more noticeable than the ones on her hand, now that he'd taken off his choker and bands.

She pulled away. "Don't. It's so ugly."

Baffled by her reaction, it took him a minute to understand what she referred to. "Do you mean your hand?"

"Both of them." She put them behind her back. "They remind me of how stupid I was."

He wanted to laugh at the irony of the situation, but he could see her scars truly upset her. Instead, he unbuttoned his new flannel shirt, a gift she'd brought him from Fairbanks.

"What are you doing? Not that I mind or anything."

He shrugged out of his shirt and dropped it on the table. "Sas? Talk to me."

He lifted her hand again and laid her palm on his chest next to his heart, just below the scar that ran above it. "Your scars are beautiful to me. They are like mine, proof that we survived."

Her gaze fell. "I only survived because of you." She tried to move her hand, but he held tight.

"Your scars are beautiful to me." He repeated his phrase,

willing her to really hear him. "They are like mine, proof that we were fated for one another. "

Her gaze lifted to meet his.

"Your scars are beautiful to me." He paused, staring into her eyes. "They are proof that you healed my scarred heart."

Her eyes filled with tears. "Oh, Sas. Your scars are beautiful to me, too. I promise to never let anyone hurt your heart again." She rose onto her toes and kissed the scar that ran horizontally across his chest above their hands.

His heart filled with happiness and he tilted her chin up, kissing her with all the love he had, his soul lifting with joy at what he'd found in her. He was open now to receiving the love she gave to him freely, not to a monster, but to a man with a future.

She broke the kiss, wrapping her arms around him and resting her cheek against his bare chest. "I love you, Sas."

He looked over her head at the book that chronicled his early life, now sitting in a place of honor on the shelf next to his old mirror. Instead of anger and guilt, he felt only peace in her arms.

He squeezed her lightly. "I love you, too, Angel."

For updates, sneak peeks, and special prizes, sign up to receive the latest news from Lexi at

http://bit.ly/LexiUpdate

Read on for a taste of Masque...

CHAPTER ONE

Cape Breton, Nova Scotia

People. Living, breathing people.

Synn MacAllistair grasped the embrasure of the parapet, his heart thudding as he stared at the vehicle crossing the stone bridge over the moat. It came to a stop at Ashton Abbey's massive gate.

He waited. The great iron grille, chained and padlocked against intruders, would be considered a significant deterrent to entering. *Open it. Damn it, open it!*

The vehicle remained stationary. No one exited the large red monstrosity.

Impatiently, he pushed away his hair as the breeze whipped it across his view. What were they waiting for? If they needed an axe to break the chain, he'd gladly provide them with one.

Another smaller vehicle rolling parallel to the west wall caught his attention. It crossed the bridge and parked behind the larger one. More people?

A man stepped from the small conveyance and shuffled to the gate. Synn leaned farther over the battlement, anxious to see if their time had come. The joyful sound of clanking chains floated up to him on the breeze.

Finally! About bloody time. He swallowed hard to keep the yell of triumph from escaping his throat. No need to scare their new guests.

The man below hurried back to his transport and, without hesitation, backed across the bridge and left faster than he'd arrived.

Synn peered down at the red vehicle, still as a brick, its black windows making it impossible to see inside. A door opened and a woman burst onto the cobblestone entrance. She bent over and spoke to someone else still inside. Her blonde hair hid her face, but her ass, covered in men's trousers, was small, her legs lanky. A woman? A woman dared enter a haunted abbey? He tried to grasp the concept.

His plan was to convince a man to enjoy the pleasures of the flesh, but there had to be a man to convince…unless a couple entered the Abbey. Couples enjoyed the Pleasure Rooms as well. If he could persuade a couple to participate in the Masque then his companions could still be freed.

Peering hard, he watched and waited. After what seemed another decade, a door on the other side of the red contraption opened. He held his breath, willing the occupant to have broad shoulders, a beard, anything to indicate a man.

A long, slender leg stretched out, a black high-heel shoe of delicate design at its end, and a feminine hand grasped the side, but remained stationary.

He growled with frustration. "Bloody hell. What am I supposed to do with two women?" He hadn't expected women. The Abbey overflowed with spirits. Only men should dare enter. How were blasted women going to help him? He paced away from the wall, but quickly returned. Could there be more people inside the vehicle?

He waited, his patience long gone, not that he ever had much, but damn, it'd been a hundred and fifty years. That would strain the patience of an archangel, something he definitely was not.

He glared as the leg moved and within a moment's breath, the woman unfolded herself from the conveyance.

Synn stared, frozen in time for once, drinking in a beauty far surpassing any painted Aphrodite he'd ever gazed upon. Her long, wavy brown hair captured the sun, shining like fine brandy. Her figure, as lush as any Greek goddess, swayed sensuously in her short dress. Her arms were bare and the smallest of noses held her dark glasses in place. He stepped back, away from the crenellation, his heart racing, his mind whirling with ideas.

He paced the length of the wall. A vision was about to enter his stone prison. A woman fit to be worshiped with every salacious touch he'd ever learned. His cock hardened beneath his pantaloons. Amazed, he stopped and looked down at it. After so many years of having no needs—for food, for sleep, for relieving himself—the last he'd expected to feel was the need for a woman. He shook his head. It defied logic. But if his body could respond, then he could participate, guide a woman through the Masque.

The creaking hinges of the gate brought him back to the wall to see the backs of the two women entering the Abbey courtyard. Two women. Vivid memories of his happier days with the prince caught him by surprise and gave him hope. As he strode across the wall-walk and down the stone staircase, his mind raced with possibilities. One after another they were discarded as he floated to the landing on the second floor. But a new plan began to form as the great pine doors opened.

~~*~~

If she hadn't been in heels, Rena Mills would have jumped over the threshold as she and Valerie pushed open the twelve-foot doors of Ashton Abbey. Their creaking sound didn't bother her. In fact, she'd be sure those hinges never saw oil for the rest of their days. They made a perfect first impression for a haunted bed-and-breakfast.

Valerie shook her head. "You love that noise, don't you?"

Rena grinned sheepishly as she stepped into the two-story stone entry the size of her parents' house and spread her arms wide. "It's perfect. I can't believe it. I'm actually going to make this happen. Can't you see it, Valerie?"

Her friend raised her eyebrow. "If you say so."

"I do." She examined the stone floor beneath her feet before touching a wall. The hard rock under her fingers was cool and rough. Her stomach somersaulted as success filled her veins. She could do this. Ashton Abbey resembled a castle and tourists would love staying here. All she needed was a little plumbing, a little electricity, a functioning kitchen, and a few ghosts. "Seriously, Val. You can see the potential, right?"

Valerie gave her a hard look. "You don't have to do this, Ree. You don't have to prove anything. That jerk is full of himself. So all your success has come while working at your family's company or at Bryce's. That's simply because you are a good event planner. Look at me. I've worked for my dad's company all my life. That doesn't mean I don't know my shit."

"It's not about Bryce. I have to prove this to myself." She wished Valerie could understand.

Her friend threw up her hands and stalked away. The

woman was too confident to have any idea how it felt to be unsure. Rena sighed. The fact was, her ex-fiancé had a point. All her jobs had been obtained through her parents or him. After two months of being out of work, this was her only option. Now she had to make her new haunted abbey into a successful bed-and-breakfast, not simply to prove she could, but because she had every last penny on the line.

As she perused the large entry with its double staircase leading to the next floor, her jubilance returned. The abandoned building was so much more than she'd expected for the price. She looked up at the semicircle windows near the ceiling, which let in sunlight, but she didn't see any spirits. "I hope the real estate agent hadn't exaggerated about the ghosts. If this place hasn't sold because it's haunted, then I better see some dead people pretty darn fast."

"Uh, Rena?"

She glanced behind her to see Valerie had stepped into the next room. Turning, she strode through the doorway to find a grand dining room with green-and-gold paisley wallpaper. She stopped and smiled. "Oh, this is too good to be true." Valerie had pulled aside one of the curtains from the fifteen-foot windows to let in the sun, and it reflected off an elegantly set table.

"Over here." Her friend stood at the head of the table, a deep frown on her face.

"What is it? Did you find something?" She started down the length of the long table set to feed twenty-four. Her stomach twitched with excitement at the sight. She stopped to look at the place setting Valerie stared at. "What am I looking for?"

Valerie shook her head. "Do you see anything unusual here?"

She peered at the setting. The silverware had an elaborate P etched into it, but other than the fact it had multiple plates as if set for a formal occasion, she saw nothing out of the ordinary. "No. Should I?"

Valerie sighed and crossed her arms over her small chest. "How long has this place been empty?"

She shrugged. "I don't know. Over a hundred years or so? From what I hear, colored lights can be seen shining from the windows at night, but there's no electricity. I guess the Abbey got lucky with ghosts and I'm going to make that work for us."

"And is there a caretaker of some sort?"

"There is one family here who has taken care of the grounds for eons. I can't remember their names, but it's an old widower and his son. Why?"

Valerie dragged her finger across the plate. "Do they take care of the inside as well?"

"No, we are the only ones to enter inside these walls in a hundred and fifty years. Isn't that amazing? Why, what are you getting at?"

Valerie lifted her finger in front of Rena's eyes. "Then why is there no dust?"

Her brain came to a halt as she grasped Valerie's point. Taking another look around the room, she saw no cobwebs, no dust, not even a chair out of place. She returned her gaze to Valerie. "Clean ghosts?"

Valerie raised her brow. "Did you read about that in your research?"

Rena picked up the plate and examined it, not comfortable

meeting her friend's eyes. "No, but I didn't exactly do research. I watched a few shows on television and discovered people will pay to go to a haunted hotel. There has to be an explanation. Maybe someone has been living here and no one realized it."

Valerie crossed the room to the windows. "You mean behind the padlocked gate?"

She joined her friend, puzzled, ready to believe in ghosts who cleaned. "What are you looking at?"

"These curtains. If they're a hundred years old, shouldn't they be dry-rotted and in shreds?"

A shiver ran across Rena's skin. "Oh, damn. This is stranger than a simple haunting." She ran her hand along the forest-green velvet of the curtain. The material, strong and thick, had a beige cotton backing. This didn't make any sense. She turned to examine the rest of the room. The chairs around the massive table also had velvet in their backs. She stepped closer to one and ran her hand over the material. The softness was irresistible…and new.

She paused. "It's as if time has no meaning inside these walls. I wonder if the place is bewitched as well as haunted!"

Valerie gave her one of her deprecating smiles. "And why is it haunted?"

She grinned. She couldn't help it. The more she saw of the Abbey, the more convinced she was that she could make it profitable. "It had something to do with the Red Death that swept through this town around 1861. I read that it could take a life within thirty minutes of exposure."

"Hmmm, that would explain a haunted town." Valerie ran her hand along the fireplace mantle. "But why is the Abbey the only place haunted? There has to be more to it than that. Maybe a monk bargained for a life and they all ended up dead?"

Even more sure now than the night she'd watched the documentary on haunted hotels, Rena headed for the door at the end of the room, the clacking of her heels echoing across the room. "I don't know, but I plan to find out. I will need a history of this place to put up on the website."

Valerie followed. "That will work. It's a good thing you're rid of Bryce. He'd find a reasonable, logical explanation for this and take all the fun out of it."

Rena stopped in her tracks, causing Valerie to bump into her. "Ugh. Thanks for ruining my mood again, Val."

"Hey, it's true. You are so lucky to be rid of him. Are you ready yet to tell me why he broke off the engagement? There's no one to overhear but the ghosts."

She faced her friend, aware that her heartache shone in her eyes, but it was too raw, too humiliating still. "I can't. Not yet. Okay?"

Valerie gave her a quick hug. "Of course. But remember, I'm your best friend and you will have to tell me eventually."

She nodded, but her excitement for the Abbey had left. "Why don't we bring our luggage in and find bedrooms? If we have to buy blow-up mattresses, I'd rather know now instead of tonight when the place is pitch black and all we have are our lanterns."

"You got it. And maybe we'll run into a ghost in the process."

Valerie's smile was contagious and Rena grinned, her upbeat spirit making a quick return. "We better, or this haunted bed-and-breakfast idea will be a complete bust."

Synn ducked around the doorway as the ladies turned toward the entry once again. He let the slender blonde pass through, but he couldn't resist touching the other one. Lightly, so as not to frighten her, he brushed his fingers across her bare shoulder.

"What?" She turned, looking about.

The scent of dusky, tart pomegranate wafted by his nose. His body responded with an overwhelming need to touch her again. He craved her smoothness like a pickpocket coveted a half-dollar. When had he last craved anything? He tamped down his own interest. It was of little importance. This woman would be their freedom.

"Rena, are you coming?"

With her smile wide and full of joy, she followed after her friend. "You are not going to believe this, but a ghost just touched me."

That she hadn't run in fear confirmed his belief she could be the answer. Rena. He liked her name.

Her hips swayed with her quick pace, her energy palpable. Would she have that kind of liveliness in bed?

As she crossed the threshold to the outside, his gut tightened in panic. She couldn't leave. Not now!

Synn ran to the open door and stopped, the memory of his last venture outside freezing his limbs in place. He couldn't leave the Abbey or he'd cease to exist. He needed to calm himself. Too much was at stake.

The women pulled belongings from their conveyance. They should have allowed the servants to do that kind of work. When they turned to enter again, he blended back into the wall, his stomach relaxing at their entrance.

The blonde dropped her bags. "Okay, I'll take the stairway to the left and you take the one on the right."

Rena glanced upward. "Great. If you see anything unusual, yell. I want to see a ghost."

"Believe me, you'll know if I see one."

As the two ascended the grand stairways, Synn followed. He glanced around, surprised Mrs. McMurray hadn't appeared yet. Not that he minded. Their two guests seemed to be open to the spirits who lived here, but he hoped they could settle in first. At least until he introduced himself, and the way he wanted to introduce himself had his cock paying attention.

Rena headed down the hallway on the second floor, opening doors and looking inside. Her mumbled words made her opinions of each room clear. Everything from "hideous" to "extraordinary" passed by her lips. Lips, full and red, with no rouge, begged for a kiss.

When she had passed judgment on all the rooms, she returned to the one second from the stairs. He tried to ignore the fact she stood outside the bedroom next to his. It appeared fate continued to play with him.

He followed her inside as she gave the bedroom a thorough inspection. He could not fault her taste. Decorated in pale yellows and deep purples, it suited her. When she moved next to the large four-poster bed, he couldn't resist standing behind her, inhaling her unique scent. Her hand touched the quilt, and he ran his fingers along her bare arm, wanting more than anything to turn her around and kiss her.

She stilled but didn't pull away. "Is there someone here?"

He remained silent, but placed his hands upon her arms and let his breath brush by her ear.

A shiver ran through her body and Synn grinned. A responsive woman was exactly what he needed. Triumph filled his heart and he brought his chest in contact with her back.

Her breathing grew rapid, but from sexual excitement or at being touched by a ghost? He bent his head to kiss her neck when a scream rent the air.

"Reeeennnaaa!!!"

She pulled away and ran across the inside balcony that connected the two stairways on the second floor.

Irritated, he tried to ignore his reborn need for a woman. Adjusting himself within his pantaloons, he followed. Who was causing problems now?

Rena came to a halt before an open doorway. Inside, the blonde stood with a candelabra held before her like a Roman shield.

"What is it, Val?"

She pointed to the corner of the room. Before the open wardrobe doors stood Mrs. McMurray. Synn silently sighed. At least Mrs. McMurray was a kindhearted soul who wouldn't hurt a three-legged cat.

Rena clapped her hands as she joined her friend. "It's a ghost. A real, live ghost."

She probably wouldn't appreciate him correcting her oxymoron, so he remained silent and invisible. He leaned against the doorframe behind the women, but where Mrs. McMurray could see him. The older woman's expression turned from concerned to relieved.

Rena approached her. "Hello. I'm Rena and this is Valerie. We are pleased to meet you."

Mrs. McMurray gave her guests a deep curtsy.

Rena turned back to look at Valerie and smiled. She had the whitest teeth he'd ever seen. She mouthed the words "she has no legs", her eyes wide with surprise.

Valerie glanced toward the older lady and sucked in a breath before nodding.

Facing Mrs. McMurray again, Rena addressed the spirit. "Can you tell us your name?"

Mrs. McMurray shook her head then lifted her gaze to him. Her pleading look had him cursing inside. He had wanted more time, but he couldn't ignore his friend's request. She wouldn't be able to vocalize until closer to the full moon. Blast.

Allowing himself to materialize, he answered for her. "Her name is Mrs. McMurray."

Rena spun at the deep voice that caressed her senses. Before her stood a woman's wet dream come to life, though as a respectable woman, she shouldn't be having wet dreams, or so she'd been informed.

The man looked as if he'd stepped out of a nineteenth-century drawing room, except his coffee-brown hair hung loose about his shoulders. She was pretty sure it should have been tied in a queue to be proper. His entire demeanor projected upper class from his sharp nose, to his angular chin outlined by a neatly trimmed beard, to his broad-shouldered stance. A rather tall stance it was too, with one snugly encased leg crossed over the other. But his eyes stupefied her. They appeared gray, ancient, yet flickered with bright shards of blue.

Valerie recovered first, brandishing her tightly held candelabra as she stepped forward. "Who are you and what are you doing in here?"

He straightened and gave them a formal bow. "My name is Synn MacAllistair. That is Synn as in S Y N N. I'm the caretaker of the ghosts."

Rena took a deep breath. She could feel her cheeks heating as his voice reverberated through her body. Sin fit him. When he moved his gaze from Valerie to herself, his intense scrutiny warmed her. She swallowed. "Uh, I didn't think anyone lived here."

His stare held hers captive. "I do."

Valerie retreated to stand next to her. "Oh really. With a padlock on the outside of the gate?"

He raised his right brow, the look of arrogance worthy of Mr. Darcy. "There is a postern gate."

Rena racked her brain. She'd heard that word before. Oh yes. "I thought only the owners of a castle knew the secret to that rear exit."

He raised his brows together. "That is true but I desi— discovered it while following a small boy around the Abbey."

Valerie crossed her arms. "A small boy?"

"Yes. The children in the neighborhood dare each other to get close to the Abbey. They want to see the ghosts, who are quite harmless to humans." He gestured to the housekeeper. "Mrs. McMurray here will become more solid as the full moon approaches and will be pleased to help you in any way she can."

They turned and stared at their ghost, having forgotten her. The older woman nodded vigorously, her white cap covering her gray hair falling to the side. Mrs. McMurray's plump frame included pudgy arms sprouting from a short-sleeved blouse and a white apron that protected her skirt, but from the knees down, she didn't exist at all.

Rena's heart pounded. A real ghost. If what Synn said was true, that the ghosts would become solid, the possibilities for her new venture were endless. Could the ghosts serve breakfast to the guests? How would she pay them? She couldn't resist asking. "Are you the one who keeps it so clean in here?"

Mrs. McMurray blushed and nodded again. She actually *blushed*.

Synn clarified. "She and a dozen maids have kept this place clean for centuries in the hopes that someone would come here to live. Do you plan to stay?"

She turned to answer him, but Valerie gave him a disapproving look. "The real estate agent didn't say anything about anyone living here."

He sighed, clearly bored. "No, I imagine he didn't. He is what we refer to as a lickfinger."

Rena chuckled at the strange word. She couldn't help it. It sounded backward.

Valerie didn't find the expression funny. "Well, you need to know, Rena owns this castle now, abbey, whatever you want to call it, and she has the right to throw you out."

Rena grabbed her arm. "Valerie." She changed her warning tone to a more pleasant octave as she addressed the sexy man in front of her. "You are of course welcome to stay, Synn. Perhaps you can help us understand the ghosts, the history of the Abbey and anything else that might be helpful." She smiled encouragingly. She didn't want him to leave.

He gave her an arrogant nod. "I would be happy to be of service. Perhaps I should start by helping you to bring your personal items upstairs as the footmen will not be solid enough to lift anything for another week."

Another week? How strange. She didn't remember seeing anything on television regarding ghosts changing with the moon. "Thank you. That would be perfect." She could tell Valerie didn't trust him. She, on the other hand, was thrilled to have him in the Abbey. Anyone who could help her succeed was welcome. The fact that the man was incredibly hot didn't hurt either.

He nodded once and held his arm out to her. She looked at her friend and shrugged, then looped her arm with his. The second they made contact, a sizzling sensation raced across her skin.

He didn't move. Did he feel it too? He gazed down at her, his face serious. "Shall we?"

She nodded, her throat having closed at his look. There was something sensual about his lips. They were strong, full and serious and made her want to taste him. Sheesh, hadn't she learned anything from her failed engagement? She needed to keep her libido under control. Men like Synn wouldn't appreciate her scandalous thoughts. Besides, who used phrases like "shall we"? He was too far out of her league. Probably from an old Nova Scotia family who could trace its ancestors back to King Robert the Bruce of Scotland.

As they descended the stairs, Rena could picture herself in a beautiful ball gown entering the foyer to meet her beau. The image was so powerful, she stopped. Could this have happened here? In an abbey?

"Rena?"

Synn had covered her hand with his and the sizzling sensation started again, but there was more warmth to it, like the tingling gel she'd bought once and threw away before Bryce discovered it. She lifted her gaze to Synn's. His intense focus unnerved her, and she looked back down at the entryway. "I can picture grand ladies descending these staircases in beautiful gowns, but that couldn't be, because this was an abbey, right?"

She chanced a quick look into his face and caught a glimpse of pain and anger in his eyes before he masked it with a matter-of-fact look.

"Actually, women did descend these staircases in grand ball gowns. The structure was built as a Pleasure Palace. The name Ashton Abbey was added as a bad joke, but there is a beautiful chapel in the back, so it couldn't have been all licentiousness and depravity."

"A Pleasure Palace? That sounds decadent." They continued their descent. Maybe women came to show off their costly dresses, play poker, and, heaven forbid, smoke cigars. "I think it would be lovely all lit up. Maybe for a charity dinner. Oh, are there any charities in town?"

As they reached the bottom, Synn unlinked their arms and faced her, his look condescending, like the ones Bryce used to give her.

From habit, she straightened herself to her full height.

He must have noticed because he quirked his brow. "I think, perhaps, you should learn a bit more about the Abbey before throwing a ball as there are many who reside here."

Her shoulders fell. He was right, of course. She hadn't seen the entire place yet and already her event-planning instincts were sending her off in another direction. She came to open a haunted bed-and-breakfast, not throw parties. She looked up into Synn's face to apologize, but his gaze made her catch her breath. Admiration shone in his eyes before he turned away to pick up her suitcase.

Stunned and baffled, she hesitated before grabbing her laptop. "I'm sorry. You're right. I need to get a feel for the place first. I hope you can help me with that."

He was already striding toward the stairs when he stopped, but he didn't look at her when he spoke. "It will be my pleasure to help you feel this place."

ALSO BY LEXI POST

Paranormal Romance

Masque

Passion's Poison

Passion of Sleepy Hollow

Pleasures of Christmas Past

(A Christmas Carol Series: Book 1)

Desires of Christmas Present

(A Christmas Carol Series: Book 2)

Temptations of Christmas Future

(A Christmas Carol: Book 3) *Coming 2017*

Sci-fi Romance

Cruise into Eden

(The Eden Series: Book 1)

Unexpected Eden

(The Eden Series: Book 2)

Eden Discovered

(The Eden Series: Book 3)

Eden Revealed

(The Eden Series: Book 4)

Avenging Eden

(The Eden Series: Book 5) *Coming 2018*

Contemporary Cowboy Romance

Cowboys Never Fold
(Poker Flat Series: Book 1)
Cowboy's Match
(Poker Flat Series: Book 2)
Cowboy's Best Shot
(Poker Flat Series: Book 3)
Cowboy's Break
(Poker Flat Series: Book 4)
Christmas with Angel
(Last Chance Series: Book 1)
Trace's Trouble
(Last Chance Series: Book 2)
Fletcher's Flame
(Last Chance Series: Book 3)
Logan's Luck
(Last Chance Series: Book 4)
Dillon's Dare
(Last Chance Series: Book 5) *Coming 2018*

Military Romance

When Love Chimes
(Broken Valor Series: Book 1)
Poisoned Honor
(Broken Valor Series: Book 2)

ABOUT LEXI POST

Lexi Post is a New York Times and USA Today best-selling author of romance inspired by the classics. She spent years in higher education taking and teaching courses about the classical literature she loved. From Edgar Allan Poe's short story "The Masque of the Red Death" to Tolstoy's *War and Peace*, she's read, studied, and taught wonderful classics.

But Lexi's first love is romance novels. In an effort to marry her two first loves, she started writing romance inspired by the classics and found she loved it. From hot paranormals to sizzling cowboys to hunks from out of this world, Lexi provides a sensuous experience with a "whole lotta story."

Lexi is living her own happily ever after with her husband and her cat in Florida. She makes her own ice cream every weekend, loves bright colors, and you will never see her without a hat.

www.lexipostbooks.com